SOUL BINDING

R. MICHAEL CARD

Gryphon's Gate Publishing

Soul Binding

Gryphon's Gate Publishing

550 King St. N.

PO Box 42088 Conestoga

Waterloo, ON

N2L 6K5

ebook ISBN 978-1-988115-86-3

Print ISBN 978-1-988115-85-6

1

THE SUN WAS BARELY ABOVE THE HORIZON AS JAIS BEGAN HIS calisthenics. The routine, which he'd built up over the last three months, loosened and worked out important muscles before the usual morning sword practice.

Once done with his stretches, he paused for a moment to enjoy the morning blooming around him. The days were quite warm here in the south, even though it was a little more than a month past the Feast of Emera, celebrating the harvest at the autumnal equinox. Back in Klasten's Green, the days would be growing cool and the nights even cooler. But the seasons had hardly seemed to change during the time he, Caerwyn, and Volf had been on the road.

Last night they had camped near a stone bridge, where the road crossed a small river. A forest sat to one side, perhaps fifty feet from the road, and on the other side, more farmer's fields. This morning, birds sang pleasant tunes, flitting back and forth, from trees to crops. The sky was a pristine blue, light and clear, save for a few clouds crowding on the southern horizon.

They were well out of the northlands now and there were

more cities and settlements down here. Not quite a week ago, they'd gone through a city which dwarfed anything Jais had seen before in his travels. Supposedly, ten thousand people lived in the city alone, not counting the farms around it, which Jais guessed would add an equal amount if not more to the population. The road they followed—paved with flat stones and well used—led to another city called Laskovic, which they would reach later today. This new city was reported to be even larger than the last, a hub of trade. The fact that such massive settlements existed boggled Jais' mind.

Caerwyn was up and tending her weapons. Volf was awake and had gone down to the creek to clean himself up a bit.

Jais drew in a deep breath and moved from stretching to exercises. He was sweating only a little by the time he was done, more from the growing heat of the day than exertion.

Caerwyn drew near and tossed him a practice 'sword,' which was little more than a straight length of wood they'd pilfered from a tree some time ago.

"Ready?" Her voice was flat, as was her expression.

Inwardly, Jais sighed at her lack of vigor. It had been months since their run-in with the wizard back north and still she seemed dispirited. Nothing seemed to be able to snap her back to her old self. Where she had once been a confident warrior, now she seemed to lack any faith in herself, despite that she still beat him at sparring three days out of five. For Jais' part, he had done his mourning for Elria. He missed the northern woman deeply, but he knew he had to move on with his life. There was no use living in the past. It was his future that worried him.

Unlike Caerwyn and Volf, he hadn't had the chance to speak to the ancient dragon in the north before it died, killed by that Holn-spawned wizard. Caerwyn and Volf knew all about their drahksani powers and heritage. He knew nothing other than what little his aunt had told him and what powers he had already discovered. Yet there remained a rather large unknown within him which he sought to explore, but without a dragon, he had no idea how to do so.

Volf approached.

"You should have probably waited until after we'd sparred to wash up," Jais chided.

Volf shrugged then rolled his shoulders, seemingly with some pain. "Perhaps, but I was stiff and sore." The lean man was sore all the time, it seemed. Volf had been practicing with them, but Jais was surprised at his lack of progress. Where Jais had picked up the basics of fighting fairly easily within only a few days, for Volf it had taken months. He was only now a passable fighter on a good day. "I wanted to wake myself up a little. It's amazing what a little cold river water will do. Though water here doesn't seem half as cold as that up north."

Jais laughed. "You come from a town called Cold River. I think anything in the south will have trouble living up to that."

Volf grinned. "Fair enough."

"Enough talk," Caerwyn said with listless exasperation. She tossed Volf a practice sword. "Fight." She wasn't much for talking these days either.

Jais squared off with Volf. He'd go easy on the man. Volf never started a match, but waited and watched. That was good, but someday he may need to start a fight and he wouldn't know any good opening moves if he never tried any.

Jais swung lazily at Volf. He thought he was moving slowly, but Volf barely got his sword up in a weak block. If Jais had put any significant force behind the strike he'd have knocked Volf's sword into the man's own neck.

Volf was very quick, to his credit, once the man was

warmed up. At that point, Jais could attack at normal speeds and Volf would be able to defend himself. But Volf rarely went on the offensive and fighting defensively wouldn't win battles. Also, his strength wasn't anywhere near Jais', and Jais found himself having to pull his strikes, so as not to knock Volf's sword out of his hands entirely.

"You're pulling your strikes," Caerwyn said astutely. "Don't. He needs to know what it's going to be like in the heat of battle."

"I'm a lot stronger than most men he'd face," Jais said, not stopping with his attacks.

"And if he can learn to counter your attacks, he'll have no problem with those others. Don't hold back."

That seemed harsh, but Jais put his full strength into the next slash. Volf's practice sword was there to block the blow, but Jais' wooden sword simply pushed Volf's sword back to hit him on his sword arm, hard.

Volf staggered to one side, falling to one knee, dropping his sword.

"Ah, ow!" Volf gasped, holding his arm with a pained expression.

Jais looked at Caerwyn, who shook her head.

"Volf, what did I tell you about hard wrists?" Caerwyn asked in a deflated yet exasperated tone. "Hard but flexible. Remember that?"

The man nodded. "Jais is too strong!"

"Then you should be...?" Caerwyn trailed off, looking expectantly at Volf to finish the sentence. She got a blank stare for her trouble. Jais knew the answer. A moment later, Caerwyn shook her head and finished. "...using two hands on the grip. If you're fighting a stronger foe you need to make sure you can resist their blows and if that means using both hands, you do it. You still think you can match him? You can't."

It was harsh, if true.

"Also, you are so much quicker than he is. Why aren't you trying to attack him? If you attack quick you could easily whittle down someone of superior strength."

Jais didn't think he was that much slower.

"Get your sword and get up. Attack him!" Caerwyn wasn't leaving room for questions.

Volf did so, though he winced as he gripped the stick—his arm must hurt. He set himself and Jais readied for an attack. This wasn't how it would happen in real life, he'd probably be attacking already, but he'd humor Volf.

Volf's sword whipped around, almost too fast to see. But the attack was at Jais' sword arm and he didn't have to move his blade much to block it. He stopped the other man's sword less than an inch from his shoulder, then saw an opening and took it. He spun his sword at the wrist of Volf's sword-arm, smacking it hard. He was already inside the other man's' defenses so Volf never had a chance to block the blow. How was that for fast?

"Cursed Shadows of Holn!" Volf swore as he dropped his sword and clutched his wrist.

Caerwyn sighed, drawing Jais' attention. She was shaking her head.

"What was that?" she asked with another heavy sigh. The question wasn't for him, but for Volf.

"I..." the slender man seemed to deflate a little. "I was just doing what you said!"

"I suppose," she said with a flat stare. "But why attack his sword arm? His sword was right there ready to defend against such an attack. There were so many other places you could have tried."

"I thought I'd try to end the fight quickly by disarming him."

"But against a superior foe, you leave yourself open if the attack fails. You need to be sure you're going to hit if you're attacking in such a way. If you aren't certain you'll hit, then… well, don't do that."

"Ah." Volf didn't seem pleased to hear this. He shrank in on himself a little more.

"If you are going to do that, make it more of a feint."

"A bluff?"

She nodded. "Give me your sword." He handed it over. She squared off against Jais. "We're going to do the same thing, slowly, so Volf can see it."

Jais nodded.

She sliced at Jais' shoulder. He blocked and pushed her blade away. Yet she was stepping in at the same time. She'd made sure her blade was knocked more back toward her than away and having moved in she was now too close for his quick counter attack. Instead, she had her blade well within Jais' guard and at his throat a moment later.

"Hunh!" Jais blinked. "Didn't see that coming."

"Then you both still need a lot of work," she said sharply. She was close, her look hard. "Your style is still raw and uncontrolled. You need more precision. If you can manage that…" She stepped away and shrugged. "Then you might just be the best warrior I've ever seen."

Oh? Really? The best? But her words before that had been on point. He was still rough. He trusted his strength and natural talent more than his training. It worked most of the time, but…

"Volf, take a break. I'll spar with Jais for a while," Caerwyn said setting herself again.

Jais did the same.

When she came at him, she didn't hold back. Flying into a series of attacks, she pushed him back, step after step. Finally, he knocked her sword down and away, stepping to one side so she was forced past him. He stopped, breathing hard.

He heard her voice behind him. "You could have cut me as I passed you there. You're missing things."

He grimaced with a wince. She was right. He could have sliced at her left shoulder as she'd stumbled past him. He sighed. "I'm tired. It's early"

"You'll be tired in fights too. You can't miss any opening." And with that she threw herself at him in a savage series of attack, pushing him back the way they'd come once more.

He heard Volf's low whistle and some exclamation as they passed him.

Jais finally dug in and stopped giving ground.

Caerwyn nodded even though she didn't relent on her attacks. He was still defending, but he wasn't going to let her push him. He wondered if she was growing tired.

Then something came over him. Some extreme sense of peace and centeredness. It was as if her attacks slowed, as if time itself slowed, everything but him. He could see what she was going to do before she did it. No, not see, it was more of an innate sense. He just knew what she was going to do.

He found his eyes slowly closing. But his sword arm kept moving. He felt the rush of wind from her blade, heard her grunts and the slide of her feet on the ground. He knew what she was doing without looking. It was amazing!

He felt his sword connect with her sword-arm, mid-fore-arm. She gave a grunt and he heard the clatter of her wooden sword hit the paving stones.

He heard her step back, away, breathing hard.

"What in Holn was that?" she asked.

Jais blinked his eyes open. "I don't know." He grinned.

"Whatever it was, it felt amazing. I could tell what you were doing even with my eyes closed. I just... knew what was happening and how to counter each attack. It felt easy and smooth." He looked down at the stone road, still blinking in surprise. Shaking his head, he said, "I've never felt anything like that before."

It felt like some piece of a puzzle had fallen into place within him. As if he'd been some ideal version of himself. It had been transcendent!

And yet... that only served to illustrate how much he still didn't know about himself and his powers. Could he even get back to that place of ease and flow again if he tried? Probably not. He let out another sigh. All it had been was a single glimpse of a larger mystery he still couldn't define. There was so much more he needed to learn.

Caerwyn's voice was a little different than her usual blasé tone when she spoke. "Take some time to think about what happened. See if you can do it again tomorrow when we spar."

"I will."

"For now, let's get some food, I'm famished."

Volf was already laying out a cold breakfast. They'd picked up some fruit, bread, and cheese in the last city and were nearly done with it.

As Jais came over, Volf held out his arm. There was a nasty welt on his wrist and upper arm. "Care to heal me?"

Jais nodded. The wounds were his fault, after all. He knelt next to the man and soothed the two wounds.

Caerwyn's tone was back to its usual spear-point sharpness when she sat. "You won't always have a healer around. Sometimes you just need to keep going through the pain to survive."

Volf eyed her but said nothing.

She looked away as she chewed on some hard bread. Jais

looked off to where she seemed to be looking. It was south, and dark clouds were gathering there. Looking back at her, he saw a similarly dark expression on her face. These gloomy moods were normal for her now. She always seemed to have that dark and cloudy feeling about her.

He wondered what it would take to snap her out of whatever dark place she was in.

2

CAERWYN ATE WITHOUT TASTING HER MEAL. NOT THAT THERE would have been much to taste: withered fruit, stale bread, and hard cheese.

She didn't like the look of those dark clouds on the horizon. It spoke to a dark place inside her soul and told her nothing good was ahead of them. As they'd passed through the towns and cities of the south, they'd heard that the rainy season was coming. Until now, they'd been blessed with many sunny days. It had helped to keep her spirits from the darker corners of the depths in which they already sat. But now...

She sighed. It had been a long trip down out of the mountains then over the lowlands. A long time away from friends. She felt a sting in her soul.

She missed Barami.

He'd been a companion, a fixture in her life for so long. And she needed him now more than ever: his blunt wisdom and strength. Untethered, that's how she felt most of the time. Tossed about like a boat in a storm with no sight of land.

What she'd just said to Volf echoed in her mind: *Sometimes you just need to keep going through the pain to survive.* It was a truth she'd lived with for three months now. Though for her it was more of an emptiness, the loss of something she'd once been. She didn't know if her doubt and uncertainty would ever lift. A part of her told her it wouldn't. But she had to hope it would. Yet hope was so very hard these days. She was still going, but more and more she just wanted to stop and rest and give up on this quest of theirs.

She just couldn't get over what had happened with the wizard up north. She'd been perfectly able to fight but had chosen not to. If she had acted, Barami would have died, but she'd been forced to choose another to die. She'd had all her power yet been powerless. She'd had all her strength but been weak. She should have done something. But all paths had led to the death of an ally. Some might say it was an impossible choice, but she'd made it quick enough. She'd saved a friend, sacrificing the woman Jais had cared for.

She'd tried telling herself that it was a battle and people died in battle. Certainly, she'd led men to their deaths before as a general in Afgen. And yet, this had been different. Those men had died fighting. She hadn't told the enemy to kill them specifically, then stood there doing nothing watching it happen. She'd been fighting too. Moreover, as much as she may have been close with some of those men, they hadn't been true friends. Elria had been more than a friend to Jais. It just wasn't the same and she couldn't seem to forget about it, no matter what she did. Elria had died and it had been Caerwyn's fault.

How was she supposed to live with that?

She'd thought herself strong enough to handle any situation, any problem, but she'd been wrong. She didn't know who she was anymore. She only knew she wasn't the same woman who'd gone north all those months ago.

A cold finger of despair traced her spine and she shivered.

Yes, it would be so much easier to give up and just wait to die. Yet she wouldn't. She had enough strength to keep going, for now.

There had been a few days when she'd come close to feeling like her old self, confident and in control, but a part of her wondered if that wasn't some lie she was telling herself. Most of the time she just felt lost and confused. At first, she'd tried not to show it. Certainly, she'd never tell Jais or Volf how she felt. But it had quickly become apparent that her efforts to hide her uncertainty were for naught. The behavior of the two men had changed toward her. They knew. She could feel their pity. She'd never been pitied before. It galled her and yet she couldn't deny her own pathos.

Searching for any break from these thoughts, she turned her attention to the south. She was not looking forward to heading farther in that direction, despite the warmth in these lands. It wasn't just those clouds and their portent of rain. They were getting close to several drahksani: three of them. She couldn't help but feel a little wary. Perhaps it was the dark clouds which hung over the lands to the south that tainted her mood, but she just couldn't shake the feeling that they should all just turn around and avoid these next drahksani. The pull was too strong. Whoever this was, they must be quite powerful. Volf agreed with her on that. Jais, of course, sensed nothing.

Whoever these drahksani were, one thing was certain: they'd have sensed Caerwyn and her companions as well. For several days, those others had been moving steadily northward, heading straight for Caerwyn's group. There was also another drahksani, who'd remained back where these three had originated. He hadn't come north. But what did that mean?

She shivered despite the growing warmth of the day. What

if these ones were like that wizard? What powers did they have? Would she find herself useless and floundering again?

Gods, she needed Barami. She'd been able to tell him anything. She could talk to him.

But she didn't have the stalwart southern warrior anymore. She had two men who were friends and yet somehow still subtly vying for her attentions. It was hard to confide in them. In a vain attempt to stop their awkward affections she'd hacked off most of her hair not long ago, leaving it a messy, spiky mop on her head.

In many ways, she was trying to push them away. She didn't want to be close to anyone right now, emotionally or physically. Even just sitting near them grated on her. She wanted to be alone, so she took her small meal and wandered away from the others.

They expected her to lead them, to be something she had been, but wasn't anymore. They kept looking to her, but other than fighting, there wasn't much she would trust herself to tell them. What did she know?

Her mood darkened and she wanted nothing more than to sit somewhere in that gloomy forest and let the eventual rains drench her.

But she couldn't.

She would keep going as she'd told Volf to do.

But that didn't stop her from feeling more and more troubled about what was to come.

So, she looked south at those dark clouds and tried to ignore the roiling anxiety in the pit of her stomach.

A LIGHT RAIN BEGAN TO FALL, PATTERING ON THE STONES OF the road and wetting the fields around them. They'd walked for most of the day and could finally see the City of Laskovic in the distance, when those three other drahksani met them on the road.

They were nothing like what Caerwyn had envisioned. She'd been expecting hard-looking men. In her mind these three had become monsters, but in truth, they looked rather harmless. At first glance it seemed to be two parents and a child. The presence of the young one instantly threw Caerwyn, especially since it was the young girl who was by far the most powerful of the three of them. All at once Caerwyn felt both disarmed and on edge.

For a long moment, the two groups simply stood there in the rain, sizing-up each other. Caerwyn was certain her group would seem the far more intimidating. Jais alone was imposing, with his great girth, even if he wasn't particularly tall. Whereas these others seemed quite normal. The most striking one of the three of them was the woman. She was beautiful by nearly anyone's definition. Even with a hood up to cover her head, waves of auburn hair tumbled out, slowly soaking up water. She had a perfect face, smooth brow and cheeks, straight but not overly prominent nose, eyes of clear and pristine blue, and full blushing lips. The way the woman's cloak fell over her, suggested a well-endowed figure as well.

The young girl was the woman's daughter, or at least some blood relation. There were too many similarities: eyes of a cold silvery blue, nose identical, lips not as rosy, but of the same shape, and though the hair was darker, it had the same full and flowing nature.

It was only after Caerwyn had studied the man for a moment that she guessed he was not the woman's husband, but perhaps... her brother? He too shared similar features. His face was refined for a man: slight nose, high cheeks, the eyes were brown, soft, but framed by a shockingly similar brow-ridge to the woman. His hair was cut short, but the color was close enough to the woman's to complete the resemblance. They were also of a height, both as tall as she, which made the woman tall and the man only slightly taller than average.

"We seek your aid," the man said with sudden fierceness. The woman gave him a harsh look, as if he was saying too much, but he shook his head at her. "They know we've been heading straight for them. We might as well be forthright."

The rains were starting to fall in earnest, the day growing dark around them.

"Perhaps," the woman said, looking from the man to Caerwyn and the others. "We can talk?" She tilted her head up a little acknowledging the rains. "Somewhere... drier?"

Caerwyn nodded to that. "There was a farm not far off the road a little way back. We could beg use of their barn. Or we could go to the city?"

At mention of returning back the way they had come, all three of the others became tense. That spoke volumes.

"Let's try for that barn," the man said. He moved up to Caerwyn and the others, then past. "I am Donallo, this is my sister Mirala, and her daughter Astria."

"Caerwyn, Volf, and Jais," Caerwyn said indicating those she mentioned.

Donallo nodded to each of them, then he kept them moving back down the road.

Caerwyn didn't know what to make of any of this. Certainly, this odd trio and their plea for help was the last thing she'd expected.

The question that grew in her mind as they all passed through the now drenching rains was simple: could she trust them?

No, she'd no longer trust anyone quickly. She'd wait and see.

~

THE FARMER WAS ACCOMMODATING AND AS THE STORM PICKED up outside, winds causing the barn-boards to creak, the six of them removed sodden garments and settled among the hay in a corner of the barn not occupied by oxen or chickens. The barn was well tended and the smell of livestock wasn't overpowering. Caerwyn, unable to relax and recline as Volf and Jais had done on the bales of hay, stood carefully watching the three newcomers as they told their story.

Mostly it was Donallo who spoke, while Mirala tended a tired Astria, who lay with her head in her mother's lap. The woman was stroking the girl's dark hair. Now that the cloaks were off, even with the dimness of the day outside, Caerwyn could see the small differences between mother and daughter. There were some more severe angles on the girl's face, compared to the soft rounded cheeks of her mother. The hair of the child was full but straight, unlike the bouncing waves of Mirala's red-brown locks.

Donallo drew in a long, heaving breath and began. "First, perhaps I should say that we are not without our faults." That wasn't an auspicious start in Caerwyn's mind. "We have done things to survive which we… regret." Donallo, from where he sat leaning against the wooden slats which separated their stall from the next—shoulders slumped in exhaustion— looked up at Caerwyn. His earnest brown eyes were searching, next to desperate. "I do not know if you have had to suffer as we have or not, but we were desperate to find some protection from the great purge." He looked away, his entire being heavy with shame. That meant he missed the flash of pain in Caerwyn's own eyes.

Oh, she had suffered greatly when the humans had risen up to rid the world of all drahksani. Her parents had been slaughtered when she was but a child, perhaps as old as Astria, no more. Then she'd been driven from her adopted father and the home she'd made for herself in the Afgenni Empire in the south by the same dragon hunter who'd killed her parents. She still had oddly mixed feelings about that man.

She hated him with a passion, and yet... he had given his life to help them when they'd fought that wizard and his minions in the north. Jais had said the dragon hunter had regretted his life, wanted to repent and repay his debts. Caerwyn didn't believe that, couldn't bring herself to believe it.

She shook off those thoughts and concentrated on what Donallo was saying. She'd missed a bit.

"—he promised to help us, protect us." Who had? She didn't ask. Perhaps that would become clear from listening to the rest. Though from the way Mirala stiffened and seemed to have a brief fit of trembling, whoever they were talking about was someone they both feared. "He was—and still is—a powerful man, too powerful. I don't know where he gets his power from, but it's unnatural, even for a drahksan." Well that didn't sound good. "He said he would protect us. Yet he was surrounded by humans, so we were uncertain at first. We soon found out they were all devoutly loyal to him. They see him as some sort of semi-divine being, some conduit to their god. The way they look at him..." Donallo shivered. "It's unnerving. They call him 'The Undying', because he's been around for generations of their kind. So, we thought it would be safe there and stayed."

Caerwyn had to interrupt. There was something she needed to know. "You say you needed protection, but you're drahksani. What powers do you have? Could you not protect yourselves?"

Donallo gave a grimace then sighed. "We tried. Our

powers are not insignificant, but in the end, we are not fighters, as I'm guessing you are." Another sigh. There was something odd with how he shook his head then, as if he possessed
far too many regrets. "I am a mind talent, but alas, few of my
powers are offensive. Mirala is a soul talent. She can inspire
fear to make enemies flee, or try to make those who aren't
overtly hostile friendlier. Of course, we're both stronger than
normal humans and our senses are enhanced, but beyond
that..." He shrugged.

Caerwyn shuddered a little.

A mind talent? Could he read her thoughts? Would he be
able to control her? Not from what he'd said, but perhaps he
wasn't telling them everything. She'd remain wary.

Even with that wariness, a part of her, the part that still
remembered being a scared little girl on the run through
wildlands, felt a certain empathy for Astria. Whatever else was
going on here, the girl didn't deserve to be caught up in it.

"What about this Lucian?" Jais said. "What are his powers?"

Lucian? That must have been the name of the 'protector'
who had taken in Donallo and Mirala.

This must be the drahksan still far south of them. His call
through the spirit-link was quite powerful.

Lucian.

Already she didn't like the man.

"He has storm powers, those are his most prevalent abilities," Donallo said. "Though he also has some fire abilities and
can even wield the foundational elements."

"Foundational?" Jais asked.

Caerwyn knew the term, but only from the knowledge
granted to her by the dragon. She answered. "The foundational elements are those which make up the world: earth,
water, and air." She added—since Jais wouldn't know, "Fire
and storm are known as the chaotic elements."

"Oh," Jais said, nodding.

Caerwyn sighed inwardly. She regretted that Jais hadn't had the chance to speak with the dragon. He, most of all of them, had wanted to know his powers and his place in this world. Though Caerwyn wasn't sure if that would truly help the man. She had been certain of her place in the world, but all of that was gone now, replaced only with doubt and darkness.

"He has all of those abilities?" Volf asked. He then let out a low whistle as Donallo nodded.

"The man is powerful. And with his cult, which follows him unquestioningly, he is a true force of chaos in this world."

"Cult?" Jais asked.

It was Mirala who answered, voice low but quavering with fear. "Oh yes. He's got them all eating from his hand. I don't know how it started, but it's a vile and corrupted thing now." She shuddered. "They claim to worship Davul, but I doubt the god condones their activities. As much as he's the god of passions and heat, the things they do..." Another shudder.

Caerwyn wanted to ask why the two of them had subjected themselves to this, but she suspected the reason. Lucian had protected them. Caerwyn knew the fear and apprehension which came from being hunted.

"You said you needed protection?" she asked. "From what, exactly? Is it still a threat to you now?"

"Dragon hunters," Donallo said stoically. "Three different ones were hunting us. We'd been on the run since the fall of the drahksani stronghold at Bulovas. Several drahksani had survived and fled in different directions. We fled east with a dragon hunter on our tail, dogging us for three years. We thought we'd lost her once we were in the Shujen lands. But another found us there and when they first caught up to us again, we fled. We lost them by taking a ship from Q'an-Tua west across the Calastan Sea to Saravia, but they found us yet again and had brought along a third from that area as well. We fled west to Rodathia, which is where we met Lucian. He…" Donallo seemed at a loss for words, shaking his head.

Mirala picked up the tale. "Those three dragon hunters came for us. His cult dealt with them swiftly enough. The dragon hunters were expecting drahksan, not crazed humans. That caused enough chaos for one to be killed outright. The other two were… saved as—" Mirala lowered her voice to a whisper. "—sacrifices."

"Sacrifices?" Volf asked.

Mirala shuddered yet again.

Donallo responded. "It's part of the ritual the cult does monthly. Someone is sacrificed and killed during a… wild revel, burned first, then torn apart and… sometimes eaten. The truly disgusting part is that usually the sacrifice is culled from the cult itself and the person often goes willingly. Yet when they do catch intruders or foes, they use them instead. Those rituals, where outsiders are sacrificed, are always a much more *festive* occasion."

"Gods," Jais breathed. "That's disgusting!"

Donallo looked at Jais then quickly away. That wasn't the first time the man or Mirala had done that. There was something about Jais that they seemed to flinch away from. It was something she'd have to investigate, but not now. Jais hadn't seemed to notice, or if he had, hadn't said anything.

"How long did you stay there?" Caerwyn asked. Her voice held an edge now. She agreed that this cult and its practices were vile—and knew this leader would be someone she would despise as well. Yet these two had lived that life, living under this man's protection for how long?

"Twelve years."

Caerwyn grimaced. As she'd thought. These two had been

complicit in that vile behavior for far too long. She understood their seeking protection but— "Why did you stay after the dragon hunters were dealt with?"

Mirala answered, her voice was low, barely audible. "We'd been on the run for so long. We just wanted someplace… safe."

"But it wasn't safe, was it?" Caerwyn had a feeling she knew where this was going.

Mirala shook her head.

Caerwyn pushed. "Who's Astria's father, Mirala?" Astria seemed to be sleeping, which was good. The young one shouldn't have to hear all this contemptible talk.

The woman didn't answer.

Donallo looked up at Caerwyn. "I think you already know."

"Lucian's."

A nod.

Donallo gave his sister a sidelong glance for a drawn-out moment, perhaps seeing if she'd say anything. Finally, she met his gaze but shook her head. He sighed. "Perhaps the whole tale is in order."

"Yes," Caerwyn said, voice harsh. "If you want our help, I think you'd better tell us everything."

"Don't be mad."

Caerwyn started. It had been Astria who had spoken. She looked over to see the girl's eyes open, looking at her. And in that moment, looking into those silver-blue eyes, Caerwyn couldn't be mad. Her heart melted just a little.

Astria sat up and put a hand to her mother's cheek. Instantly Mirala seemed to relax, tension flowing out of her. Then she wept softly, but even that was short-lived. "There, now," Astria said, in some odd parody, the child comforting the parent.

Caerwyn looked back to Donallo, who had been watching Astria as well. When their gazes met again and Caerwyn could see the grief in his eyes once more—now that the anger was gone from her—she relented just a little. Whatever these three had been through, it hadn't been easy on any of them.

She felt some of the pent-up, irritated tension leave her, her shoulders falling.

"Please," she said softly. "Go on."

Donallo nodded and continued his tale.

3

VOLF FOUND HIMSELF LETTING OUT A BREATH HE HADN'T known he'd been holding. Something had just happened between Caerwyn and the new trio; something to do with the girl. Caerwyn had relaxed and relented a little and Volf found himself now able to do the same.

He'd been ready to help these three the moment he'd met them. There was an air about the small group, one of desperation and urgency. He felt no trap, as he suspected Caerwyn had. He'd deferred to Caerwyn's battle instincts and waited until they'd heard the story from the three of them. Now he was quite certain these three posed no threat. No, the threat was this Lucian, still well south of them.

Volf's gaze kept being drawn to Mirala. Despite the dark day and the lack of light in the barn, he could see her well enough in the dim and diffuse light. He recalled how he'd been taken with Caerwyn the first time he'd seen her: tall and stalwart and unlike any woman he'd ever known. Well Mirala had captured his attention in a similar way. She was of a height with Volf himself and certainly the most captivating woman he'd ever met. Those piercing blue eyes peered out from an angelic face, framed by perfect waves of auburn hair. It was a good thing the woman seemed preoccupied tending to Astria. Otherwise she probably would have noticed Volf's fascination.

Caerwyn no longer wanted a child and she'd made it abundantly clear that she didn't need a man for anything. She'd pushed Volf and Jais away these last few months and Volf hadn't quite known what to do with himself. He had initially followed her, gone where she'd gone, taken by her commanding attitude and fierce nature, but she lacked both of those qualities now. He'd tried to talk to her, but social skills were not his strength. He hadn't had many people to talk to for most of his adult life.

All of that had made it just a little easier for his attentions to shift toward Mirala.

"It was clear when we met Lucian, that he was Domassi." Donallo said. "We were—"

"Sorry, did you mean drahksani?" Jais asked, just a moment before Volf was about to voice a similar question.

Donallo quirked a brow. "No, Domassi." The man looked around at each of them for a long moment. "Domassi drahk-san," Donallo repeated. "Do none of you know what that means?"

It was Caerwyn who answered. "Our education in all things drahksani is a bit lacking."

What was odd, was that it shouldn't have been. Both she and Volf had received much information on the drahksani race from the dragon they'd met up north. He'd thought they'd known everything they needed to know about the race, yet it seemed there was still more to learn.

Donallo drew in a long breath, eyes a little wide with concern. "Did your parents not tell you of such things?"

Caerwyn's tone had just a hint of an edge to it when she said, "We're all orphans."

"Oh, I'm so sorry to hear that," Donallo said softly. "Apologies then. Allow me to explain." He pursed his lips for a long moment, looking away, seemingly in thought. "Perhaps I'd better go back a bit further." He blew out a breath and drew himself up. "Long ago, when the drahksani were still young as a race, there was a schism among them. It began with siblings, a brother and sister. Domira and Palanir. Domira believed that the best way to help humanity was to rule over them. Be benevolent kings and queens and keep the humans in line with firm laws. Palanir believed that the best way to let humanity thrive was to let them rule themselves and instead be protectors and advisors to humanity; to stay out of their way for the most part and remain neutral in their affairs. Drahksani began to divide themselves up by which doctrine they followed. And, of course, as time passed, both beliefs became a bit... skewed. The followers of Domira, or Domassi as they became known, often became tyrants more than benevolent rulers. They began to believe they were superior and meant to rule humanity. Some thought humanity no more than slaves to be used. The Palassi—followers of Palanir— well, most of them followed a fairly hands-off approach, only helping when humanity needed it, becoming well known heroes and defenders. But even some of them became reclusive, leaving humanity entirely to itself. Others became quite militant, warring with some of the more tyrannical Domassi."

Donallo grimaced. "I don't know if either side was right. We were a part of a collective of drahksani who had remained mostly apart from humanity. We'd built up our own small kingdom, called Bulovas. There were many humans who lived among us and saw nothing wrong with our way of life. It wasn't them who turned on us during the great purge, but neighboring kingdoms, who sought our land or feared our powers. They banded together and brought a massive army against us." Donallo grimaced. "Some of us wanted to fight them. Others wanted to flee and find some other place to live. Mirala and I chose to flee. We didn't want to fight."

"Which is why, when we found Lucian and he had a... stable, if odd relationship with people, we thought it would be safe. And he did deal with the dragon hunters who came after us, but... when we saw how, we were a bit concerned."

"A bit?" Jais scoffed. "From what you said, he murdered them and his people *ate* them!"

Donallo nodded, sighing heavily. "Yes, we should have known then that this wasn't a good place to settle. But we'd been on the run for nearly three years and were tired and at our wits' end." Another heavy sigh as he looked down at the hay-strewn floor. "We both turned a blind eye to such things, hoping that perhaps they might change, that we might help to change them. But that never happened." Donallo turned to Mirala. "Did you want to take Astria for a bit of a walk around the stables?"

Mirala nodded faintly and rose, drawing her daughter up by their joined hands. "Come on, sweetie, let's stretch our legs a little," Mirala said and led Astria away.

Donallo shuffled a little closer to the rest of them and lowered his voice as he continued. Oddly Volf noticed how Donallo still kept a safe distance from Jais. There was something in how he and Mirala looked at Jais. It was odd, and Volf could see no reason for it.

"For a long time, we were treated as special, on a level with Lucian, and as such we were exempt from the... activities of the humans in Lucian's cult. But then we began to talk to a few of the people and even Lucian himself. We thought we were being subtle, hoped to change things, if slowly." He shook his head. "We should have kept quiet, or just left. Lucian got angry and told us things wouldn't change, and perhaps we needed to get a taste for the rituals to better understand them. He demanded we attend one of his... revels." Donallo's voice became hard to hear, barely a whisper. "They were orgies, dressed up as something formal, a part of the ritual they had every month. It seemed this part, at least, had been going on ever since Lucian had started the cult. The sacrifices... they had come later. Anyway, we seriously considered leaving then, but we were still too scared. We thought... just one, perhaps we could do that to see what it's like, perhaps it's not what we think." Another heavy sigh. "It was exactly what we thought. Hundreds of naked bodies writhing in a fit of passion, as dictated by their supposed god Davul. Mirala, being an empath, was a bit overwhelmed by the heightened emotions around her. It wasn't painful, nor unpleasant, far from it, but she was overcome with ecstasy and blacked out, losing all memory of the events. When I caught up with her afterward she was dazed and elated still. It took her some time to recover and come down. I must admit, I too was a little overcome. Though I don't sense emotions, the myriad thoughts which were bombarding my senses made it hard for me to concentrate. From what little I recall, I was a semi-willing participant. Perhaps Lucian knew that would be the case, or perhaps he just wanted the event as an excuse... but..." He trailed off.

Volf didn't know where the other man had been leading, but apparently Caerwyn did. "Lucian found Mirala during the revel and coupled with her?"

Volf nearly choked on his next breath. How vile!

Donallo nodded. "We didn't know until much later, when the pregnancy began. At first, we didn't know who the father might be, given how the conception had occurred. It was only after the birth of Astria that Lucian made his plan known. He'd made it very clear to the other men at the revels that Mirala would be for him only. He knew he was the father and it was clear once Astria was born, that he was correct." Any energy and vigor seemed to drain out of Donallo then, his shoulders fell, posture limp. "He had us then. He made sure to keep Astria close. He wouldn't let the girl go and he knew Mirala wouldn't either."

"So, how did you get her away from him?" Jais asked.

Donallo looked up at Jais and seemed to flinch back as if struck.

"What?" Jais asked. "You and Mirala have been acting weird around me since we met. What is it?"

Donallo turned away. "You... you look a lot like someone who helped Mirala and I. He was the one who made it possible for us to escape with Astria. We... shouldn't have left him behind."

"Who?" Jais asked.

"His name was Andrei," Donallo whispered, seeming near to broken by whatever memories were plaguing him.

Oddly, it was Caerwyn who knelt next to him. "You don't need to tell us any more if you don't want to. We've heard enough for now." She placed a firm hand on the frail looking man's shoulder. "I'm sorry I pushed you. We've all been through horrid things we should never have to retell or relive."

That was true enough.

Since Donallo seemed to be finished, Volf rose to find Mirala and bring her back. It was clear now why Donallo had sent Astria away. That wasn't something the girl should hear.

He found Mirala and Astria at the far end of the barn crouching and making clucking sounds to get the chickens to come closer. The girl seemed a natural and had one of the animals up in her arms, stroking it. The bird didn't seem to mind in the least.

"We're done," he said softly. "You can return now." Mirala rose and regarded him, eyes full of sorrow. Volf felt compelled to add, "I'm sorry."

She nodded.

Astria put the chicken down then stood.

"Why don't you run back to the others," Mirala said to her daughter. The girl nodded and walked sedately to the far side of the barn. Mirala watched her go, made sure she was where she needed to be, then turned to Volf.

"I can't imagine what you must think of me. Allowing such a thing to happen. Then remaining trapped with that man for nine years."

"Did he…" Volf had been going to ask if Lucian had forced himself on her other times, but thought better of the highly inappropriate question. Yet Mirala seemed to understand.

"No. He never tried to… be with me, after that, and never made us go back to the revels. He had enough women to sate his desires. In truth, I think he only wanted the child. He had —" She shook her head. "No he didn't." Those words weren't for Volf, she'd been talking to herself and she looked up at Volf and apologized. "I'm sorry, I'm making no sense. What I had meant to say was that he hadn't had any children, any true drahksan children of his own. I believe he wanted one, and in doing so, also found a way to keep my brother and I close. He appreciated our abilities especially when dealing with others. It was a boon to know what trade partners and allies were thinking or feeling."

"You make it sound like he was a king or governor."

"He is. His… cult, has grown to the point of being a small city. He rules it like a king, actually more like a god to those depraved and lost peoples." She shuddered.

"Oh."

Mirala wrapped her arms around herself. She'd left her cloak hanging to dry back where the others were.

"Are you cold?" Volf asked. "I could get your cloak." Though it would still be wet. With the heavy clouds blocking the sun and the rains bringing a splash of cooler winds, he too was a bit chilly. In truth, this would still be a pleasant spring or fall day back in Cold River.

"No," she said softly. She looked up, those clear blue eyes, like twin pools of summer sky, regarded him for a long moment. "You're a good man, Volf," she said softly. "I can sense it."

He blinked. He wasn't sure where that had come from. He tried to be as good as he could be.

She gave him a faint smile before heading back to the others.

He stood there for a long moment pondering her words, then he too headed back.

THE RAINS STOPPED BY EARLY EVENING. NONE OF THEM WISHED to move on at night, so they remained in the barn, laying blankets and bedrolls on the hay to make their beds. It would be more comfortable than sleeping on the ground.

Volf had the first watch of the night. Even though they were in civilized lands and there wouldn't be much of a threat of beasts, Mirala and Donallo were worried about some of Lucian's cult following after them. So, a rotation of watches had been set among them, to keep an eye out for trouble.

Volf was exhausted. Caerwyn had insisted on maintaining their routine of an evening sword practice and Volf had thrown himself into it fully in a vain attempt to impress

Mirala. Yet his skill was far from that of Jais or Caerwyn—though the two of them had been impressed with his renewed vigor to learn. Donallo had joined them. He carried a sword and it seemed he knew how to use it well enough. He couldn't defeat either Jais or Caerwyn, but when he'd faced off against Volf, he'd won three of four bouts. Volf had gotten in a lucky hit winning one. Yet he felt like he was learning, if slowly, which was good. He had a reason to fight now, something he hadn't really had before. The few times he'd been in battle, he'd been trying to stay alive, nothing more. That was a very compelling motivation in that moment of combat, but once the heat of a fight had passed, just fighting to survive seemed somehow a distant and lack-luster goal. But to protect someone else... someone like Mirala.

Gods how she consumed his thoughts.

He found himself looking over at her slumbering form several times as he kept watch, standing by the open door to the barn. They'd opened it to let in a breeze to dispel the stale air within. With his night-sight—able to see as if it were day—he scanned the hills around the farm, but saw no threats.

He found his thoughts drifting to Mirala more and more, even if he wasn't looking over at her. The plight of the woman and her family was compelling. It was odd. He'd originally been quite consumed with Caerwyn and when she'd told him of her desire to have a child, he'd wanted to help her with it. Yet after more than three months with her, around her every day, she felt more like an older sister to him now... and a standoffish one at that. He still admired her and found her fascinating, but he was a little glad she'd not pursued a child with him. It would have made things odd between them. He was fairly certain he'd just been captivated by her commanding, martial nature and the fact that she was a drahksan, like him. With Mirala... well he wondered if he was caught up in her beauty. Certainly, she was the most attractive woman he'd ever seen. Yet there was far more to her than that. Her strength, having fought to survive through horrible situations as long as she had. And her caring, raising a daughter on the run, that couldn't be easy. He found himself admiring these qualities as well.

With a heavy sigh, he sank down to a sitting position in the entranceway, growing more tired as the night wore on. It was nearly the end of his watch. The moon was close to where it needed to be for him to wake Caerwyn.

"Volf!"

He started awake.

Gods! When had he fallen asleep! A quick look up at the moon showed him it was well past the end of his watch, well into the night.

"Sorry," he said, turning toward the voice. Mirala stood over him, looking concerned, even a little hurt. He could understand why she might feel that way, since he'd fallen asleep while supposedly protecting them. "Don't worry, no one's out there, we're still safe," he said to reassure her.

"No, we're not!" she scolded him, her voice strained. "Astria's gone!"

4

LUCIAN SEETHED WITH RAGE, BUT KEPT IT CONTAINED. IT would do him little good. He hadn't built the empire he had by being quick to act.

In the distance to the east, the sun was just above the horizon and its light spread out on all before him.

He leaned on the thick marble railing of the balcony outside the office of his estate. From here he could see the entirety of his small city, which huddled along the mouth of the Tiska River, where it emptied into the Calastan Sea. The estate had been built atop the highest hill with a good view of the river, the sea, and the settlement. The city had started as a camp nestled next to the river. High, jagged hills to the west and north-west curved around to protect the area. There were a few small farms on this side of the river, more on the other side, where flat lands spread out along the coast. Most of their supplies came from trade—either down the river from inland, or over the sea—as well as fishermen and a few industrious herders who plied their trade up the sides of the hills around the town.

Lucian had built this city: Rodathia. It was his. The people were loyal to him, thought him a god. Referred to him as "The Undying" because of his long life. Yet all of that could be taken from him...

He still couldn't believe his own son had betrayed him, well, the man wasn't his blood, not truly, but Lucian had raised him since he was a babe! Then there were those two conniving foreigners. He hadn't thought they had the guts to take Astria away from him!

Yet they had, and now they'd joined up with three more drahksani far to the north, near the city of Laskovic. That worried him.

He'd come out here to wind-talk to the group he'd send after his daughter and her wretch of a mother.

He summoned the high winds, those that blew cold and fast. A moment later, he felt a down-draft of near-frozen air surrounding him and spoke into it. "My friends and follow-ers," he said, keeping his voice level, unaffected. It was how he began most of his addresses. He made sure he wasn't giving away any of his misgivings. "I need to warn you that those you seek have met up with others like them. There are now five drahksani, in addition to my daughter, you will have to contend with. This will make your task that much harder, but I have faith in you and the powers I have bestowed upon you. These others are nowhere near as powerful as I am. I know you will prevail. Take care my friends. Use caution and guile, and remember: all of them can die, except for my daughter, she must be returned to me alive and well."

There were two among the group who would be able to speak to him in a similar manner. He waited for a moment and indeed Syasha—one of his most powerful minions, a druhi among the hierarchy of the cult—responded to him. Her voice was lithe and supple, much like Syasha herself, on the cold breath of wind which came to him.

"Thank you, Undying One. We will proceed with caution. Fear not, your daughter will be returned to you soon."

Then the wind dissipated.

Would she?

He'd awoken that morning to discover that his daughter had vanished from the spirit-link. He couldn't sense her. It was most disconcerting and yet another element which stoked his rage. He knew Mirala would never let the child die, but what else could this mean? He was aware of drahksan who were able to mask their spirit-link, but that had never been one of Astria's abilities. If his sense of these three new drahksani was correct—he had spent a good deal of the previous day reaching out to them through the spirit-link to feel their abilities and level of power—then one of them did have the ability to mask himself. Perhaps that was how the group was hiding Astria from him. It seemed the most logical explanation. Yet it still troubled him.

From the information he'd gleaned about these three newcomers he hadn't sensed any great level of power among them. They were all of muddled-blood, impure, their drahksan heritage mixed with human over time. Lucian's line was pure. He was fourth generation drahksan, tracing his lineage back through his parents and grandparents to the first of those born from the eggs of dragons. Of the few remaining drahksan left to this world, he was—most likely—the most powerful. And yet, three upstart mutts along with the two of purer blood who had recently fled from him... together they might pose a challenge for him. Though that would be only if he didn't have his minions nearby. He had been bestowing power upon the most loyal of his followers ever since the god Davul had chosen him as his vessel upon this world.

It was still something Lucian couldn't quite fathom.

In truth, he hadn't thought any of the gods truly existed.

He'd begun this cult in the name of Davul of the south-winds because it suited him and the powers he'd then possessed. Lucian had always been strong in the realm of storm; he could summon raging winds and lightning, hail, rains, or so much worse. Since many in these lands had worshiped Davul to begin with, he'd used their foolishness against them, claiming to be the god's right hand, sent to build up the most powerful nation in the world. The people had eaten it up, especially since he'd focused the religion on the outpouring of passion. His ritual orgies had been a fixture in these lands for over three hundred years now. But a little over a hundred years ago, something had changed.

He'd been contacted by some higher power. He had no way to describe the immensity of influence he'd felt upon that touch to his mind and soul. He'd known in that instant, that the gods were indeed real. Davul had reached out to him, giving him expanded powers over earth, air, fire, and water, primal abilities... *and* the knowledge for how to bind these powers to certain precious stones: diamond for earth, pearl for water, ruby for fire, sapphire for air. He'd used that to begin rewarding the most loyal of his followers with rings imbued with power. Now he had a small army of minions, completely faithful to him and empowered with elemental rings to do his bidding.

He hadn't been able to create any rings with his own powers over storm. Only the powers given to him by Davul could be passed on to others.

Lucian had no clue why Davul had chosen him for such a reward, but he wasn't about to question it. He had obeyed—to a point—the voice which spoke into his mind. It seemed the god didn't much care about the few instances when he had done his own thing instead. Though, to be fair, the god's wishes were mostly in line with his own, and the more gruesome requests, the sacrifices, were something with which Lucian was more than happy to oblige.

He turned his face up to the heavens to speak to his god now. *Davul, most holy of the gods, Sovereign Southern Gale and Master of Passions, I seek thee.* The titles and flowery language weren't required, but Lucian had always had a flair for the dramatic. He'd insisted on such extravagant names for himself when his followers addressed him.

Yes, my loyal son? The voice was deep and resonant, echoing into his mind, filling him with its power and authority. Lucian shivered at the sensation.

There are those who threaten my power. The drahksani who had been loyal to me have betrayed me and now two of them ally with three more from the north. I may need more of your power to repel them from our sacred lands.

Lucian got a distinct sense of displeasure.

Odd. It was the first time he'd sensed anything like that from the divinity.

I have given you all the power I can. You possess realms of drahksani ability far beyond your own and have many minions to aid you. If you are not able to protect yourself, perhaps you are not worthy of such gifts.

Lucian went a little cold. *Am I not your most loyal follower?* he prodded.

You are but one follower. That was also something new. Were there others upon whom Davul had bestowed such gifts? *And you have lost my loyal daughter, your own child. Even now she resists me. This cannot be, Lucian. Return her to my fold and you shall have all of my power at your command. I can still sense her, even though she is hidden from you. I shall contact you again soon with more instructions on where and when to retrieve her.*

Oh, so that was it. Interesting. This was the first time

Davul had ever made such a focus on Astria. It was true the god had been urging him to make sure Astria was fully engaged with Lucian's choice of religion, to bring her closer to Davul. But now it seemed the truth came out. Somehow, Astria was more important to the god's plans than Lucian.

This was a disturbing realization. Lucian did not much like being overlooked in such a way, but at least he now knew the mind of his god.

I await your command, my lord. She will worship you. It is my promise.

Make sure she does. Then the god was gone and the sense of power engulfing Lucian with it.

So, the god was more interested in Astria than himself.

Lucian could use that.

But first he needed his daughter back.

This might change his plans. He'd need to talk to Syasha. He summoned the high winds to wind-talk with his minions once more.

After that he'd go down to his dungeons, to visit the man who had once been his son. A little torture always helped to make Lucian feel better.

5

ASTRIA DIDN'T KNOW WHERE SHE WAS GOING. SHE KNEW THE lands around her well enough, could sense the structures within the earth, the rise and fall of the hills and where the forest ended. Her water sense told her where the small stream she followed joined with a much larger river not far ahead. The air around her was moist, thick with the potential for rain, though the heavy clouds overhead were holding off for now. It would rain shortly. She wasn't much concerned; she could keep the waters from bothering her. Yet, as much as her senses could give her a clear picture of the lands around her, she still didn't know where to go.

She'd run away from her mother and uncle and those other drahksani, but had no real sense of direction. She just knew she needed to get away from her father… and distance herself from her mother to protect the woman, to protect all of the others. They would all be safer without her nearby. She didn't like it, but that was the way it had to be.

She missed her mother and Uncle Donallo already. They had always been there to help her, even after she'd mostly learned her powers. Though, to be fair, it hadn't been that long since the day she'd finally felt... comfortable with what she could do.

Though comfortable wasn't the right word at all. These powers, everything she could do, it all felt so wrong, too much. She didn't want any of it, but at least now she knew how to control the various abilities well enough to survive on her own.

Even if she didn't want to be on her own.

"It's safer for them," she said aloud to reassure herself that running away had been the right decision.

And yet...

What would she do? Where would she go? She'd have no one. And that... that made her feel so very alone.

"It's safer," she said again, a whisper, jaw tense, tears welling. "I had to."

But where did that leave her?

With her multitude of powers... and nothing else.

She had always possessed a heightened awareness. Her childhood had not been like other children's. She'd been far too cognizant of the ebb and flow of power around her—both the power possessed by people, and those of the drahksan and Davul.

Yes my child? She'd made a mistake; thinking of the god could summon him easily enough. She should have been more careful with her thoughts. *You really should return to your father. He is worried for you.*

Go away! I don't want you here! She surged her mental powers to keep him out of her mind and was able to push him out... for now.

Yet still some distant thought of the divine being echoed back to her. *You shall need my power one day, just wait!* Then laughter, which slowly faded as the essence of the god grew more distant.

Astria shivered. It was never pleasant when He contacted her.

She stopped when she came to where the stream met the river. Concentrating for a moment, she reached back along her path, feeling through the earth to the places where her light footsteps had disturbed the mosses, grasses and dirt. She expended a little effort, to put all of that to right, erasing her passage through the forest.

Next, she summoned her water powers and stepped out onto the burbling waters of the river. The watercourse wasn't that wide, perhaps a dozen feet across at this point, but she could sense where it joined with a greater river not far downstream; the Tiska River, which passed by Rodathia.

Rodathia.

It had been her home her entire life, now she fled from it.

Where would she go? That question plagued her constantly.

For now, she only thought to go north, away from the only home she'd ever known; away from the people who loved her.

A shiver coursed through her, but she drew herself up, resolute.

Stepping upon the water as if it were solid as earth, she moved out to the middle of the river and began to walk upriver, knowing she'd be harder to track this way.

As the morning progressed, the skies cleared. She could sense another storm on the way as the brisk upper winds pushed clouds around, but for now, she'd enjoy the sun. It shone down on her through the gap in the trees created by the river and also twinkled up at her, reflecting off the rushing waters. It wasn't long before she removed her cloak and hung it over an arm.

She pondered, as she walked, how poor Volf must be feeling. Mother would be mad at him for falling asleep during his watch—and letting Astria get away. But it hadn't been his fault. She wished she could tell her mother that. Astria had feigned sleep, all the while calming Volf's emotions to dull his senses until his natural exhaustion made him succumb to slumber. Then Astria had risen and gone to the man. She'd touched him, taking his hand. It was easier to steal someone's powers if she was in physical contact with them. She knew she'd need Volf's ability to go unseen and undetected to get away from them all. His shadow-walk would also come in handy to travel significant distances quickly. Though she didn't need that one as much. She could earth-shift or wind-walk to move fast as well, although she hadn't yet mastered true flight—as her father had. It didn't much matter since wind walking tended to use less energy and was nearly as fast. Once she was clear of the forest, she'd try wind-walking. For now, she was happy with just her water-step.

A part of her felt bad for leaving. She knew Mother would be worried. They would come looking for her. But she knew it had been the right decision. They wouldn't have to worry about protecting her if they were set upon.

"They're safer," she repeated; her mantra.

And she would be alone... although... perhaps she could make her way north, to where those other three had come from... and visit the dragon! That had been a startling revelation to learn. Admittedly, she'd had to sift fairly heavily through their memories to find it. She knew Uncle Donallo wouldn't read them so deep, not initially, but Astria had been too curious. She was quite adept at using her uncle's abilities, having acquired them from him long ago, and having used them often. Through that, she'd learned a lot about the three strangers.

She hoped Caerwyn would ask Uncle Don and her mother for help with her thoughts and feelings. There would be a lot the two could do to ease the troubled mind and soul of the woman. Astria also hoped that Uncle Don would tell Caerwyn how he felt about her. It had been clear to Astria that her uncle had been quite taken with the warrior-woman the moment he saw her. He'd never shown much interest in other women and the fact that he'd warmed to Caerwyn so quickly had to mean something.

Volf and Jais were interesting, but still just 'boys' in so many ways. As much as it might be odd for a nine-year-old to think of men in their early twenties as 'boys', it seemed the best descriptor for them. It wasn't that they weren't tough or strong or capable, they were just... inexperienced. They'd seen some of the hardships of life, but only within the last few months. Astria had been living with that odd heightened awareness of hers since she was three—six years now. It had been a hard and trying life so far. She'd been forced to get stronger, wiser, smarter, and do it all at an age when other children were still playing in the mud.

A part of her mourned the loss of her childhood. Even now looking at the muddy banks of the river, a part of her wanted to stop and be carefree and get muddy. She honestly didn't know how it would feel, if it would be fun or just... dirty. She'd never had the chance to find out. Perhaps she'd give herself that opportunity in the future. But first, she had to make sure she was far from her father... and her mother.

Her heart constricted.

A tear traced her cheek. She sniffed it away.

She'd learned to be hard. She didn't much like it, but knew it would keep her safe for now; safe from Lucian and... that god.

She'd had 'that god' in her head for far too long now. He was often tricky, sadistic, and cruel. That wasn't pleasant to live with. Yet she'd been living with the divinity long enough to know how to block him out. Her uncle's powers helped. It had been the initial reason she'd stolen those powers.

Stolen wasn't a good word. It wasn't like they couldn't use their own powers when she did; she just acquired the same abilities at the same time. And after years of working with them now, she was getting to a significant strength. That's how she was able to push the god from her mind most of the time.

She had used those same powers to see into her father's mind. She'd wanted to understand him. She'd seen all the horrific things he'd done, the people he'd killed—as sacrifices or in so many other ways—and how that vile god had affected him. It seemed that her father had always been obsessed with power, but he hadn't always been a cruel man. He'd formed his 'cult' to keep people in line, true enough, but he had never hurt any of them. It hadn't been until 'that god' had contacted him, about a hundred years ago, that everything had changed. It had happened slow enough that neither Lucian nor his followers had really noticed the changes. A cult devoted to passions, who'd had their 'rituals'—where no one died—only on the solstices and equinoxes, had slowly transformed into one which sacrificed people... once a month on the night of the new moon.

Astria had been truly shaken by the transformation she'd seen in her father. It had been over a hundred years for him, but she'd seen it in the span of a few minutes and couldn't make sense of it at first. When she finally had, she'd gone to her mother that same day and told her they needed to get away from the man.

She tried to put these thoughts from her mind as she moved through the forest. The trees were lovely. She focused on them and the river over which she walked. Pausing over calmer waters, she peered down to watch the fish swimming beneath her. That brought a smile to her lips.

Though, that smile soon faded.

Too much weighed on her. Too much, bogging down the mind and soul.

She shivered and sniffed back more tears.

As the afternoon waned, she found a pleasant glade near the river to rest. She ate another meagre meal of berries, which was enough to quell her rising hunger, though she hoped she'd find something more filling on the morrow.

There she slept, laying her head on the tufts of earth, without any care for wildlife or her pursuers. She'd used a bit of her mother's power to instill the area with a strong feeling of disinterest. Anything or anyone who came here would simply leave again, not interested in what lay here. She made sure to sink enough power into it to hold it overnight. Then she slept, or… tried to, but dark thoughts whirled within her mind. She conjured images of her mother and uncle being set upon by Lucian and his minions… all the while her own voice whispered over the horrid scene: 'They're safer… safer'.

6

JAIS GREW MORE FRUSTRATED AND CONCERNED. HE HAD GROWN up tracking all manner of animals through the forests around his home. Finding one girl should have been easy! Yet she'd left hardly any tracks and was infuriatingly hard to follow. Already, three times today, he'd lost her trail and led the others the wrong direction for far too long.

At the moment he'd left the others in a clearing—the last place where he'd seen any sign of Astria—and gone in search of more evidence of her passing. He came to a stream and knelt next to it. Looking along the narrow break in the forest created by the creek, he thought he spotted something. He rose and stalked carefully along the rocky banks of the small watercourse to the branch he'd spied. It had indeed been broken off at the tip, fairly recently. There was even a small tuft of fabric caught on the end of the twig, which hung precariously from the rest of the branch. Astria had been here.

Thank all the gods, another good lead.

He knelt again. There was some mud along the side of the stream, but even though he was certain she'd had to have stepped there, he could see no prints. Had she been floating along? This was what had been making it so difficult to track her. At least now he had a fair idea where she'd been heading. He could guess that from here she'd probably followed the stream for at least a little while.

He'd go get the others and bring them here, with Volf's shadow-walk, it wouldn't take them long to make the trip.

He sighed as he rose. He knew he was falling behind in tracking her. She would be well ahead of him by now, even with her shorter legs and a child's stamina. It was already late afternoon. He was growing more and more certain he wouldn't catch up to her today. Not without a miracle.

He backtracked as fast as he could to the others, but found his mind wandering as he slipped through the forest.

All day he'd been distracted. He didn't know why it bothered him so much that Caerwyn seemed to be keeping close to Donallo, talking quietly with the other man. No, he *did* know why. It was because there was some faint spark of life in the woman that hadn't been there in months. Somehow Donallo had brought out—at least a bit of—the old Caerwyn. And Jais was angry and jealous because of it. He could recognize his own feelings well enough. He wasn't proud of them, but he knew exactly where they were coming from, after having most of a day to mull it over. He wasn't angry with Donallo, just the opposite, really. He was happy the man had found some way to reach Caerwyn.

No, Jais was angry with himself. He'd always been fairly good at judging people's emotions. He'd known how Caerwyn had been feeling, but he hadn't been able to help her. He should have tried harder to snap her out of her dark moods. Yet he didn't even know what he could have done. Which was the main reason for his anger and frustration on that matter. He should have found some way... and he hadn't. Which is why he was a little jealous of Donallo. The man had known

Caerwyn for a day and already he'd found some way to help her. It probably helped that he was a mental talent. Seeing into her thoughts would go a long way to knowing how to help her, or so Jais assumed. He tried to shake off those thoughts and feelings. They weren't useful for anything.

But he only found himself contemplating other odd matters. There was something odd in general about Donallo and Mirala. Well, not about them, so much as how they reacted to Jais. As good as Jais was at reading people, he'd picked up a lot of small signs and signals from the two. They looked at him and felt shame. Last night they'd said it was because he reminded them of someone they'd left behind, but he found that hard to believe. It wasn't that he didn't trust them. Sure, they might have left someone behind to some terrible fate. But could that person really look so much like Jais? Most of the people in these parts had darker skin than he, a well-tanned, bronze skin-tone. That and there were few people of his build. He'd never met anyone with his girth who wasn't drahksan.

That thought stopped him in his tracks.

Had the person they'd known been drahksan?

In that moment Jais really wished he could connect to the spirit-link like every other drahksani seemed to be able to do. Yet from what he'd heard the others saying there was only one other drahksan they could sense within any significant distance... and that was Lucian. Did that mean this other drahksan was dead? Or was the one they left behind not a drahksan at all? There were too many questions and he suspected there was far more to the tale than the two were saying. They still acted oddly around him, those sidelong glances filled with regret.

He reached the camp and took a moment to take in the scene, as the others looked to him. Caerwyn was still with

Donallo, close. One of the man's hands was touching her temple next to her hairline in front of her left ear. The connection seemed far too intimate for Jais' liking. Neither looked ashamed when they looked at him though, well Donallo was no more ashamed than normal.

Mirala was pacing, fidgeting. Volf was nearby leaning against a tree looking weary and dejected. The man had been trying to apologize to Mirala all day, but she'd had none of it.

"I've found another marker," Jais said. "Volf, do your thing and follow me."

The four of them were ready in an instant and up behind Jais. Now came the disorienting part. Volf was warping everything around them so they could move faster, but Jais had to lead them. This meant retracing his steps through the forest at speeds which made his mind ache. He'd gotten good enough at it, now that they'd done it a few times today. Yet still, by the time they came to the stream, he had a headache and needed a moment to steady himself.

Once the disorientation had passed, he nodded to the others and moved on, saying he'd return once he'd found more markers. They settled by the creek.

He'd see what else he could find before it was too dark to continue. Unless she'd stopped to sit in one place for a long while... he was fairly certain he wouldn't be finding Astria today.

7

THE SOFT BURBLE OF THE STREAM AND THE LATE-DAY SUN— which shone down directly upon them through the narrow crack in the trees above, following the creek's path—were both pleasant sensations as Caerwyn closed her eyes to let Donallo work.

She was surprised how much she'd opened up to him. Perhaps it was his easygoing manner and disarming smile that made it easy to speak to him. Perhaps it was her lack of history with him, which just seemed to make any interaction a little freer and open. She didn't know. He was adamant that he hadn't been using any abilities to force her to open up, though he had said he'd skimmed her thoughts a couple of times. She'd felt a little odd about that, but the fact that he'd been open about it and worried for what he'd found had dispelled most of her concerns. She was still hesitant. The idea of being manipulated by anyone, even a friend, was loathsome to her. So, she'd had her own immunity to the magic of other drahksani active for most of the day.

After talking with him for that long, she'd found just a hint of her old self returning. It was some breath of confidence, or perhaps a lessening of the doubt, or a bit of something to fill the hollow sensation within her. She didn't know exactly what it was, but she felt better than she had in months! It was the only reason why she felt she could allow him to take a deeper look within her thoughts.

But by all the gods, how that idea terrified her. She was ready to clamp down her magical barrier if she even suspected any foul play by the man. More than that, though, she was shaken by the idea of having those old thoughts and memories dredged up once more. And yet...

When he'd started to reach within her mind, before Jais had returned and moved them, she hadn't felt anything change at all. They'd only had a few moments before being interrupted by Jais, but it hadn't felt bad.

So, when Donallo leaned in once again, now that they were settled by this stream, she felt ever-so-slightly more at ease.

His voice was soft and low, comforting. He was repeating what he'd said when he'd begun last time. "I will start only with surface thoughts. I'll let you know as I work deeper. Tell me if you start to feel at all uncomfortable and we'll stop."

She nodded as he brushed back her short-cropped hair at her temple with a light touch.

And once again, she noticed... nothing.

He gave a light laugh. "You don't trust me. I don't blame you. From what Mirala said, you've suffered some deep trauma. Even just on the surface, I can see it. Your thoughts are constantly returning to trust, manipulation, and something to do with the north... and a wizard? And... oh!" His hand left her temple. "I'm sorry Caerwyn. For an instant you thought about something you were trying not to think about. Yet I still caught a bit of it."

She opened her eyes. He was close, those soft brown eyes,

in his kind face, about a foot distant from her own. He seemed sorry.

He lowered his voice. "You thought about... the dragon."

She nodded. Of course she had. She kept her voice low as well, yet added a heavy dose of lethality when she whispered: "I hope I can trust you with that information. If you do anything to indicate, you aren't worthy of my trust... I will end you." She gave him a nasty smile. "You've probably seen enough of my thoughts to know that is not an idle threat and I have the means to follow through on it."

He nodded but didn't seem concerned at all. "I'll do my best to prove myself worthy of such knowledge." His gaze on hers was sincere, intense, unwavering.

"Good," she said softly.

"May I continue? Are there other things I should know?"

She shook her head. "No, that would have been the only secret that wasn't truly mine to keep. You may continue."

He nodded and reached for her temple again. She closed her eyes and tried to still her mind.

She felt the brush of his fingers, then his low words: "I'm going to seek your memories on this wizard, are you well with that?"

No.

"Yes."

"Are you sure?"

Of course, he could read her thoughts. "No, not at all, but if this is what it takes to get me back to normal, then I'll do it."

"Let me know if I touch anything I shouldn't, and I'll back out again."

Oh, she would.

Now, she did feel something. Thoughts she'd kept suppressed were brought back to her. She shuddered, but to reassure Donallo, she quickly said, "It's well, keep going." She just hoped this would actually help her in some way.

"Oh, gods..." Donallo breathed the words, full of sympathy. "I'm so sorry!"

Even just those words, as she felt the scene from the dragon's cave flash through her mind, were soothing to her. For a heartbeat only, she relived the memory of having to choose who would die at that crazed man's hands. The helplessness of knowing that no matter what she did, someone would die. Then... the dragon's death as well.

Donallo's hand lifted away. "I think that is more than enough," he whispered.

Caerwyn heard soft footfalls drawing near. She opened her eyes again to see Mirala standing over her. The woman was looking down in concern.

"You were experiencing..." The woman seemed lost for words. Then she knelt next to Caerwyn. "I can help sooth your emotions, if you'll let me."

Caerwyn nodded. She would very much appreciate that.

Mirala touched Caerwyn's hand and instantly Caerwyn felt a warm, comforting sensation fill her, driving away the fear, doubt, self-loathing, and so many other dark emotions.

Caerwyn drew in a long breath as it happened and by the end of that inhalation, felt substantially better. She blinked. In truth, she felt far better than she had in months!

"Thank you," she said to Mirala, capturing the woman's hand to give it a quick squeeze. "Thank you."

Donallo was sitting on his haunches before Caerwyn. "There's a lot there to work with. I may need some time to sort it out. But if you'll let me, I would like to help you with this, to put these thoughts to rest, as best you are able."

"Yes, I would like that." So very much. But she had to ask. "Why are you helping me? You've only known me for a day."

Donallo and Mirala shared a look. It was she who answered. "It's what we do. It's what our gifts are best suited for."

Just as Caerwyn's were best suited for fighting... for protecting others.

Protecting.

She shuddered.

Mirala's hand, still grasped within her own, clutched hold a little tighter and Caerwyn felt another surge of soothing within her.

"What was that?" Mirala asked.

"I think..." What did she think? It was still a mostly unformed thought. She needed time to figure it out. "I think I need a little time alone, thank you, thank you both." She smiled up at Mirala, then nodded to Donallo. Mirala released her and Caerwyn rose.

"If you need anything we're here," Mirala said with a faint smile. It must have been difficult for the woman to find any sort of peace or joy with her daughter still missing.

Caerwyn nodded again and moved a little way off, down the stream.

What had she come across within her thoughts? It had hit a very sensitive spot within her when she'd thought of... protecting people.

There it was again, that faint shudder and tension at forming those words in her mind.

Why was she so caught up with that word? Was it something Donallo had dragged up from her memories?

Caerwyn sat slowly to try to figure out her own thoughts. So much was dancing around in her head at the moment, so much of the past.

What did this all mean? Why did she react to thinking about protecting people?

She concentrated on that word: protection.

Protecting others… Another shudder ran through her. She saw Elria in her mind's eye, someone she hadn't been able to protect.

And with that simple thought a great weight of knowledge cascaded down upon her. She realized that her entire being had been formed around the idea of protecting people.

And it had started when she'd been so very young.

She hadn't been able to protect her parents, but she'd been just a scared little girl. She'd run away and a part of her had hated herself for it. That same part, sometime later on had hardened with the certainty that she would never let such things happen to herself or those she cared about ever again.

Slowly, as the sun sank in the sky and the shadows lengthened and darkness descended, Caerwyn put together the varied pieces of this epiphany she'd had.

She'd made some form of inner vow, to protect others. It was why she'd trained so hard once she'd been adopted by her foster father, the Afgenni Prince. It had formed the core of who she'd become as a general. It had suffered and become harder still when she'd lost most of her men the day she had saved Barami's life so long ago. She'd not known it, but she'd vowed then and there to protect him too, just as he had made the same vow for her. *That* was why leaving him in the north had been so hard on her! She couldn't keep the vow she'd made to him… one which she hadn't even known she'd made!

It was also why what happened with the wizard had hit her so hard. She hadn't been able to protect everyone. And for whatever reason, that group of people had been so much more important to protect, including the dragon.

And when she'd failed that day, she'd lost her faith in the one thing which had formed her entire personality and purpose!

"Oh, gods," she breathed heavily. "Ohhhh!"

For a moment she just sat with this full realization falling into place for her.

Had it been Donallo's searching within her mind that had revealed this?

Perhaps.

It might be that his digging into things she'd wanted to hide from herself had jarred this piece of knowledge loose.

For a long time she sat with what she now knew.

Night fell.

This all made so much sense! And as much as this knowledge had added a significant weight to her mind and soul... she also felt... hope. For the first time in months she thought perhaps she could see some way out of the darkness in which she'd been mired. The solution was blatantly before her now: she couldn't protect everyone. She couldn't accept that, not yet, but at least she now knew what it was she had to accept, what would lift her from her current state.

"Gods." She blew out a long, steadying breath.

She needed to talk to Donallo again.

Now.

She rose and turned to where the others were, running into Donallo. They bounced off each other harmlessly, both flinching back in the same instant. In the growing dark, she hadn't seen him.

Then they were both talking at once, their words muddled. Caerwyn hadn't even been entirely certain what she'd said.

Donallo paused, expectant.

"I was coming to see you," Caerwyn said. It sounded inane to her ears now that the words were out.

He gave a half-smile. "And I you. Mirala said that despite your request to be alone, you were going through something profound and perhaps might need someone just… to be nearby."

Yes. So very much, that was exactly what she needed. She wanted to embrace him… or Mirala, they were both just so understanding! Caerwyn didn't understand why or how these people cared so much for a complete stranger.

Caerwyn found herself nodding, and suddenly emotions she'd kept repressed for so very long were welling up within her: yearning for contact and comfort, vulnerability, fear of being truly alone.

"Thank you," she said, though it wasn't easy to speak, as she was growing more and more choked up. She did step in then and embrace him.

He remained still for a time before his arms slowly moved to wrap around her, chaste and supporting.

He whispered, for they were quite close now. "If you want to talk about whatever it is you're going through, I'm here." He wasn't even reading her. He didn't know what she was going through. He expected her to tell him, to let him in. He was a true gentleman.

She choked on a sob then. For a moment she tried to keep back the tears, as part of her looked harshly upon such weakness. But another part, which had been buried for so very long—a part that sounded so much like her mother's voice—said that it wasn't weakness to fully express one's emotions. So, she wept.

There they stood, Donallo holding her, for a long time.

The moon shone brightly down upon them when finally she'd cried herself out and she'd released him. She knew she must look a mess, eyes red, nose running, yet he smiled to look upon her.

"Feel better?" he asked.

She nodded. "And I think I will tell you everything, but I

need a little time to let it settle and understand it myself." She gave him a weak smile. "I've had a rather big realization and I just need a little time to let it... settle a little." She was repeating herself.

He nodded.

They stood there, together, in the growing dimness. Caerwyn, looking upon this man—who she had only known for not more than a couple score hours—finally saw him. Gone was her mistrust of him. He was what he claimed to be, an honest and good man, who only wanted to help others. She was sure of that now.

"Donallo, I—" She cut off sharply as she thought she heard something. It was quite distant. She cocked her head to one side to listen more intently.

Donallo did the same thing.

"Did you hear that?" she asked softly, still trying to hear the sound again.

"No, but I sense minds out there in the forest, approaching from the way we came."

Somehow Caerwyn knew this couldn't be good.

"I can go see who it is," she offered.

He shook his head. "No, I'll have a better sense of their minds in just a moment if they get much closer. I'll know who they are and what they want."

So, she waited, there in the darkness, with a man she was coming to admire greatly, even if he wasn't a warrior.

8

Mirala couldn't sit, nor stand still. She paced along the bank of the small creek, her steps light and easy. She'd always had a natural balance and grace, which could have been how she was made, or a part of her drahksani heritage. It didn't truly matter, but she could easily move over the wet and mossy stones without slipping or falling.

Astria was out there somewhere, alone. Mirala was fairly certain of that now. The girl hadn't been taken, she'd run off on her own. It had been a simple process of deduction once Mirala had thought about it. Astria was powerful in her own right. The only one who'd be able to take the girl by force would be her father. No human would have been able to steal her away. And it would have had to be a human since she felt no other drahksani around. There was the faint possibility that someone like Volf, with his ability to hide his spirit-link, might have taken Astria, but that seemed unlikely. There were few enough drahksani left in the world as it was. For another like Volf to have just happened upon them, would be nearly inconceivable.

But that didn't explain why Astria had vanished from the spirit-link herself.

Unless...

It had been a suspicion Mirala had held for some time now. It seemed absurd, but it would explain a lot. There were things the girl could do, which she shouldn't be able to do. She'd had powers come out of nowhere, like the sudden ability to hide her spirit-link. It would all make sense if Astria was somehow able to... borrow and use the powers of others. Yet, as far as Mirala knew, there was no precedent for such a thing. None of the drahksani realms of power held such an ability. Yet it would explain so much.

Astria had always been odd. As young as three years old she'd seemed far too aware of things around her. She hadn't played with toys or dolls. She'd wanted to learn and under-stand the world. She'd spent a lot of time with teachers, or following Mirala and Donallo around. She'd started to say things which made no sense, things she shouldn't have known. The most recent had been when she'd come to Mirala to tell her that her father was evil and they needed to leave. That had shocked Mirala profoundly. Not because she didn't already know this, but because of the blunt simplicity of the statement of truth from a nine-year-old girl. If Astria had somehow been using her uncle's abilities she'd have been able to find out about Lucian quite easily.

The implications of Astria being able to borrow people's powers like that was... not one Mirala wanted to consider. It would be a shift in everything she'd ever known about drahksan.

"Mirala." The soft, tentative voice broke her from her thoughts, but only served to raise her ire. Volf had been apol-ogizing all day. It seemed she was about to have another bout of it.

"Mirala, I'm so sorry." There it was. Volf drew close beside her. She didn't look at him. That would only encourage him.

"Go away, Volf. I don't want to hear it. Not now." That was the truth. She still blamed the man for letting Astria get away. Even if Astria had run off all on her own, which meant that—potentially—the girl had put the man to sleep. Mirala didn't want to think about that option, even if it seemed more and more likely. The girl must have subdued Volf then stolen the man's powers to remain hidden. Mirala had no idea why Astria would do that and was so very worried for her. It meant Volf wasn't to blame, but still.

"Volf, please just give me some room. I'm... I'm not upset with you... anymore. I just need some time and space. Please."

He nodded and slipped away, ever quiet.

Mirala sighed and finally, drained and tired, sat on a large rock next to the stream. She put her head in her hands and tried to calm herself. She dug deep within herself to bring peace to her emotions. She could help others with such serenity easily, but for herself, it always seemed that much harder to find.

"Astria, please, come back to me." She whispered the words, but also sent them out on a wave of emotions. She hoped her daughter would feel the emotions associated with the words and heed the call. Astria would be able to respond with her own powers over emotion, though Mirala didn't know if the girl knew how. Yet Mirala suspected there was little that girl didn't know about her own powers.

Mirala sat there in the darkness, waiting.

When Jais had said that he could track Astria, that he'd grown up as a tracker and forester, Mirala had had hope that they'd find Astria quickly. But it seemed Jais wasn't as good as he claimed. He kept losing Astria's trail.

Mirala was glad the bulky young man wasn't sticking

around though. It hurt far too much to look at him. She'd been shocked when she'd first seem him. There had been a moment of hope that perhaps Andrei had survived the confrontation with Lucian in the south, but then she'd seen the differences between Jais and Andrei. As much as the face was nearly identical, along with that shaggy, unkempt hair, the build was different. Jais was shorter, stocky, where Andrei was tall, though just as broad. The dissimilarities seemed so minor compared to the similarities. Mirala couldn't understand how this man from the north could appear to be so similar to Lucian's son.

Though that wasn't the truth. Andrei wasn't Lucian's son. He'd been adopted and raised by the man, but he wasn't Lucian's blood. And the horrible thing was, Lucian had killed the boy's parents when Andrei had been just a babe, then taken the child to raise as his own. Lucian had some sick fascination with having drahksani children. It had caused the man to steal and raise Andrei, then had prompted him to have a child with Mirala.

Mirala didn't want to think about that. It always disgusted her. As much as she loved her daughter, she never wanted to think about how the girl had been conceived or who her father was.

"Someone's coming!" Donallo said, drawing near. Mirala hadn't looked up, but she knew that voice and could hear his running footfalls.

Mirala's first thought was that Jais was returning, but Donallo sounded too worried for that to be the case.

"Who is it?" she asked finally looking up. Donallo looked genuinely distressed.

"It's Syasha and a group from the cult. They've come for us!"

"Lansus have mercy, no!"

Donallo nodded. "They'll be here shortly. We must prepare."

Mirala had been trained in a little sword work and hand fighting, enough to defend herself against any average attacker, but she was no warrior. She could project emotions into people, but that had differing degrees of success, depending on the person and their dedication to their cause. She was more effective if she could touch someone, but she wouldn't want to get that close to an attacker.

She looked past Donallo to Caerwyn, who was strapping on a shield, ready for battle. Volf had his sword out, taking a few test swipes, loosening up. Donallo knew how to use the blade at his hip, but something told Mirala this fight wouldn't go well in general.

She reached out through the spirit-link to Jais, who was some distance away. She sent an emotional call through the spirit-link to the man, but she didn't know if he'd receive it. Apparently, he had some block to the spirit-link.

She rose slowly. "I'll do what I can," she said softly.

"They're coming!" Caerwyn called out. Mirala could hear several people moving quickly through the woods. A moment later, the enemy's attacks became evident. The air grew chill, freezing, blasting down on them. Earth rose up, rumbling beneath them, and water surged from the stream to stab out at them with frozen spikes.

Mirala evaded these attacks with her usual grace, but even as she was going to push fear at the attackers, she felt something.

It was distant, but she knew what it was the instant she felt it. *Do not worry for me, Mother. I will be well on my own.* Astria's response to Mirala's emotional sending, stunned her. It didn't come across in words, so much as a certainty of feeling that Mirala could interpret easily.

Yet she'd stayed still for too long.

A lance of icy water stabbed up at her from the stream. Suddenly time slowed as Volf touched her, extending his shadow form around her and shadow walking with her. Yet, even with his enhanced speed he hadn't been able to fully get out of the way of the attack as well. She watched—in slow motion—as the ice-spear caught Volf, a glancing blow on the shoulder, spinning him around.

Time resumed its normal pace as Volf screamed and fell.

Gods! Volf!

She wanted to tend to him, but first needed to deal with these attackers. She spun and pushed fear at them with everything she had.

9

Volf didn't have Jais' ability to heal, but he knew he'd heal faster than any human. Yet that didn't stop his injury from hurting like the blazes of Holn. The ice had only stabbed across the side of his shoulder, taking a chunk out of the top of his arm, but his blood still flowed freely. He pressed his opposite hand to the wound to try to staunch the bleeding and gave a clipped cry at the pain this pressure caused. Yet that agony spiked his awareness, suddenly alert.

He'd saved Mirala, that's all that mattered.

Gritting his teeth, he rose, removing his hand and wiping it on his shirt to clean away the blood so he could draw his sword. At least it had been the shoulder of his offhand that had been hit.

Yet even as he drew his sword, the elements were rising up around them all once again: earth, water, and wind, with gouts of fire, lighting up the night.

He released a wordless cry of fury as he threw himself at the attackers.

The sane voice in his head yelled at him to run, that he

wasn't a warrior. No, he wasn't, but he had a lot of tricks he could use.

He slipped into his shadow-form and shadow-walked two steps, bringing himself to where Mirala was hiding behind a tree, cringing as one of the attackers pulled gouts of fire off a torch into his hand to throw at her. The tree behind her smoldered with a few flames licking up the opposite side.

With a couple more steps he reached the attacker and struck out, stabbing with all his terrified fury.

He knew it was coming, and he hated every jolt and jar of his arm as his blade slid into the attacker, a woman with flame-red hair. She cried out in alarm and staggered back—off Volf's blade—dropping her torch before going to her knees. Then she fell, limp and lifeless.

Volf raced back to Mirala.

"Are you well?"

She nodded. "I only scared one away with my fear. You need to help them!" Mirala pointed.

Volf turned to see Caerwyn and Donallo fighting side by side, but not doing well. They tried to advance, but the earth slid out from under them—though both had exceptional balance and remained afoot—or rose up to batter at them from all sides. In addition, icy winds howled down on them and frost rimed their hair and eyebrows. That couldn't be comfortable.

He took a step toward that fight, but a bout of weakness took him and his legs faltered. Perhaps he'd lost more blood than he'd thought. He began to fall, but was caught suddenly by strong arms.

"Take a moment," Jais said beside him. Volf felt his wound close and heal. "Regain yourself, then join us. See if you can't sneak around them and at least distract them." Then Jais released him and Volf found he could stand on his own.

Jais drew both his swords and slipped into the forest, perhaps to try to get around behind the remaining attackers.

"Do you know how many there are?" Volf asked turning back to Mirala, who was drawing up cautiously behind him.

"There were only six. One I scared away, one you dealt with. The other four are there."

Volf nodded. Well now it was four on four and his shoulder was healed. He was starting to feel good about surviving this fight.

JAIS HAD BEEN RETURNING TO THE OTHERS WHEN HE'D BEEN temporarily overwhelmed by some strange call for help from Mirala. Then he'd heard the sounds of combat. Apparently, he'd arrived just in time. He still couldn't quite believe Volf was heading towards the fight—wounded as the man had been. Jais' estimation of the man had just risen.

Jais could move quietly through the forest when he wished and used that skill now to try to get behind the attackers.

He didn't know what he'd done that might have alerted them, but it must have been something, as the earth beneath him suddenly rose skyward, sending him flying high through the trees. He collided with branches, some firmer than others, most no match for his dense frame. Still, by the time he landed he was well cut up and bruised. He groaned as he rose. His head ached. It had met, quite unpleasantly, with several thick branches and at least one tree trunk. He raised a hand to his head to try to stop it from spinning.

Some tremor in the ground below him gave him the barest of warnings. Jais dove to one side to avoid being tossed again. Yet this time the attack was different. Two slabs of earth on either side slammed up to crush him—had he remained where he was. He kept moving, trying to be light on his feet. It was clear to him now that if someone could control the earth, they could probably feel where he stepped upon it. He jumped, grasping branches and clinging to trees. He didn't know if that would help him avoid the earth-bound attacker or not, but it was worth a try. It seemed to work, as no more earthen attacks came at him.

He took a moment to catch his breath and heal himself. Then he was on the move again. As much as possible he swung through the trees back to where the fight occurred. Luckily, he had a surprise attack he could use once he was close enough to see one of the attackers.

Jais spoke with his father's spirit within his sword: *Are you ready, Father?*

I am, came the eager reply.

THIS MAGIC WAS DIFFERENT. CAERWYN'S IMMUNITY TO drahksani abilities didn't seem to apply to the powers these people wielded. It was something else. She didn't have time to ponder this at the moment though. The down draft of frigid air upon her hadn't ceased and Caerwyn shivered despite usually being quite warmed by most fights. She'd managed, though it hadn't been easy—and she was already quite well fatigued and battered from attacks of earth and air—to get close to one of the attackers, a woman. This one seemed to be surrounded by some shield of strong winds. Caerwyn's attacks slowed as they drew near the woman, as if moving through water. She had to push hard for her attacks to hit home. She'd scored a couple light hits, but that shield was keeping most of her attacks at bay, especially as she grew more and more weary.

Donallo, thankfully, was nimble and quick, which seemed all that was saving him. He'd managed to close distance with another of the attackers, one who controlled earth. Donallo's dance around the man was all that was keeping massive slabs of stone from crushing him. It also meant, however, that he wasn't doing a whole lot of damage at the moment, having to concentrate on defense. And there were still two other attackers working away on them as well: another wielder of earth and air each.

Caerwyn had also surmised, from the way her opponent was barking orders, that the woman before her was the leader of this group. If she could just take the woman down, this fight might end!

She commanded Davlas to fly around behind the woman. Yet the wind-shield of her opponent must have fully encompassed her, as that attack was pushed to one side as well. Davlas would be mostly useless in this fight. If Caerwyn was going to get through that swirling mass of air, she'd have to do it with brute force.

Yet before she could act, the woman shifted her attack. Instead of blasting wind down on Caerwyn, she blasted it directly at her. Suddenly bits of debris, dirt and small stones, flew at her, peppering her face.

She couldn't see for a moment, before recalling one of her powers she rarely used, one which had been revealed to her by the dragon in the north: echolocation. She could use the sounds of what was happening around her to determine where things were. She closed her eyes and focused on that. Turning slightly, she knew her attacker was directly in front of her.

Caerwyn surged her strength. She would pay for this with fatigue later, but it was needed now. She drove through the winds and struck at the woman. Suddenly that shield wasn't so hard to get through. Her next two slashes cut ribbons off the woman's cloak and clothes, though the woman was deft enough to avoid most of the damage from the blows.

Caerwyn pressed her advantage.

A part of her felt a rush at this fight. She might not be her old self, but this... this action, defending and protecting others, using all her abilities to fight a worthy foe, this was what she was meant for.

With that sense of purpose, she pushed onward. The woman before her was dancing back now. The blasts of wind at Caerwyn ceased. She hoped this meant her assailant was weakening. Caerwyn opened her eyes once again and lunged in, keeping the pressure on, raining down blows upon the shield of air around the woman. A few more slipped through, but again, only succeeded in shallow cuts. That said, the woman wasn't looking so good anymore.

Then a blazing beam of light lit the night somewhere off to Caerwyn's right. She paused. Was that an enemy? The answer came to her quick enough. No, she'd seen that before. It was some special attack of Jais' father's sword. Hopefully that meant another enemy was out of the fight.

"Davul's Mercy!" This from Caerwyn's attacker.

Caerwyn whirled about to see the woman flying up through the trees.

"Suur's sweaty sack!" Caerwyn swore. She'd really wanted to finish that woman but wouldn't be able to fly after her.

She turned and ran back to help the others before exhaustion took her.

She arrived in time to see Volf and Donallo both working on one of the men, the same one Donallo had been fighting earlier. Even as she watched, Volf scored a slight hit on the man's back, which distracted him enough for Donallo to run him through.

Yet one more remained. Caerwyn only just spotted the enemy through the trees. He'd been hiding and was readying an attack now, arms outstretched toward where Volf and Donallo stood.

The man wasn't that far away, but there were a lot of trees between Caerwyn and the attacker. She'd have trouble getting there quickly, but...

"Davlas!" she called out and the spear followed her mental command, flying through the trees toward the man. His concentration was on the other two. So, he was probably surprised to have her spear skewer his head, or more likely he never had time to be surprised at all. He fell limp. The forest became eerily quiet.

That was it.

The fatigue Caerwyn knew would come hadn't hit her yet. Her blood pumped hard from the thrill of the fight. That same part of her that had rediscovered her purposed earlier latched on to this heady sensation and Caerwyn found herself genuinely smiling for the first time in what seemed like a lifetime. She was full of life and energy and actually felt a spark of joy!

And she knew exactly who was to thank.

She hurried over to Donallo. He was quite surprised to find her lips on his, as she threw her arms around him. The kiss was fierce, and full, and passionate, though more from the ardor of battle than anything else.

His eyes were wide when she drew away.

"Thank you!" she said, her face close to his. "Thank you so much! Without you, I never would have... It doesn't matter. I'm feeling more like myself than I have in ages and that's because of you."

Some distant thought bubbled up to her in her fervor. Something she'd wanted, then denied herself. For a moment her mind battled itself as to whether she'd say anything. But in the end, she decided she wouldn't deny herself any longer. The battle-fervor that filled her drove her to decisive action. She kissed him again, quickly, then stepped away, taking one of his hands as she did.

"Come with me, I need you to help me make a child."

10

JAIS MADE HIS WAY SLOWLY BACK TO THE OTHERS, FEELING drained. He'd used a lot of healing on himself and a little on Volf. He could go on, he was far from exhausted, but he was hoping most of the others were well enough.

He arrived at the edge of the trees in time to see Caerwyn throw herself at Donallo.

That stunned him, as it seemed to stun Donallo as well. That kiss she gave the man… Jais didn't think she did that sort of thing. She'd always been methodical and calculating, not passionate… well not like this anyway.

Then she was taking Donallo's hand and Jais caught her words. "Come with me, I need you to help me make a child."

Jais blinked.

Really?

Now?

With him?

Why?

What had Jais missed?

Yet it seemed Donallo had some shred of decency within

him. The man resisted Caerwyn's pull and released her hand. "No, Caerwyn."

She spun back on him. "Yes, and now, before I collapse into a sleep I probably won't come out of for a half a day! I want a child again. You've seen my thoughts. You know how I so wanted one once. And right now, I want it with you. You've done so much for me, and well yes, this would be for me as well, but I'm fairly certain you'll enjoy it."

Donallo smiled and there was a hint of mischief in that grin. "I'm sure I would, yes. But you're fragile right now and still excited from the heat of battle. If this is something you really want, then it can wait until you are a bit more sound of mind. If you still want it then..." He hesitated, letting out a long breath. "Then, we can talk."

Gods!

Jais turned away, teeth grinding. He stalked a little way back into the forest. He couldn't bear to hear any more. Everything he'd heard just made him cringe. He was so angry and frustrated and...

"Ugh!" He let out the quiet grunt through his clenched teeth.

Why did that man have to be so... chivalrous and... civilized! It would be so much easier to hate him if he'd been crass and selfish. And Jais wanted to hate Donallo in this moment.

And why was Caerwyn throwing herself at the man? She'd known him for little more than a day! What had he done to help her? Jais had been off searching for the man's niece all day, and in that time, somehow, Caerwyn seemed to have been brought out of whatever funk she'd been in since the north! Why couldn't Jais have helped her like that? Caerwyn hadn't ever let him close enough to even try to help her! What was it about Donallo that was so special?

Jais' head snapped up as he realized... Donallo could read

minds. Maybe he could affect them too. Maybe he had somehow manipulated Caerwyn into... No, if he'd been the manipulator, then he wouldn't have refused her offer. It genuinely seemed like he'd helped her! And all in just one day!

Jais stalked a little farther away from the others. Right now, he wanted to be alone. Perhaps this was his place, his fate, to be alone, always on the outside. He didn't know who he was, like it seemed Donallo did, and perhaps Jais never would. He would always be wondering, wandering, uncertain, unable to be with...

He stopped, frozen in the woods at that last thought.

To be with... Caerwyn.

But then... that wasn't really anything new, was it? He thought back. It wasn't easy in this state of heightened emotions, so he tried to calm himself a little. This was important.

When he'd met Caerwyn back in Klasten's Green he'd been focused on Alnia. He'd been quite smitten with the girl he'd known his entire life and she'd been intent on him as well. Yet even through that, when he'd gotten to know Caerwyn, he'd felt a certain... something. It had started as a kinship. She was like him, drahksan, different. His aunt had been telling him he was different his entire life, that he'd never fit in with the other villagers—of which Alnia was one. And that had turned out to be true. The town had turned on him as soon as they'd discovered he was drahksan. Well, all but Alnia. She had truly loved him, but she had died in the fight against the krolls.

Gods, how he missed her.

And afterward, when Caerwyn had told him she wished for a child, he'd found that idea... appealing. But Caerwyn hadn't wanted a man to take care of the child, no family, no connections, just the child. And Jais hadn't understood that.

He'd declined to give her what she desired because he wasn't sure he could keep himself that separated from the child. He didn't understand why Caerwyn wouldn't want to be... with him. And yet, some part of him had realized then that the idea of being with Caerwyn was far from unpleasant. Alnia had been soft and warm, whereas Caerwyn was hard and cold, yet what they shared was an impassioned desire and intelligence. It was that which had appealed to him. Add to that the sense of unity he felt with Caerwyn and for a while he'd considered her an ideal mate. He had been content to wait until she wanted, not only the child, but the husband to go with it.

But then...

Then he'd met Elria, the dronnegir woman of the north. She had been part Alnia, soft and warm of body, and yet part Caerwyn, hard and fierce of spirit. She'd seemed ideal and he'd felt a certain kinship with her as well. She shared his ability to heal, though she'd come by it differently. But like him, she was generally outcast from 'human' society. He had only known her a short time, but in that time, he'd come to think he could spend his life with her. Caerwyn had not changed her mind about wanting a husband, and Jais had begun to wonder: what if she never did?

But that was then, before Elria had died as well.

And yet...

He was starting to see a pattern. Perhaps it was just... who he was. He loved fiercely, throwing himself into such things with abandon, whether or not it was wise. It was something he knew about himself, even if it didn't help him right now.

After Elria's death, he'd mourned for some time, months. When his emotions had settled, he'd become concerned for Caerwyn, so maudlin and unlike herself. She was a fixture in his life, despite having only been a part of it for a few months. It seemed he'd known her forever. Yet he'd not been able to help her. She'd not let him, and if he was honest, he hadn't pushed her too hard either.

He sat heavily, knees close, elbows on knees, head in hands.

A heavy sigh escaped him.

He hadn't truly realized when they'd been travelling south, but it was clear to him now, that he'd admired Caerwyn since he'd first met her. And now... she was more. But she hadn't wanted him like that, and still didn't as far as he knew.

And now it seemed he'd waited too long to speak his mind. Now she seemed to have designs on Donallo.

Though in truth, perhaps that was just to give her a child and nothing more as well. Had she really changed? If she hadn't... perhaps it would be best for Donallo to oblige her in that desire. Jais was still fairly certain he'd not be able to keep his distance from his own son or daughter. He'd want a part in raising them. He wanted a family.

A part of him knew he should just tell Caerwyn how he felt. Even if she still didn't want the same thing, at least he'd have been honest and up-front with her.

But he couldn't bring himself to do it now.

He was too tired and she seemed to be as well. The question that plagued him as he sat in the dark with thoughts and emotions churning within him was: Would there ever be a right time?

No, the real question was: would he ever be brave enough?

And that... he just didn't know.

11

ASTRIA WOKE EARLY AND WAS ON HER WAY QUICKLY, WALKING once more along the river. As such, she emerged from the forest just as the sun was cresting the horizon in the east. It was a beautiful clear day.

Beyond, to the north, lit by the new-day sun, were fields and scattered farmlands. She was well to the west of the main road. Out here, there were only a few villages dotting the country-side.

She left the river and struck out across the fields.

Without warning, winds suddenly gripped her tighter than any bonds, a giant fist of air holding her, and she was lifted off the ground.

She yelped in surprise and fear, even as she realized what was happening. This was her father. She'd thought herself hidden from him with Volf's Shadow-form, specifically the part which hid her from the spirit-link. Yet he must have used some other means to find her. The cocoon of air spun her slowly to face her father as he strode from behind some trees at the edge of the forest.

She went cold, trembling. Her father's temper was not to

be raised. She'd run away and had no clue what he'd do to her now. Her gut churned with unabashed terror.

"You have been a very bad girl, Astria. You will return with me to Rodathia, to... Davul. He has plans for you and I mean to make sure I am a part of them."

That was the last thing she wanted. Yet, even as her fear sought to overwhelm her and she struggled against the windborne restraints, she knew it was useless. Her father's stormhold was too strong. For a moment she thought to use her powers against her father, but dismissed that idea as soon as it came. She might have had her elemental powers her entire life, but he'd had his for longer. He was stronger than her, though not as much now as he used to be. She knew her power now nearly rivaled his... but it wouldn't be enough to get away from him.

She could try to use powers he didn't possess, her own soul abilities, or her borrowed powers from Uncle Donallo, but in truth there was little they could do. Both of those powers tended to need subtlety to work. They were better for indirect influence, when a foe wasn't expecting a fight.

She was caught, helpless, and at that her terrified trembling only increased.

"Father, please I—"

"No excuses!" he snapped. She flinched at the heat of his words. Her heart pounded with dread, not knowing what would happen next. "You will return with me and you'll like it!"

She knew that tone and knew the best thing would be to submit. Through her frenzied fears a part of her mind knew she'd just have to wait for her chance to get away from the man once again.

"Yes, Father, as you wish."

"Good, I'm glad you know your place, girl." With these

words Lucian lifted from the ground and brought her with him as he rose higher, above the trees. Then they were moving swiftly, flying on rushing winds which hurried them through the sky. The forest blurred below them and was gone far too quickly. Their speed was intense. In just two hours they passed over all the lands which it had taken her and her mother and uncle days to traverse. The morning was only just fully in bloom as they touched down at the governor's estate overlooking Rodathia.

Astria was still bound by air, and she was kept that way and made to follow along behind Lucian as he entered the estates.

If you had not run from me, or returned as I'd asked, you would not be a prisoner now. She flinched, startled at Davul's sudden intrusion, so frayed were her nerves with fear and dismay.

Tired and hungry, Astria didn't want to spend the energy to push the god out of her mind. Instead, she used this opportunity to discover more about the being. After the voice had first come to her, she'd studied everything her father had on Davul. What she'd found hadn't matched with the sense which accompanied this voice. She'd had a theory for some time that this being wasn't Davul at all, but something using that god's name. Lucian had bought into the fraud, but she hadn't. So, every now and then, she tried to tease out what she could from this being.

I am sorry, master.

That's more like it, my child. Though I sense a duplicitous nature within you. It will take more than the right words to win your freedom.

What must I do?

Do you wish to know only to free yourself, or do you wish to serve me fully?

My father serves you so willingly, what will be his reward?

A chuckle. *Ah, now we get to the heart of things, yes? As it is with all mortals. You want to know what you'll get from the bargain? What about power, unlimited, untold power.*

My father's power is not unlimited. He controls a few thousand people in this city, no more.

The being's tone was subdued a little. *Such power takes time to accumulate. I have been working with your father for a hundred years and we had to start slowly. Soon, very soon, there will be great power to be had for those who are loyal to me.*

I could have my own kingdom, ruling many thousands of people? She didn't really want that. Mostly she wanted to be left alone, but that didn't seem to be her fate. She was curious what the god would say to this, however.

The voice was arrogant yet soft, when it responded. *So much more than that, my child. This whole world could be yours!* An interesting reply.

Would not the other gods have something to say about that?

Another hearty laugh. Which was a very interesting response, not what she had expected. There was a sense behind that laugh, a superiority, a feeling of unfettered authority. And when the laughter died, there was a bit of a moment, just a tiny hesitancy, but she felt it. The god didn't have a quick answer. When he did speak it was with that same arrogance once again. *They will not challenge me.* Yet Astria got the sense that the god had chosen those words very carefully.

Interesting.

Then it would seem I have little choice. Oh, she had a choice, but for now she'd play along and see where this led. *I am yours to command.* She hadn't said anything about whether she'd follow those commands or not. *What do you wish me to do?*

It is good to hear you so willing to be of service. I have a plan for you, my child. I will illuminate it in time. For now, do as your father commands. I am, if nothing else, patient. Again, she sensed a hidden meaning behind those words.

She felt the presence of the being leave her. She allowed herself a brief sense of respite. She was still her father's prisoner after all.

To her father, she said, "You can release me, I will not resist."

He grunted, then said, "Not yet. There is a lesson that must be learned."

Astria had never angered him like this before. He'd never said such things to her, only to his minions and their punishment was always severe. She began to tremble once again.

"And what about Mother and Uncle Donallo?" she asked. "You aren't going to hurt them, are you?"

"I will have to punish them for their disobedience, but for your sake I will keep it light."

"You're going after them?"

"Oh, no. They will return to me willingly, seeking you. Of that I am certain. Which is why I must keep you very safe until that happens. Especially with these new interlopers helping them."

"You won't kill them, the new drahksani? Will you?" That was the last thing Astria wanted. She'd run away to avoid anyone else getting hurt.

"They will volunteer for sacrifice in the coming months."

"Oh, Father, please, no!"

"It is the will of Davul. And I thought you said you wouldn't resist?" He glared back at her with a suspicious look.

"I won't run away again, I promise, so you don't have to sacrifice them."

He waved a hand dismissively. "Davul must be appeased, and that is the end of it! Besides, they will save the lives of our people, taking their place in the sacrifices. It is a boon. You will come to see it as such, my daughter, if you are to follow Davul as I have."

Well, she certainly didn't want that. But there was little she could do in her current state. She just didn't know how to go along with what her father and that god were doing—if only to gain her freedom—without being drawn into the horrible things they did. She didn't know enough, which meant watching and learning and hoping she'd know what to do before someone died.

She tried to sound subdued and submissive when she asked, "Where are we going?"

"To visit your brother," Lucian said with a hint of cruel mirth.

"Andrei? He's alive?" Amidst all her fear and dismay, there came a faint light of hope.

"Oh, yes," Lucian chuckled. Something in the way her father said these words dashed her hopes like so much shattering crystal.

Astria knew Andrei wasn't her real brother. The young man had been taken from his parents—whom Lucian had killed—almost twenty years ago. Since then Lucian had raised him as his own.

And it had shown.

Andrei was a brute: large, tall and built like an ox. He'd been Lucian's enforcer and right-hand man ever since Astria could remember. Her first memories of the man were as a brat of a child. He'd been thirteen but looked younger. Yet he'd still been big for his age, nearly as tall as Lucian, and already starting to put on muscle. He'd only grown since then, a little taller than Lucian now, but far broader through shoulders and chest with thick arms, and legs like tree trunks.

Astria felt bad for Andrei. He'd been lied to his entire life. He'd thought he was the son of a tyrant and acted as such, becoming a bully... that was until her mother and Uncle Donallo had shown Andrei the truth.

It had happened through a series of events, which had begun with Astria's own pillaging of her father's mind. After that, she'd gone to her mother to tell her they should leave. Astria had known it would never happen while Andrei was around to hunt them down. So, her mother had dream-walked into the slumbering minds of both Lucian and Andrei to find some weakness to exploit. It was through that, she'd discovered Andrei's true parentage. Donallo had then taken the image from Mirala's mind and together they'd shown it to the young man.

Astria had sneaked along when they'd done so, hiding outside the room, peering through the keyhole. She'd seen the large man break down. He'd said a part of him had always known, that he'd hated what he'd been doing and what he'd become. He'd told them that to make up for his life of oppression he would help them all escape.

Andrei had stayed behind when the three of them had run away. He'd kept Lucian busy, giving them time to make it as far as they could. They'd all assumed Andrei was dead. Certainly, none of them could feel him through the spirit-link. Yet it seemed that wasn't the case.

"Where is he?" she asked.

"In a special place, not even your parents had known about. And... here we are now!" Lucian had dragged her along behind him, still floating and held by unseen bonds of air. They had descended deep beneath the estate into the rocks of the hills below the building. It was damp down here, but clear and clean. Tunnels, it seemed, ran all through the area. Lucian had taken her to a heavy iron door.

"Long ago, Davul revealed to me that encasing a drahksan entirely in cold-forged iron would sever them from the spirit-link. I had this room made for just such a purpose." Lucian drew out what looked like a key: it had a larger end to hold, which seemed like that of a key, but the other end, where there should have been tines and protrusions, there was nothing.

After a moment of concentration and a deep breath from Lucian, Astria watched the end of the key transform. It was metal, and he had powers over earth. He was changing its shape. When the transformation was done, he put the key in the lock and turned it.

As her father opened the door, Astria panicked. If he was going to keep her in here, her mother and uncle wouldn't know where she was. She'd been continuing to hide her spirit-link using Volf's shadow-form. It was why she hadn't sensed her father's presence that morning when he'd surprised her. She dropped that now, and as she was dragged along behind Lucian, sent a quick sense-message to her mother: *I am alive, Father is hiding me, come!*

Then Lucian was closing the door behind her and the sprit-link, which had so momentarily connected her with her mother and uncle, and the other three drahksani, was gone.

But she was reconnected with Andrei.

Her heart wrenched. Poor man! Through her soul-sense, she could feel his pain, absolute and all-encompassing.

"What did you do? He is your son!"

Andrei was held like she was—or so she assumed—floating aloft in an unseen binding of air. He was not well at all, and barely seemed conscious. Heavy bruising covered his face, as did large areas of swelling. One eye was swollen shut, the other, barely much better. Parts of him had been burned, hair singed away on his head, the charred edges of clothes around burns on his body. Blood dripped from the man, keeping a slow, wet beat in the puddle beneath him.

Astria gagged at the horrid sight.

Lucian laughed. *Laughed!* Of all things. She knew the man had done awful things, but never seen how much he delighted in them.

"He needed to be punished. And since I know he heals so quickly, I needed to make sure I kept up the punishment until he was exhausted. And continue to keep him so wounded so he doesn't have the strength to escape." The man actually seemed giddy about this.

"But he's your son, my broth—"

Lucian spun on her, tone rising, face contorted with hatred. "He is nothing of the sort! I don't know how he found out, probably that meddling mind-talent Donallo. He's never been my son, and he turned on me quickly enough, despite my raising him these eighteen years! He is a betrayer and a fool!" Spittle flew from her father's mouth as he frothed at this tirade. Lucian calmed himself, shaking his head and drawing a breath. "Luckily for you, I know you are my daughter. You will also need to be punished, but if you mean what you say in coming to Davul, then it shall be nowhere near as severe as this."

Lucian was quick and strong. The hand that reached out to slap her across her face did so almost too fast to see. She was left with a stinging cheek and turned head, ears ringing from the strike. "I think that shall be enough for now."

She looked back at her father slowly, tears in her eyes, which she didn't have to force. Never once before had he hit her. She was suddenly terrified at what else might have changed between them. She began to shake once again.

Her father must have seen her reaction. "Good, you know your place. But I think I will leave you here to watch your so-called-brother's suffering as I put him through another round of beatings, and you shall remain here until I deem your punishment completed." Lucian drew himself up and smiled. There was no love or joy in that expression. "Now watch carefully, my child. I want you to understand what a real punishment looks like, so you know never to betray me and Davul again." With that he turned.

Large stones, which had been scattered around the iron-clad room, rose from the floor and flew in to strike Andrei. He screamed, and Astria joined him,

"Father, no!"

But Lucian was too far gone into the ecstasy of torture to hear her.

12

VOLF, DESPITE HIS OWN FATIGUE, HAD BEEN UP EARLY. THOUGH, not early enough. It had taken him a long time, after waking, to interpret what he was feeling. A strange sensation, which he finally identified as a connection to another drahksan through the spirit-link. But it had felt so odd because he'd never encountered anyone moving that fast before. And once this realization hit, he was very glad to know they were moving away from where he and the others were camped, since the only other drahksan in the area—which they could currently identify—was Lucian. And this one certainly felt powerful enough to be the evil man Mirala and Donallo had described. The fact that he was moving away from them was a bit terrifying in the implication that he had potentially been near them sometime in the night or early morning. That thought shook Volf.

The group had had someone on watch, keeping an eye out in case more of those elemental wielding goons found them. But the one who'd been scheduled for the early morning watch had been Jais, who wouldn't have felt any drahksan coming or going.

As the others woke, he told them of what he had sensed. No one was happy about the idea that Lucian might have been so close to them. Mirala and Donallo were particularly suspicious of what the man might have done.

Then had come a rather odd moment when, having only felt one drahksan to the south, suddenly there were three!

In that moment, Mirala had cried out. "Astria! No!"

Then all three they sensed through the spirit-link were gone and Volf could sense no drahksani to the south at all. That thought was frightening. Did Lucian have some way to hide himself? He didn't have much time to ponder this though, as Mirala was close to raving.

He went to comfort her, as did her brother.

"Are you certain one of those three was Astria?" Donallo asked. "I felt them for such a short time, I couldn't identify any of them." There was something else in how the man had said 'any of them,' which caused Volf to wonder if Donallo knew who the third one was. Perhaps this mysterious 'Andrei' they were so ashamed of leaving behind?

"Yes, she reached out to me, an emotional sending. I know it was her. She said that she is alive and that her father was hiding her. Oh Gods, I can't... how did Lucian find her!"

Volf wanted to embrace the woman to comfort her, but Donallo was there first, holding her with a brother's affection, trying to calm her down.

"If there is one good thing in all of this, at least now we know for certain where Astria is," Donallo said softly. "And we now have allies who might help us to get her back." With that Donallo looked around at the others.

"I'm in," Caerwyn said, and Volf noticed how self-assured she seemed. She'd spent a lot of time with Donallo yesterday. Had that helped her to break out of the dark place in which she'd been? If so, he was happy for her. And the way she was looking at Donallo... was quite intriguing. There was a fire in her eyes now that hadn't been there in some time, and it seemed to burn a little brighter when she looked at Donallo.

Volf found himself responding as well. "I'll do whatever you need," he said. He hoped Mirala heard him. As much as he knew he was no warrior, he also knew he wanted to fight to help and protect her... and her daughter. There were precious few things in this world for which he'd willingly put his life on the line. He'd just decided she was one of them.

And yet his own soft words seemed lost and overwhelmed by Jais' voice: "And where you go, I go." Oddly this seemed directed more at Caerwyn than anyone else. She quirked a brow at that, but then her attention was back on Donallo. That meant she didn't see Jais' shoulders slump when her gaze left him.

Interesting.

"We have to be smart about this, though," Donallo said, and with those words seemed to take control of the situation. "I'm sorry, Mira, but we can't just run in there after Astria. We need a plan and we need to be well rested. We're all still tired from the fight last night. Rushing to meet Lucian in such a state would be a bad idea. With his minions and their power, we'd be hard pressed to defeat him. We need to wait and rest... and besides, we have no way to get there fast. It's probably a good four or five days walk back to Rodathia."

Volf could speed up that trip. With his shadow-walk he was certain he could make the trip in a single day. Before he could say anything, Mirala spoke,

"It's only about two days to the river."

"A good point and a better idea." Donallo nodded.

"The river?" Caerwyn asked.

"The Tiska," Donallo answered. "It runs through Laskovic, the city where we met you. It would be about two days to return there, faster if Volf moves us. Once there, we can take a riverboat down river. With the current it would only be about another full day of travel to get there, but we'd be able to rest along the way."

"Then let's go," Volf said. He was tired, but he'd be able to get them that far, he was certain.

"No," Mirala said softly. She slowly extricated herself from her brother's embrace. Her eyes were red, though her cheeks were dry. "Donallo is right. We're all tired." She shuddered. "And as much as I want to get Astria back more than any of you, we need to rest now. She's his daughter. Lucian won't harm her." Again, there was something in how the woman had said 'her' which made Volf wonder. But before he could ask, Caerwyn seemed to have heard it as well.

"Only her? For a moment, I sensed three drahksan in the south. Do you know who the other was? Do we need to be worried about them? Are they an ally of his, or someone else Lucian would... harm?"

Mirala and Donallo shared a long glance. Finally, Donallo said simply. "Andrei."

"The one who looks like me?" Jais asked, moving closer to the group of them.

"Yes," Donallo said. "And now that we know he's alive, that is perhaps something we need to discuss, but Mirala is right. We all need to rest and..." Volf noticed something in Donallo's eyes when he looked at Caerwyn then. It seemed he might have some of that same fire that she had for him. "Caerwyn, we should work with you a little further. We'll need you all at your best if we're to face Lucian and win." Volf's gaze was drawn to Jais as Donallo and Caerwyn shared a glance. Jais' jaw seemed to twitch. Things were getting heated here. That would make things interesting.

He turned his attentions to Mirala. Oddly she was looking at him. "Might we have a moment?" she asked softly.

Volf was stunned but managed a nod.

She stepped a little way from the others and he followed along behind her.

She turned to him and sunlight caught her auburn locks, highlighting the red, setting it on fire. "I wanted to thank you. Last night, you took that attack meant for me. That was very brave." His ego puffed up a little bit. Though it deflated with her next words, "And very stupid." She sighed heavily and looked away for a long moment. When she spoke again, she was still looking away. "I am an empath, Volf. I was distracted by the loss of my daughter for most of yesterday, but now I can sense clearly enough how you feel about me." Her gaze fell to the side, not meeting his.

Volf went a little cold on the inside. What was she trying to say? For a brief moment, he'd been happy that she knew how he felt. It meant he was spared the awkward words of trying to tell her. And yet, how she'd said it made his heart constrict.

"We hardly know each other Volf. And I'm in no place to know how I feel about anyone. All I know right now is that I must get my daughter back from that madman. I know you're a good man and I'm sorry that I blamed you for letting Astria escape. I know now it wasn't your fault."

It wasn't? What did she know that he didn't? He was fairly certain it had been his fault, falling asleep on watch. "Mirala, I—"

"No, please allow me to finish." She looked up into his eyes then. Her own were still red-rimmed, and he could see the moisture clinging to the corners. She smiled, but it was a sad smile. "I had a husband once, some time ago. And when he died, a part of me died with him. I'm not ready for anything like that, and I honestly don't know how I feel about you. Perhaps once this is all over and we're well away from this place, then..." She shrugged. Her voice was quiet when she added. "Even I, who can sense, and project emotions don't know how they will play out for myself or others. That is all up to the fates." She reached out to place a delicate hand on his chest. "If you're willing to wait, then perhaps we'll see? That is the best I can offer."

He swallowed around a lump in his throat and nodded. "Yes, I'll wait," he said, though his voice was choked up with emotion. He didn't want to sound broken-hearted, he wanted to be certain and sure for her, show her his feelings were true. But... were they? He'd only known her a couple of days. Perhaps waiting would be best.

He nodded again and turned away. He needed some space, needed to think. He didn't go back to the others but wandered a little into the forest. Yet he couldn't get her words out of his head:

I'm not ready...

I don't know how I feel about you...

Perhaps once this is over...

Well if that's what she wanted, then that's what he'd give her. Time and space... and he didn't know if he could get Astria back on his own, but he was sure as Holn going to try.

Despite his fatigue, he slipped into his shadow-form and cut himself off from the spirit-link.

He heard a distant voice call, "Volf?" But then he was moving, using his shadow-walk to swiftly slip through the forest. As tired as he was, he didn't know how far he'd get. All he knew was he would get Mirala's daughter back, somehow. He had stealth and guile on his side. Perhaps that's all it would take. If none of the enemy knew he was there, perhaps he'd be able to slip in and out undetected and free the girl.

He didn't know, but he was going to do his best to get her back.

He'd show Mirala he was a man worthy of her. He'd do whatever it took.

Even if it meant his own life.

13

CAERWYN'S HEAD SNAPPED TO ONE SIDE AS SHE FELT VOLF vanish from her spirit-link.

"What's he doing?" she said softly.

Mirala came running up to join them. "I think Volf is going to do something stupid."

"Sounds like Volf to me," Jais said sardonically.

Caerwyn shot him a look. The stout young man seemed dejected. When her gaze met his, he opened his mouth to say something, but Donallo interrupted him.

"What he's going to do, he'll do. We can't stop him now." The man sighed as Caerwyn's gaze shifted back to him. "Our plan remains the same. Rest and travel. Meet Lucian head on when we're at our best and—" A shrug. "—perhaps we'll have a chance."

"You make the man sound all-powerful?" Caerwyn asked. Certainly, she'd felt the swift moving drahksan that morning, having no clue how anyone could move that fast. It seemed impossible. Yet with even four of them against him, he couldn't resist them all, could he?

"It's not just him, remember, it's those minions as well. We had enough trouble fighting six of them, and he has dozens surrounding him in Rodathia."

"Oh." She grimaced. That changed things substantially. "Are they all that powerful?"

"No," Mirala answered. "Those were some of his elite minions. The one you fought was Syasha, one of his druhi."

"Druhi?" Jais asked.

Donallo grimaced. "They are his seconds in the cult, his… captains, if you will."

And she'd gotten away. She could still potentially be around for another fight. Great. "How many more like her?"

"Three others; there is one captain for each of the elements other than storm: air, earth, fire, and water." Donallo's voice was grim.

"And there are twice as many treti—the next level down within the hierarchy of the cult. Then there are struvrti and piati as well. Those are everyone who make up the leadership of the organization. Perhaps forty or so, in all? We battled only six and were hard pressed. And two of them got away." Mirala did not sound hopeful. "We may not have to fight all of them, but I am quite certain Lucian will have many around him when we arrive."

"What if we didn't try to fight him?" Caerwyn asked.

"And leave Astria?" Mirala's eyes grew wide.

"No." Caerwyn raised a hand to stop that train of thought. "No, we go, but our objective is to free Astria and this other drahksan."

Mirala looked a little confused. "That might work, but Lucian would pursue us. We would have to face him at some point."

"But." Caerwyn tried to sound hopeful. "If we get those others, who may also be willing to join the fight—"

"Astria is too young to—"

"Of course, but perhaps that other drahksan could fight. And I'm sure even Astria, if pressed, would resist, but that's not the point. If we get them away and Lucian comes after us, he may not bring all his minions. We'd have more resources and he'd have fewer."

Caerwyn looked from Donallo to Mirala. They were considering this. Finally, Donallo nodded. "It's a good plan." Then he sighed heavily. "And perhaps it's time we told you more about this other drahksan, Andrei." Donallo's gaze shifted to Jais. The young man held the intense look with steely eyes. Donallo broke that off and turned to Mirala. "Are we certain?"

Caerwyn didn't know what that comment was in reference to.

Mirala sighed, nodding. "Look at his sword. There has to be some connection."

"My sword?" Jais asked, putting his hand over the dragon-fire pommel-stone of his father's blade. "What about it?"

"How did you come by it?" Mirala asked careful, cautious.

Caerwyn wondered where this all was headed. She knew well enough the sword had been a gift from the gods—Asavi in particular—given to Jais before their fight with the krolloc back in Klasten's Green. Before that, it had been Jais' father's blade.

Jais said simply. "It came to me by magic. It was my father's."

Donallo nodded. "Then we were right."

"Right." Jais was getting more and more worked up. "About what?"

Mirala stepped over to the young man and placed a hand on his shoulder. She must have used something to calm Jais as he seemed to relax a little. "We believe," Mirala began slowly. "That Andrei… is your brother."

Caerwyn's eyes went wide. She caught her mouth gaping and closed it. She hadn't expected that.

"But..." Jais was blinking. He seemed to be in shock. "How...?" Jais managed to stammer after another long moment.

"You noticed how we looked at you." Mirala motioned to a large stone on the ground. Jais nodded, sitting. Mirala joined him on a log nearby. Caerwyn and Donallo remained standing. "We said it was because you reminded us of this man, Andrei. You do. It's uncanny. He is taller and younger, but otherwise... your faces are so much alike, and your general build is near to identical. We didn't really understand this until we saw your sword."

"My sword?" Jais seemed limited to only short phrases, he was still stunned.

"It's quite unique, wouldn't you say?" Donallo said. Jais looked up at the man and nodded.

Mirala picked things up from there. "Well up until a few months ago, a sword identical to that hung on the wall in Lucian's study. I highly doubt there are two such blades, especially since that blade mysteriously disappeared from where it hung a few months back. Was that about the time it came to you?"

Jais nodded.

None of this felt good; Caerwyn could feel it in her bones.

"As we thought." Mirala sighed heavily. "That sword belonged to Andrei's father... your father as you say. It was taken from the man when Lucian... killed him and your mother, roughly eighteen years ago."

Jais just kept nodding, eyes distant, unseeing.

"What happened?" Caerwyn asked for the stunned young man.

Donallo took up the telling. "We don't know all the details.

I was only able to glean a few images and thoughts from Lucian's mind when I tried to read him. I was trying to be careful, so he wouldn't know I was doing it, which meant I didn't get a complete picture. From what we can tell, Jais' parents came to Rodathia eighteen years ago, having heard about Lucian's cult. They were Palassi drahksan. They fought to protect humans, even during a time when humans were trying to kill us all. They sought to free Rodathia from Lucian's control but didn't count on the people there being so loyal to him. They fought him, and lost, surprised by Lucian's minions in the end. Yet Lucian sensed that there was still another drahksan nearby." Donallo sighed. Mirala took it from there.

"He found your brother, Andrei. He'd been just a babe, only a few months old. Your parents had hidden him before they'd gone to face Lucian. Perhaps they thought Lucian would be easy to defeat. They'd left him in the care of a kind farmer up the river a little way, outside of Rodathia. They must have thought they'd be returning for him soon enough, but they never did.

Lucian had always wanted a fully drahksan child and took Andrei to raise as his own. Your father's sword was hung in Lucian's study as a trophy." Mirala leaned over to lay a hand on one of Jais'. "I'm sorry, Jais. This must be a lot to learn all at once."

Jais nodded. When he spoke next, his voice was breathy... sounding more than a little lost. "I'd assumed my parents were dead, but I never knew..."

Mirala looked up at Caerwyn and Donallo. "Why don't you give me some time with him? I'll see what I can do to soothe this revelation."

Donallo nodded and turned to Caerwyn. "I think perhaps we still have much to talk about as well, yes?"

That was true. "Yes."

He led her a short distance away and they too sat on the rocky banks of the stream to talk.

Donallo waited, silent.

Caerwyn drew in a long breath. "You know about what happened... with the wizard, up north." He nodded. "Well, something hit me yesterday, and hit me hard. It has to do with protecting people." She swallowed around a lump that was growing in her throat. None of this was easy to think about, and it seemed it was harder to say the words. She blew out a long breath then drew in another one. "Perhaps I should start from the beginning. I don't know if it's something you saw when you were in my thoughts or not, but I lost my parents when I was young, around Astria's age I'd guess."

"Oh, Caerwyn, that's horrible," he said softly.

She grimaced. "You don't know the half of it. I was alone and on the run from dragon hunters and living off the land in the forest. I became a wildling for a time, scared of civilization, of people. But some part of me knew I couldn't remain scared forever. I think it was the same part of me that... eventually decided I'd never let anything like that happen to myself or those I cared about. I made a vow, not out-loud, but in my heart, that I would protect myself, protect those I loved, and anyone else in need."

Her grimace deepened into a full frown. "But I didn't really know I'd decided that, it just became a part of me and formed how I lived my life." She hung her head for a long moment. After a few breaths, she felt ready to go on.

"I was adopted by a prince of Afgen a few years later, and through him, I got to train and become strong and obtained a position of power, where I could actually follow through on my inner vow. I was a general and I was constantly protecting people, my own men, and those of the empire we served. For a long time, life was good, I was doing what my soul felt was right... then things changed. I was forced to leave that home by a dragon hunter and that... tore at my soul. I realize now a part of what I lost in that moment was the sense of being able to protect the empire, but that didn't impact me as hard, since I knew I was leaving good men and women in place to do as I had done. No, the first real test came when I met Jais."

She hadn't thought of this yesterday, but it occurred to her as she was speaking. The whole incident at Klasten's Green had hit her harder than she'd thought. "Together we tried to save his village from dozens of krolls and a krolloc. We—"

"Sorry, did you say... a krolloc? With how many krolls? You and Jais alone?" Donallo was wide-eyed astonished.

Her frown became a weary grin. She breathed a tired laugh and nodded. "Indeed. Though we did have a little help. Jais' aunt helped a little, as did another village girl with no powers at all—so very brave that one. And finally, we had Barami, a friend from the south who had come north with me."

"Ah, yes, he featured prominently in your thoughts."

"I'll bet he does. He is a good man. You'll be the first I've admitted this to, but I'm a little lost without him."

"I didn't see his fate amongst your thoughts. Is he still alive?" Another question was implied through Donallo's words—*if he is alive, why is he not with you now?*

"He found love in the north and stayed there."

Donallo nodded. "I'm still a little stunned that you faced a krolloc and so many krolls."

"Whenever I think about it, I'm a little stunned as well."

"Perhaps we won't have as much trouble with Lucian as I'd thought."

"Let's not get ahead of ourselves," she said. "We were lucky with the krolloc, that's what it came down to. The three of us were near death when we were done, and we'd only been able to do what we did because of a little help from the gods themselves."

That got a brow raised from Donallo, but he didn't ask. That was good, since Caerwyn wasn't sure exactly how she'd explain what happened in the Festorium before the fight with the Krolloc.

"Anyway, that's not the important part of the story. What happened was that the village, when they found out we were drahksani, turned on us, even on Barami—who's human—for consorting with us. They fought us, tried to kill us. I hadn't realized it until now, but I think that started to shake my faith in myself. I know it sounds odd to say, but when the people I was trying to protect became the enemy, that threw me. I didn't know how to process that, and I don't think I fully did." A heavy sigh. Here it came.

"Then came the events in the high north. I was put in a position where no matter what I did, someone I needed to protect would perish. More than that, as you know, I had to choose someone under my protection to die. That... that broke me." Her voice quavered and she had to clamp her jaw shut for a long moment after saying that to keep her composure. After several deep breaths, she was able to go on. "I didn't know it at the time, but I realize now that in that moment I had betrayed the core of who I was. I had broken my vow. That caused everything that had happened to me since the death of my parents to flood back in, and I was that scared little girl again." She took another long moment to simply breathe, jaw taut, teeth not quite clenched, but close. "I've been so lost since then. I didn't know who I was anymore."

Donallo reached out to her, putting a hand on her shoulder. He said nothing, but the look in his eyes was of under-standing, not pity. Gods, but that was good to see.

"I can't protect everyone," she said slowly and it stung, but at the same time released something within her soul she'd clung to for so very long. It was some shred of that vow which she'd clung to after it had been torn from her. She let out a shuddering breath then repeated, "I can't protect everyone. Gods, it feels horrible to say, and yet, just a little... liberating."

Donallo moved to sit on the log beside her. "You are coming to terms with a truth, around which you had built your entire life and your being. That is never easy, and yet once you see the truth, it will make you stronger." He sighed. "There is little I can do for you in this moment. I am capable of erasing memories within a mind, but I would never do such a thing. It would change the person. Mirala is the one who is good with emotions. She could help you deal with your emotions as you go through this."

Caerwyn put a hand on Donallo's leg. "Even just your presence helps. I... I don't think I could have told any of this to Volf or Jais. At least, not for the first time. I will tell them, but just having someone who wasn't trying to fix me, who was willing to sit and listen and that was it... It means a lot to me, thank you."

And she was certain now of something further.

"I am no longer affected by the heat of battle, Donallo. My passions are cooled. Yet... I would still ask more of you, if you're willing."

"A child," he said softly. His lips pursed and he sighed.

Her voice became just a little throaty as she said, "Yes."

And yet, his expression was one of regret.

"Will you not help me?"

Another sigh. "Caerwyn, I have seen your thoughts, and perhaps there are a few I know even better than you do. Why do you ask this of me?" Before she could answer he held up a hand, forestalling her response as he spoke again. "What I mean to say is: why not ask Jais?"

She raised a brow.

Jais didn't want to help her with this. That, and he was still so young. He'd seemed so uncertain when she'd finally asked him back in Klasten's Green. He wasn't the man Donallo was. Donallo was much older, wiser, and more experienced.

Her thoughts were so tumbled about from his question that she said nothing.

Donallo spoke again a moment later. "I know he has feelings for you. He thinks about you often."

"Does he?" She blinked.

"It was you who rejected him, told him you didn't want a husband, didn't want a man to help raise the child. Tell me, has that changed?"

Had it?

She was quite astounded to discover... she wasn't sure. She had always been firm on that point before, but now... So much had changed. Did she want a man? Did she need a man? No, those were two different questions. She was still certain she did not need a man to 'complete' her. She didn't need anyone... but did she want someone? That had been a firm 'no' before, yet now... she couldn't answer.

She let out a long sigh. "I don't know anymore. I'd thought... well somehow it just seemed much easier if I had a child with you."

"Because you don't really know me. It would be easy to push me away afterward." He grimaced. "I'm not sure that's what I'd want either." He shook his head. "Caerwyn, you are in such a fragile place right now, and this is a huge decision. Perhaps—"

She cut him off in a harsh whisper. "No! I don't want to

wait. We're going to face a powerful drahksan in a few days. I could die, or you could, or…" She trailed off.

"Or Jais," Donallo finished. That had been exactly what she'd hesitated to say.

Gods, did she have feelings for him?

As much as she hated to admit it, Donallo was right. She just didn't know herself right now. She thought she knew what she wanted, but perhaps time would change that. Waiting would be the wisest solution, but she felt so much anxiety over the future. After what happened to Elria, the one thing she knew was that death was always an option, ever so close, especially for a warrior like Caerwyn.

She growled, rising, unhappy about all of this, feeling even more unsettled now. Even though a part of her knew waiting was right, the whole situation frustrated her. She felt anger rise within her. A part of her knew it was juvenile, stomping her feet over not getting what she wanted, but her emotions were just a little too tense and volatile at the moment, so that's just how it was going to be.

"Fine!" she said and stalked away from Donallo.

Behind her, she heard his resigned sigh, and that made her even more furious.

14

JAIS' THOUGHTS WOULDN'T SETTLE. AT LEAST HE WAS CALM. Mirala had settled his emotions, but that only seemed to make him concentrate more on the whirlwind of thoughts going through his mind.

He had a brother.

He drew out his father's sword.

"Oh!" Mirala gasped. She'd been saying something. He hadn't heard.

"Sorry," he said. "I just... my father's spirit is within the sword. I can communicate with him, and I don't know why he never mentioned..."

Father?

Yes Jais? There was only a moment of pause before the voice in his head let out a surprised, *Oh!*

Exactly. Why did you never tell me I had a brother? Jais was trying not to add too much accusation to his mental tone.

I... I didn't know!

What? How could you not know? But it was only then that Jais recalled his father's spirit telling him—on more than one occasion—that he seemed to lack the full memories of who he'd been in life.

Even now the memories are hazy and hard to recall. I am... limited here. And yet, I... seem to recall a bundle of cloth, wrapped tight and held close to your mother's chest as we walked. He was so new. I never really knew him. I... I died only a few months after he was born!

Now it was Jais' turn to feel sorry. Jais' father hadn't known his own child. He'd died before he'd had the chance to do so.

I'm sorry, Father. I... I was just so shocked. I needed to speak to you, find out the truth.

It is true, yes. I am sorry you had to find out like this, Jais. There was genuine remorse in his father's tone.

Jais looked up at Mirala. "He never really knew his own son."

We made a mistake leaving you behind. I hardly knew you, either. There is... a lot I regret. I'm so sorry, Jais.

Jais returned a sense of understanding but had to remove his hand from the weapon after that, the combination of his father's emotions and confusion, mixing with his own, was making it hard to focus once again.

He felt another wave of soothing energy flow into him. "That is horrible, Jais. I'm so sorry, for both of you," Mirala said softly.

Jais gave a heavy sigh as he set his sword aside. All of this was a lot to take in. "Tell me about him," Jais said softly. He looked up at Mirala. "You knew him well, didn't you?"

She grimaced and nodded. "I did, but for most of the time I knew him, he was Lucian's tool, a brute. Lucian used him to bully and intimidate his followers into falling in line."

"Oh," Jais said, shoulders falling a little. He shook his head. "Here I was hoping that he might be able to tell me more about our parents or who we really are, but it doesn't sound like he knew any of that either."

"No. He didn't even know he wasn't Lucian's son until we told him and that was only a few weeks ago."

"Truly?"

Mirala nodded.

Jais let out another sigh, running a hand over his face. "And when you did tell him…?" He didn't really know what he was asking.

Mirala seemed to know though, for her answer was what he'd been hoping to hear: "He was a different man, almost instantly. It did take a little to convince him, but Donallo went into Andrei's own memories and drew out an image of his mother and father from a time when he was only a few months old. The memory had been deeply locked away. As soon as Andrei saw that for himself, he knew. He said he'd felt like he'd been living a lie his entire life. He knew it wasn't right, doing what Lucian asked, but the man was his father." Mirala reached out and touched Jais' chin to lift his head so their gazes met. "He was full of remorse. He's a good man at heart, Jais, like you." Her lips pressed together tightly, but she nodded to herself. "Perhaps too good of a man."

Jais raised a brow. "What does that mean?"

"He… when Donallo and I wished to escape with Astria, Andrei said he'd stay behind and guard our flight. He would face Lucian and stall the man from following after us. We never quite knew what he did, but we could sense his and Lucian's essences close to each other for a while, through the spirit-link. Then… Andrei's suddenly vanished. We thought him dead. But even if something else has happened and he's still alive, it seems more than likely that he did not fare well in that engagement. He sacrificed himself for us. He'd only known his true parentage for a few days and he was ready to give everything for us." It was her turn to look away. Her hands were folded tightly in her lap.

Suddenly she rose. "We should go," she said firmly and looked around.

Jais joined her. Caerwyn and Donallo were nowhere to be found.

"I'll see if I can... Oh!"

"What is it?" Jais asked, curious at her odd expression.

Mirala sighed. "They might need a moment. Caerwyn is working through some things." She blew out a breath and met Jais' gaze and quirked her head to one side. "You have feelings for her, don't you?"

Jais hoped he showed nothing through his expression, but it was little use to hide it now. That's what he got for talking to an empath. There was little use in denying it. "Yeah." He felt compelled to go on. Since it didn't seem like they were leaving right away, he sat once again. Mirala joined him. "I've only just realized how I felt. I'd been distracted by other women... and Caerwyn was always so distant! When we first met... she wanted me to give her a child. And yet she didn't want to be married, didn't want me to be a father, just give her a child! How can one ask that and not expect the other parent to want to help! I..." He sighed heavily then and felt some of his frustration drain out of him. Both he and Caerwyn had gone through a lot since they'd met only a few months ago. "I understand her a lot more now. She doesn't need anyone and doesn't want anyone in her life, not like that. Still, I don't think I could just... lay with her and not have it mean... something. Is that so odd?"

Mirala shook her head. "No, that's not odd at all." For a long moment she simply looked at him.

"What is it?" Jais asked

She gave a half-hearted smile and another shake of her

head. "Nothing. I was just... I think both you and Caerwyn need to talk."

"Oh?"

Mirala grimaced. "I cannot sense thoughts, I don't know what she's thinking, but she is in turmoil at the moment. That is all I know. And you... you love her, don't you? If so, you need to tell her. That is all I know."

He sighed. It was true. It must be if that's what Mirala was feeling. Even if he hadn't been willing to claim such certainty himself before. "Yes, I do... and you're right, I should talk to her. I was going to today, but then... with finding out about my brother and... Volf... everything just got complicated."

"I don't know if I'd advocate doing it now," Mirala said. "Caerwyn is... worked up. But I'll leave that up to you. Either way, we need to be leaving soon. We have a lot of travelling to do."

That much was true. But there was a little more Jais wanted to ask her first. "Before that," he said raising a hand to forestall her. "Do you know what Andrei's abilities are?" Perhaps if they were the same as Jais, he'd learn something.

"I don't know everything. He is exceptionally strong, as I'm guessing you are as well. He fights like a demon and can heal himself and others. His senses are exceptional, like all of ours. Other than that, I couldn't say for certain."

Jais grimaced. That didn't help much. Though now he was more eager than ever to go south. He wanted to free this man —his brother—and find out more about his kin... perhaps that would finally reveal to Jais who he really was.

15

CAERWYN SPLASHED WATER FROM THE STREAM ON HER FACE TO cool herself. It was cold and refreshing. She took a sip from the waters as well, lifting her hand to her mouth and drinking deeply.

Yet the waters seemed to do little to calm her heated heart. She told herself she was angry at Donallo, at everyone, the world, but some part of her knew she was only truly upset with herself.

She shook her head. She couldn't get her thoughts or emotions straight. What did she want? Was it a child? Was it a man? If so, who did she want? Was it Donallo? Or was it Jais, as Donallo suggested?

Perhaps this was why she'd always been so certain she didn't need a man, because it led to feelings like this. Perhaps she'd go back to that.

But then... would she ever have a child?

What did she want? It all came back to that question.

And right now, she just didn't know.

Heavy footfalls behind her signaled someone's approach. It

could only be one person, both Mirala's and Donallo's treads were much lighter than this.

"Jais?" she asked without turning. He was the last person she wanted to see right now. As much as her anger might be at herself, she just knew, if she saw him, she'd lash out. "Please let me be, just... go away." She swept her still damp hands back through her short, spiky hair.

"I want to say something," he said. His voice was firm. He wasn't going to leave. "Caerwyn—"

"Jais, just go! Please." She didn't want to speak to him now. Not yet.

"Caerwyn, I can't. I need to—"

She'd tried the nice way, and if he wasn't going to leave, she'd make him. Rising, she rounded on him. "I don't care what you have to say. Go away!" Gods, it felt horrible to say, but that shame only made her angrier, more resolute in pushing him away.

"Caer—"

"No!" Her mind whirled for what would make him flee the fastest and it found a horrible solution far too quickly. "I slept with Donallo!"

Where had those words come from? She'd meant to shock him, hopefully get him to go away, but she could see how those words cut into his soul.

His face went pale, mouth agape. Yet he didn't run off.

"I..." But she couldn't apologize now, and her guilt only made her more flustered. "Just... go..." she stammered as she felt a significant blush rise to her cheeks. She still couldn't believe she'd just said what she'd said.

"I... Caerwyn, no, I love you. I want to give you... whatever you want. I..."

Gods! That's what he'd come to say? And she'd... Oh Holn! Well she knew she couldn't take it back now, it would only sound false. She could see the pain in his eyes. She didn't know what to say and that only made her more upset and frustrated. She clenched her jaw. It seemed silence would be her only response to this unexpected outpouring. Finally, he shook his head with a sour expression. "But I can see that's not how you feel. I'm such a fool." And with that he turned and stalked away.

The heat on her cheeks remained as she spiraled to ever increasing heights of shame and anger. She let out a tooth-clenched growl of frustration, fists balled so tight they hurt. Why did he have to be so infuriating!

Yet she knew she'd caused this whole mess.

That only made her angrier.

Mirala found her. Some time had passed, but Caerwyn hadn't moved, stuck in place, uncertain, confused, and livid.

Mirala took one look at her and sighed, shaking her head. "Jais came to you, didn't he?" She didn't wait for Caerwyn to answer. "I told him now wouldn't be a good time." Another sigh, heavier. "Can I help?" she asked.

"Right now, I don't know what I'd do if I wasn't furious," Caerwyn said, a tear welling in one eye. It fell, tracing a line down her cheek. Her words were true. She felt like she'd be empty without this anger. She'd driven Jais away just as he'd tried to tell her how he felt. She didn't know if that could be mended. She didn't even really know if she wanted it to be.

"If you change your mind, let me know," Mirala said, then added, "We're leaving soon, you should gather your things."

Caerwyn nodded.

She moved, reluctantly and went to her pack, making sure she had everything. Once she was ready, her emotions were already starting to drain, leaving an empty, hollowness within her once again. She joined the others and thankfully Jais wasn't with them.

Sensing her unspoken question, Donallo said, "Jais is scouting ahead. Said he needed some space."

"Good," was her only reply.

The brother and sister shared a look, heavy with regret, then began their trek.

Great, now everyone pitied her!

That brought the anger back with a vengeance.

VOLF HAD RESTED FOR PERIODS ON HIS RAPID JOURNEY SOUTH. Even with his shadow-walk, it had taken him the entire day to reach Rodathia. Lucian's estate was unmistakable, sitting on a high hill over the small city. Volf had known he needed to rest before he went in, so he'd made sure his shadow-form was firmly set, and would remain in place while he slept. Then he'd found an out of the way spot to rest.

Now, as the new day dawned, he prepared to go in.

Volf easily balanced himself in a crouch atop the ten-foot wall which surrounded the estate and surveyed the scene before him. The hill continued up such that the estate itself—atop the rise—was still perhaps a few dozen feet above him in elevation. It commanded a great view of the city and river-mouth. The building itself was two stories and perhaps fifty feet to a side, seemingly roughly square in shape. There were many windows and balconies all around the building. The grounds were sprawling over the hillside, with beautiful gardens and small treed areas. Guards roamed the compound. Volf didn't know if they would have the same powers as those who attacked him and the others in the forest. He hoped not, but also hoped it wouldn't be an issue, if he remained in his shadow-form.

He stayed there long enough to get a sense for the routine

of the guards then dropped from the wall to walk across the lawns at the farthest point between two patrols. He made it to the house with ease. Now came the laborious part: searching the entire house for Astria.

Moving slowly and carefully, he did a room by room search. He couldn't risk lowering his shadow-form to try to use the spirit-link to sense Astria's location, and if she was still somehow hidden, that would only reveal his own location to Lucian anyway. Instead, he listened at doors for long periods, even trying to project his sight into rooms. Though he was unable to project his sight well to places he didn't know. For seeing on the other side of something like a door, it was doable, but only gave him a limited point of view. But at least it gave him a sense for whether the room was occupied and whether he could enter.

As the day drew on and he progressed through the large house, he began to wonder if he'd be able to get close to Astria. There were limitations to his shadow-form. He still had to open doors to move through them and if there were guards outside of where Astria was being kept, they would probably notice a door being opened. Yet the more he searched, the more he found no such situation.

He did, however, find Lucian. He didn't know the man, but it seemed likely that the well-dressed man sitting in a vast study behind a large desk was the drahksan in question. Volf didn't enter that room, only saw it using his limited far-sight from the other side of a door. That was enough to tell him he didn't want to go in there.

And yet, by the end of the day, he still hadn't found Astria.

He was growing tired, so he left the estate once again to sleep in peace in a farmer's barn down the hillside a short distance, feeling frustrated and angry at his failure.

LUCIAN LEANED ON THE BALUSTRADE OF HIS BALCONY AS THE night deepened. His gaze searched the darkening hillside.

Are you certain? I felt nothing? he asked his god.

Davul had said that he'd felt a presence in the house that day.

I am certain of it, my servant. Another drahksan lurked within these walls for some time today. It took me a while to feel it and identify it, but I am certain now that's what it was.

Am I in danger?

I do not believe so. If you had been, then I believe you'd already have faced the unseen foe. No, if he didn't come for you then he is most likely a scout, nothing more.

Lucian nodded. *And do you have a way to share this gift of sensing the unseen?* he asked.

Not yet, no. But if I sense it again, I will let you know and direct you to the source.

As you wish, my lord. Lucian didn't like leaving his fate in the hands of another, but he would have to trust Davul for now. He would not sleep well knowing someone had been about in his estates, but then, perhaps a session of torturing Andrei would help him relax.

VOLF WAS BACK IN THE ESTATE THE NEXT DAY. HAVING searched all the easy-to-get-to places the first day, today he had to be much more cunning. He followed people into rooms, using his ability to shrink and narrow parts of himself to slip through slightly open doors. In this way, he saw rooms he hadn't seen the previous day, ones where people had been present. It was also how he found the entrance to the cellars.

Truly daring, at the top of his game, he'd slipped into Lucian's study. The trouble was that the man was present in the room for most of the day. But at one-point Lucian had had a few visitors, and Volf had slipped in with them. From there he'd searched the suite of rooms carefully, finding the door to the cellars off one of the main rooms. He used the ring the dragon had given him to silence himself and the area around him, then he slipped through the door.

From there, he'd moved into darkness.

The gloom was no hindrance for him, he could see well in perfect darkness, though he'd not be able to discern any colors. Behind the door he'd opened was a long, straight stairwell. Since Lucian's study was on the second floor, it descended a fair distance before there was any sort of landing.

There were many layers to the underground area. The first seemed to be on the same level with the estate's regular cellars, there was even a secret door leading to those rooms. Volf risked opening it—to see if it would make a better way out than having to go back through Lucian's study—after using his far-sight to check the other side. The storeroom he'd found had been quiet. There were stairs leading up, which he'd ventured to check. They led into the kitchens and there was a door to the outside not far from where the stairs came up. It would be a much better way out. He'd sneaked back down and closed the secret door behind him to keep looking around.

On Lucian's side of the secret door, was another storage area, but for much more valuable and disturbing items. Chests filled with gold and gems, skulls on plush cushions in boxes of glass—labelled with names and dates. Weapons, some more ornate than others, as well as other prized possessions.

The next level down, was more disturbing still, a torture chamber with various gruesome instruments, many stained with blood and worse. This deep, the entire level was cut directly from the stone of the hill under the estate itself, the stairs were no longer wooden, but carved from that same stone. It was quite cold, and moisture met in small pools along the corners of the rooms and halls. These weren't caves, but had flat walls and ceilings which met at perfect corners. The smell in the torture chamber was foul and Volf tried not to linger.

The next level down Volf found a long hallway with several rooms off of it. The first door he came to was closed and locked, but some of the others were open. He crept to the first open one. Within was a room, perhaps twelve to fifteen feet to a side and just as tall. It looked quite odd within. The walls were overlaid with sheets of thick iron, which looked like nothing so much as heavy scales, but on the inside of the room. The plates were on every surface, even the back of the door.

Odd.

Volf went back to the room which was locked and stretched out his hand for a moment. He'd never been formally trained as a thief. In his sneaking around at night, he'd seen others who were. They used special tools to undo locks. He, however, didn't need such things.

Pressing his index and middle fingers together, he made them shrink and elongate. They slipped into the key-hole and could feel around inside for tumblers. He made sure to press on each of the oddly shaped key-hole structures, before attempting to turn his hand to the side.

The lock opened.

Volf smiled.

He slid quietly into the room… and gasped in horror.

He'd found Astria, sure enough, and another man, probably the one Mirala and Donallo referred to as Andrei. Volf wasn't here for him, but the large man surely seemed in need of rescuing. He was badly bruised and bleeding, seemingly barely conscious. Both the man and Astria were held in the air by unseen forces, seemingly trapped, held tight.

"Is someone there? Volf? Is that you? Close the door, quickly!" Astria called out.

Volf didn't quite know why she'd insisted on that, but he closed the door and made his way over to her. As bad as Volf felt for the battered young man, he didn't think he'd be able to carry that large body out of these dungeons. He was here for Astria and that was who he'd free.

He strode over to her and reached out to touch her. He'd be able to include her in his shadow-form with a single touch. But his arm was flung violently away, as if by some incredibly strong winds. It snapped his wrist back so hard it stung and Volf yelped with the pain, holding his hand.

So that's what was holding Astria in place, some force of wind.

Interesting.

Well he didn't need to touch someone to include them in his shadow-form, touch just made it easier. He needed information, and she'd be able to see him and talk to him, if he included her in his shadows.

He stretched out his form around Astria and she blinked, giving a gasp of shock.

"I'm here to rescue you!" Volf said with a smile. "Don't worry."

Astria regarded him. "Are you able to remove the winds around me?"

Ah... "No."

She grimaced and seemed to shrink in on herself a little. "Then I fear you will not be able to free me. Also, even having closed the door, Lucian will know it was opened. He'll know someone's here. You need to flee, quickly."

Damned Holn-spawned shades! He felt his jaw tighten; teeth clenched for a moment. "I am sorry." He felt his own heart constrict. He'd failed Astria and Mirala. "How can I get rid of these winds holding you?"

"You need a ring, from one of my father's disciples. It must have a wind-stone set in it."

"A ring?" Was that all that was needed to free her? He could get a ring. "What's a wind-stone?" It sounded quite oxymoronic.

"There are four precious gems set into the rings, one for each element." How did this girl know so much? Now wasn't the time to ask. "Ruby for fire, diamond for earth, pearl for water, and sapphire for wind. Find a ring with a blue stone in it." That was much easier to understand.

"I will, Astria, and I'll return for you."

"You must save Andrei as well."

Volf shot a glance at the other man. "I can't. I wouldn't be able to get him out of here."

Astria turned quite serious. "Volf, he is my brother, if not by blood then by spirit. He helped my mother and uncle escape the first time, that's why he… suffers as he does. I can't bear to think of him left here. I will not go without him."

Stubborn girl.

"Then I will not be able to free you," he said a little dashed. He raised a finger. "Not yet anyway. I'll return with the others. Together we'll be able to get you both out of here. It may be a few more days still. Can you hold on for that long?"

"I will do what I can." She was grim, but by all the gods, this girl seemed more stalwart than he himself.

"I am sorry, I must leave you now."

She nodded.

Volf withdrew his shadow-form from around her.

Well, that hadn't gone as expected.

He retraced his steps and left the cellars as quick as he dared. He didn't need or want to search any deeper than he had.

As he reached Lucian's storage area, he heard steps descending from Lucian's study above.

Holn-shadowed luck!

"I know you're here." The tone was playful, superior, drifting down from above.

Volf froze. Was Lucian talking to him?

Shades and Shadows!

"Are you the shadow-talent I sensed coming south? Very smart of the others to send you ahead to scout. But you are finished now, my friend."

Volf's heart went cold. Lucian knew he was here. But how?

It didn't matter. He bolted before Lucian reached the bottom of the stairs.

He left through the secret door to the regular cellars, then used his shadow-walk to speed himself up. He hoped Lucian wouldn't be able to follow as he ran as fast as he could away.

And yet it seemed mocking laughter followed him even past the walls of the estate.

16

LUCIAN MADE HIS WAY DOWN TO THE DUNGEONS. DAVUL HAD made it clear that the intruder had left in all haste. This was evidenced by the door to the room where Lucian had kept Andrei and Astria being closed, but not locked. Lucian had sensed a short period when his spirit-link with his daughter and Andrei had been re-established and that had piqued his interest. It had been about then that the god had informed him of the intruder.

Upon opening the door, he found both his captives right where they should be.

He went to Astria, who was more likely to give him useful information than Andrei. "I will end your punishment now, my daughter, and allow you to move about the house with only an escort, if you answer my questions truthfully."

"I will, Father." Her tone was repentant, but he suspected she was just acting that way to get out of her restraints.

"This door was opened not long ago. What happened afterward? Who was here?"

"There was a voice that spoke to me, Father. He said he would free me, but he couldn't. He said he could not undo the wind that bound me, then he fled. I don't know where he went or what he intends."

That sounded reasonable, and yet…

"Was this not someone you and your mother met when you went north?"

"His voice sounded familiar. Perhaps it could have been one of those three, but I was only among them for a short time."

What say you, my lord, is this the truth? he asked his god.

Not entirely. She knows the man better than she is letting on. Give her one more day where she is, then release her.

As you wish, my lord.

"Davul does not think you are being honest with me," Lucian said. "Think long and hard about how best to obey your father and your god, my daughter."

Astria's shoulders slumped, hope draining out of her. "I will, Father. I am sorry."

But was she really?

He decided to test her once more before he left. "Before I caught you, you were hiding your spirit-link. How did you do that?"

And there it was, the flash of concern and deceit on her face before she answered. "I don't know, Father. It must have been some new ability I discovered."

"You should have no access to the shadow domain. This is not some new ability!"

Astria flinched away at his anger. "Please, Father, I know nothing more!"

That was a lie and they both knew it.

Lucian felt no remorse as he hit her, a hard slap across her face, leaving her cheek bright red. Perhaps that would teach her to lie to him. "I'll come back when you're ready to tell me the truth." Then he spun on his heel and left.

By the time he'd returned to his study, his mood had settled a little. He sat heavily in his high-backed chair and considered the four rings laid out on this desk: one of air, one of fire, and two of earth. These represented some of his most powerful minions, now dead,

Syasha and Kalia, the one other survivor of the attack against the drahksani, had reported in that morning, and also returned the rings of the fallen minions to him. Lucian was not surprised to hear of their defeat, though he conveyed his extreme disappointment. He'd ordered her to return and given her the names of a few others to bring with her.

The trouble was, he'd only had four druhi and eight treti, his highest-level minions, before that attack. The loss of four treti was significant. He was about to uplift four more to that station, but they would be new to the powers of their rings and might not be at full capability when needed. He'd just have to hope they were.

The other disheartening news from Syasha's report, was the power and combat ability of these new drahksani. It seemed they were all capable fighters. Syasha had said that the one she fought had been able to cut through her wind-shield, and Syasha had the scars to prove it. She'd told of beams of light fired through the forest and the incredible resilience of the warriors she'd faced.

Lucian wondered how well he'd be able to deal with these newcomers. He already knew that Mirala and Donallo were little threat to him. He was stronger than they, older, and as much as they might be able to peek into his mind or sense his emotions, they would not be able to affect them to any significant degree. No, it was these warriors who would be the real threat. He hadn't faced strong physical and combat talents since Andrei's parents. That fight had been far closer than he liked to admit, especially since they had been weaker muddled-blood drahksani.

There came a knock on the door.

"Enter!" he called out.

Syasha and Kalia entered, with two other struvrti—third level disciples. They stood in a line before his desk, silent and waiting. This was the sort of obedience he expected from his daughter.

Lucian rose, taking up the four rings.

"Syasha, you did well to survive and return to me. Now I know the strength of these foes. The loss of the others is lamentable, but it gives me an opportunity to try something I hadn't before, something which may be needed in the coming days. To you I give, the ring of fire. This would normally have been given to a struvrti whom I wished to advance to treti, but I believe that with its powers combined with yours over air, you will be a truly formidable foe."

Syasha seemed a bit shocked. This was the first time Lucian had ever given two rings of power to any one person. It wouldn't be the last.

He handed her the ring. She placed it on her finger. The metal of the rings was imbued with a little earth-based power, such that a ring would size itself to a new bearer. She surveyed her hand, now with a ring of sapphire and one of ruby, nodding with a smile.

"I also increase your rank. You were always one of the strongest of my druhi and are definitely the most powerful now. I proclaim you to be Pruha-Druhi, first among my seconds."

"I am honored, Undying One," she said with a bow of her head, standing a little taller.

Lucian moved on. "Kalia, despite your flight from the fight, I see promise in you. I am elevating you to the rank of treti, but—!" He let that word hang in silence for a moment. "You will keep your current ring as well. To you I give the ring of air. May you use it well to defend me and keep our people safe."

"Thank you, Undying One," the woman said as she received the ring. She slipped it on and smiled at the sapphire and pearl she now wore.

The last two were both men, brothers actually, and both struvrti who had served him well. One possessed a ring of fire, the other of water. He'd picked them for that specific combination and their loyalty.

"Viktor and Veles, you have both served me well in the past. I promote you both to the rank of treti and give you these rings of earth. May you use them well to defend our city against all foes."

The two brawny men took the promotions stoically and put on the rings, having to wait a moment for the bands to resize for their thicker fingers.

"Thank you, Undying One," the two said in near unison.

"Now, go, practice with your new powers. There may be foes on the way and I will need you all in good form as soon as possible. Syasha, gather the other druhi and return here at the toll of the evening watch. I have more I'd say to them."

The four nodded and left.

Lucian returned to his desk and considered what he'd done. It was a gamble, giving two rings to one person. He'd already asked his lord if it would be possible to use such powers in combination. Davul had told him that opposing elements could not be used together: fire and water, earth and air. But any other set of two would work well. Lucian now had one of each possible set to see how it would work out.

This meant he was sacrificing the number of his followers with powers, for a few with greater powers in general.

He surveyed his minions in his mind. Syasha would be the most powerful, then would be his three other druhi, even though they only had one ring each. Then would be the three others he'd promoted today, with powers of a treti and stru-vrti combined. After them would be his four remaining treti. And still he would have nine remaining normal struvrti and over twenty of his lowest level minions, the piati. Yes, he was confident that with all of these minions nearby, those four or five drahksani would not stand a chance against him.

He smiled and relaxed a little.

He just had to prepare a fitting welcome for those inter-lopers. Davul had shown him a few ways in which he might be able to detect invisible intruders. So, he would begin to lay some traps for his foes. Soon, they would come to him and he would be more than ready for them.

And that thought pleased him immensely.

17

CAERWYN KNEW VOLF WAS COMING. HE'D NOT BEEN HIDING HIS spirit-link since evening had set in. That made sense, since he'd need it to find them. So, when Volf appeared from the shadows of the night, she didn't start or flinch.

"Hello, Volf," she said stoically. "Where have you been?" Though she had a pretty good guess. These last few days she'd had trouble keeping her temper, even with Mirala's help. There was far too much for her to process between her personal revelations and her confounding emotions around Donallo and Jais. She was still upset with Volf for running off, but her lingering frustration and ire at him faded as she saw how dejected he looked.

He sighed. "I failed in my quest, but I have news for everyone."

At least he was still alive and seemed well. "Come on then."

She'd been standing watch, a short distance from the copse of trees where the others had made camp. She'd wanted to look at the stars, without the light of a fire disrupting her vision. The wash of tiny lights in the heavens was truly beautiful. She wasn't sure she'd ever appreciated their simple, sparkling beauty.

For a moment, before Volf had arrived, as she'd looked up at the stars, she'd forgotten about everything and been... content. Yet now her emotions flooded back and she was awash in uncertainty, shame, and anger once more.

She turned and led Volf through the tight cluster of trees to the clearing where the others had made camp.

In the days since Volf had left the four of them, they had made their way quickly to Laskovic. Caerwyn had set a grueling pace for them, knowing they could rest once they were on a riverboat. They'd made it to the city in one day of hard travel and booked passage on a boat leaving that evening. That night and the next day, they had floated downriver with the swift current, making good time. They'd been let off on the bank not far from where they now camped just an hour or so before sunset. It had been shortly after that, that they'd sensed Volf's approach.

And in all that time she'd not spoken more than a handful of words to Jais, nor he to her.

"You've made it a long way in a short time," Volf said as they passed through brush, beneath the heavy branches of the trees above, now blocking out the stars.

"We were lucky to catch a riverboat leaving just as we arrived. It was carrying grains downriver to Rodathia. We slept on the sacks. It was surprisingly comfortable, though I'd not want to make a bed of such things. The fact that it was moving even as we slept helped."

The light of the fire had been visible, filtering through the brush, as they'd made their way into the small forest. Now they broke through the last of the bushes and the small clearing was lit well by the orange flames. Mirala was curled up on her blankets. Donallo and Jais talked quietly. They turned.

"Welcome back," Jais said, tone harsh, grating. "Where did you jaunt off to?" He'd been miserable the entire trip south and it seemed that hadn't changed in the last hour. He was even snipping at Volf.

"It's a long story and we should wake Mirala."

Donallo rose to go to his sister, but she sat up on her own. "I'm awake, hadn't fallen asleep yet."

Volf and Caerwyn settled around the fire, joining the rough circle.

Jais kept his distance from her. She should say something, but didn't know what might come out, given her own unbalanced state. Mirala kept glancing back and forth between them and shaking her head. Caerwyn knew she and Jais would need to talk eventually. She just hoped she hadn't killed off any hope of a friendship between them with her unfeeling and thoughtless words up north. Yet before they spoke, she'd need to figure herself out. And that seemed far more of a process than they all had time for.

Volf spoke. "I had been feeling... useless after that fight with Lucian's minions."

"Volf, you killed one of them, you were far from useless," Donallo said, but Volf seemed not to hear the man and went on.

"So, I thought, perhaps with my stealth and speed, I could sneak into wherever Lucian was keeping Astria and free her."

"Oh, Volf!" Mirala said, then pressed her lips together.

"And as you can see, I failed." He sighed heavily. "She is bound up in some sort of personal prison of wind."

Mirala let out an audible breath. "A storm-hold. It's one of Lucian's favorite tactics to disable his foes. It's nearly impossible to escape from."

"As I found out," Volf said, massaging his wrist. "I reached for her and my arm was blown aside, wrenched so hard it still hurts." He shook his head. "Astria seemed... she's one strong girl. She knew I'd be able to do little, but she told me that if we got a ring of wind from one of Lucian's disciples, we might be able to free her. She said we can tell a ring of wind because it will have—"

"A sapphire, yes," Mirala said, finishing the thought. "But those won't be easy to get either."

Volf didn't seem too upset though. "Perhaps, but at least we know where Astria is and how to free her. That is something, isn't it?" After a moment he added, "Although..."

"What?" Jais asked.

Volf had his lips pressed tight, shaking his head. He seemed reluctant to go on. Finally, he said, "I... I don't know how, but Lucian seemed to know I was there! I never came out of my shadow-form, and yet he spoke to me, as if he knew where I was! How...?"

Donallo let out a heavy, audible breath. "I might know the answer to that."

All attention turned to the man. Donallo lowered his head to his hands and sat there for a long moment, before looking up to speak. "I probably should have told you sooner, but... somehow, Lucian seems to be getting the support of a god, Davul."

"What?" That was from Mirala. Apparently Donallo hadn't told her this news either. "I know his cult worships Davul, but I didn't think the god would truly reciprocate?"

Caerwyn reeled at this news. Davul? The South Wind. The Heat of Passions. Why would the god be helping a man like Lucian, even if the man's cult was dedicated to the deity? Many people worshiped gods without the god actually helping them in any tangible way. As far as she knew, the gods were distant beings who cared little for mortal affairs. The fact that a god was helping this man directly... it was absurd!

"A god?" Jais said incredulously.

Caerwyn shared that sentiment. As much as she, Jais, and Barami had received mysterious help, before their fight with the Krolloc, from the statues of the gods in the Festorium, she still didn't truly believe in the gods. She didn't question the magical statues. There was magic in the world and that could lend itself to many mystical things, like that Festorium. But the gods, personally taking an interest in mortals... That was another thing all together.

Caerwyn had to ask, "How much help is the man getting from him?"

Donallo drew in a long breath. "Before I learned this, I was like you. I didn't think much of the gods. They were distant things. Perhaps this isn't a god, but some other powerful entity that is manipulating Lucian. Yet I've been in Lucian's mind. I know he speaks with this being and believes it's Davul." Donallo drew in another steadying breath, which made Caerwyn wonder what was coming next. "To your question, Caerwyn, I think we told you that Lucian has powers over all of the elements, foundational and chaotic. What we didn't say before—because Mirala didn't know and I found it hard to believe myself—was that it was through Davul that he gained most of those powers. He'd always had his abilities with storm, but the other elements, they came from Davul, or whoever or whatever this being is."

"How can we go up against a god?" Volf asked, sounding— as Caerwyn was starting to feel—hopeless.

"Even if it isn't a god. Something that can grant powers like that! It's..." Jais stammered for a moment but no more words were forthcoming.

"This being isn't all powerful. It has given Lucian power,

yes, but the impression I got, from being inside the man's mind, was that his connection to the being was limited and it didn't seem to act in this world directly, only through Lucian."

"Still!" Jais said, shaking his head. "How can we go up against that?"

"I think you're forgetting," Donallo said softly. "We don't have to. All we need to do is get Astria out, then run. We don't have to face Lucian. We can leave him to his god and just grab Astria."

That was true, but Caerwyn was suddenly recalculating their chances of even doing that.

"Please, we must try," Mirala said imperatively.

"Of course, we will," Volf said, seemingly doing an about face. He'd certainly gotten over his surprise and fear of this 'god' situation quickly.

Mirala smiled at him.

Caerwyn could see how the man lit up at that smile. Ah, so that was it. He was captivated by the woman.

"We'll do what we can, what we must," Caerwyn said stoically. They had previously agreed to do just that, and the presence of a god didn't change their objective, just how hard it would be to achieve.

"Thank you," Mirala said.

Jais was shaking his head. "This is crazy, but I guess that's what we do now... crazy."

And it was settled.

∽

MIRALA DREW VOLF AWAY FROM THE OTHERS, A LITTLE INTO the forest.

"You're a fool, you know that?" she hissed at him. Gods,

she couldn't believe he'd run off to try to rescue Astria on his own. "You could have gotten yourself killed!"

"I was ready for that." He seemed stoic.

"And what good would that have done anyone?" Her tone was still harsh and her voice still low.

He shrugged. "What good can I do otherwise?"

"What, while alive? There is a lot you can do!"

He shook his head slowly. "Feel free to tell me. I can't see it."

"What do you mean? You're brave, if tending toward the foolhardy side of valor. You're dedicated to your friends, even to helping others who you hardly know. That's not nothing. That's more than most people would do."

He grimaced. "Sure, but…" He lifted his hands in an exasperated shrug. "What am I really? I don't even know." He gave a harsh laugh. "I've spoken with a dragon and yet I—"

"Sorry, say that again? You've spoken with a what?" She was fairly certain she'd heard that right but didn't believe it. Gods and dragons? What was going on with this world?

His eyes went wide. "Oh, Holn. I can't even keep a secret anymore either!"

"That's a pretty big secret to keep. A dragon, really?"

He returned to his grimace. "Yes, but it's dead now."

"Oh." She wasn't sure how she felt about that.

"And what I was saying was: even though it showed me all of my powers and gave me this ring to add to what I can do, still… what am I? I don't want to be a thief, and yet that seems all my powers are meant for. I can sneak and hide. What use is there for such things in normal society?"

"We're drahksan. None of us fit into normal society."

"You know what I mean!"

She did. She at least could help people with their emotions and take away some of the pain from harsh realities and harder pasts. That's how she could help, and wanted to help. Yet with Volf, what he was saying was true. If he wasn't going to be a thief, then how could his powers really help people?

Maybe that didn't matter. "Look, Volf, did you ever stop to think that your powers don't define you?"

He quirked a brow in question.

"Let me ask you this. If you didn't have these powers, who would you be? What would you want to do?"

"I... I don't know. I've never thought of it like that before."

"Perhaps you should start."

He blinked a few times. The idea was clearly hard for him to comprehend.

She raised a hand to cup his cheek. "Volf, you have a large heart. That much I know even from the short time we've been together. You care deeply. Consider that." She let a little emotional soothing drift into him from her hand and he seemed to calm a little.

Standing there, near him in the dark forest, with only the flickering flames of a nearby fire, casting the angles of his face in sharp relief, she had to admit to herself that he was a fairly handsome man.

Erith—her first husband—had been a tall and slender man like Volf. Though that was where the similarities stopped. Erith had had dark hair and deep brown eyes, as opposed to Volf's blond and blue. He'd also been quite sure of himself, where Volf seemed so very fragile, especially in this moment. Erith's powers had been with spirit, a charismatic man, who drew people together and bound them to him or each other. He'd had some minor powers over light as well, which was another contrast to Volf. And yet... in both of their eyes she saw a caring, overflowing heart.

She'd told Volf she didn't know where she stood in terms of how she felt about him, and that much was still true. She would still want to wait until these trying times were done and she had her daughter back... and they were all safe. But after that, she could now see the possibility of Volf in her future.

She removed her hand from his cheek, only to slap him lightly. That shocked him, and he seemed a bit hurt.

"That's for running off without telling anyone and trying to do everything on your own."

He grimaced at that.

She reached that same hand around behind his head and pushed it a little toward hers as she leaned in and gave him a peck on the cheek. She lowered her tone, whispering in his ear: "And that's for caring so much and trying to free my daughter... all on your own."

When she pulled away, he seemed even more stunned, if anything. She moved her hand down to his chest and soothed his emotions once again. "You'll find your way, Volf. Just stop assuming it's your powers that define you. It's not. You get to choose who you are, and who you will be."

She left him there, returning to the others.

He emerged from the woods a short while later. She could sense his emotions still in turmoil. Hopefully he'd taken some time to think about what she'd said.

Just as she would take some time to consider how Volf might fit into her life... once this mess with Lucian was over.

18

JAIS COULDN'T SLEEP. HE HADN'T BEEN SLEEPING WELL AT ALL since…

He still couldn't believe Caerwyn had…

His emotions rolled and roiled within him and he couldn't find peace, even with Mirala's help. As much as he wanted to hate Donallo for having been the one to give Caerwyn what she desired, he couldn't. In fact, he was starting to understand why Caerwyn had chosen the man, even if he didn't like any of it. Donallo was—it was hard to describe, but Jais thought he'd found a good word for it—unattached. He seemed to live separate from everyone, and yet always living for them, giving to them. He was selfless in the truest sense of the word. He wanted nothing for himself, only to help those around him.

Jais stubbornly clung to his hatred for the man, even as he found a growing respect. It was just one of the conflicts and dichotomies warring within Jais. He loved Caerwyn—that hadn't changed— and yet in this moment, he couldn't stand to look at her. He was, at the same time, happy to find out he had a brother, a family, and terrified that he might lose that brother before he ever got to know him. He was also excited about the battle to come, though he feared what they faced: a powerful drahksan, apparently backed by a god! He was torn this way and that, and couldn't find any sense of calm.

So, he rose and left the camp; moving through the brush to stand just beyond the forest and look up at the stars. He used to stare at the night sky as a child and wonder about all those dots of light. Myth and religion said that each was a splinter of Mirh, the Lord—or Lady, depending on which religion one followed—of Light, sibling of Holn, and master of all the gods. A being of pure brilliance and truth.

Truth.

He could use some of that right now. Some semblance of something that made sense. The world just seemed so confused and in turmoil.

Is that why my parents left?

He drew out his sword and put a hand to the blade. *Father?*

Yes, son?

Tell me about the Palassi?

Donallo had told them all about the division among the drahkan, the Domassi and Palassi, but Jais wanted to hear the words from his own father.

Ah, yes, of course. I should have told you about us long before now. There came the equivalent of a sigh from the spirit of his father. *I've apologized before. Everything here, in this strange place, is so jumbled. I can't seem to recall anything specific unless and until you ask about it. I'm so sorry, Jais.*

It's more than some people have. At least I can ask.

True. Now, as to the Palassi. They... we were committed to helping humans thrive on their own, helping them only as needed to defend against tyrants and greater threats, like krolls and other powerful beings.

Like gods? Jais asked.

Gods? No, we never fought any gods. They were always distant things. We never even saw so much as a dragon in our time. You've exceeded me in that capacity. Why do you ask?

Because the god, Davul, seems to be aiding our foe. He's given him powers beyond what he should have and allowed him to give those powers to others, to humans as well.

That's madness! Davul, helping evil men grow in power? That makes no sense.

Exactly! And yet our allies say it's true. Or at least that some greater being is influencing the man.

I know not of such things. Again, I am sorry, Jais. But I can tell you more about the Palassi.

Yes, please do. I'm sorry, I keep interrupting you.

The Palassi were generally kind and benevolent. A few among us were more militant... If I'm honest, your mother and I were among the more... passionate of the Palassi. We should have listened to your aunt and hidden ourselves instead of trying to restore humanity's faith in drahksani. But that wasn't how we thought in those days. We were passionate about fighting injustice, about defending those who couldn't protect themselves. That's what it meant to be a Palassi, at least that's what it meant to us.

Jais responded, *I think Caerwyn and I are a lot like that. We both seem drawn to protecting people, even if it's to our own detriment.*

That sure sounds like Palassi to me, son.

Thank you, Dad. He got the sense of a smile from the spirit in the blade.

But that moment of peace and certainty lasted only a few heartbeats before Jais' mood fell again.

What is it? his father asked.

So, I know that I'm driven to protect, that I'm like the Palassi, and yet, that seems to be all I know about myself.

With Caerwyn having made it clear that she wanted nothing to do with him, he knew now that he'd only ever have himself to count on. One thing had been made clear to him these past few days: yet again he'd fallen into a pattern and yet again it had torn out his soul. He'd needed Caerwyn's validation, her 'yes, I love you too, Jais.' He'd been waiting on that, hoping for that to make him whole. He'd thrown himself into relationships with Alnia, then Elria, and had used that as a means to define himself. He was who loved him. And he'd hoped Caerwyn would be the next one to define him. Yet she'd made it clear she didn't want him around. So, where did that leave him? Who was he on his own?

He hadn't had the dragon to tell him, and now he was adrift without a woman to cling to. Well maybe he didn't need one. But if that was the case, then where did he even start?

Son, I think you know far more about yourself than you think.

Oh?

You don't need the world, or anything outside of you, to tell you who you are. You don't need a dragon or a woman. Only you can define who you are, and I think you already know at least some of it.

Do I? Then why is it so hard to figure out who I am?

Perhaps you just need some time alone, quiet, to search within yourself.

I'm not likely to get much of that in the near future.

Well, perhaps when you do, use it. Think back on your life. What are the patterns? What drives you? What are you good at? What do you so desperately want to be good at? What does that tell you?

Could that be it? Was it that simple?

The spirit of his father laughed in a soft, understanding way. *Oh, I didn't say it would be easy or quick, just that with time and dedicated thought, you can figure out who you are on your own.*

Perhaps he could. He'd just need to find the time to consider all of that. *You've given me a lot to think about, thank you, dad.*

You're welcome. Any time, son. Another sensed smile from the spirit.

Jais sheathed the sword and stood for a moment longer looking at the stars.

I already know who I am. It sounded odd to say in his mind, incongruent with the turmoil and uncertainty within him.

Well, perhaps he'd find some time and figure it all out. He just hoped he'd have that time. He was going to face a madman and a god. He needed to concentrate on surviving that first. Then he could think about who he was.

19

CAERWYN WAS DISTRACTED, WHICH WAS THE LAST THING SHE wanted as the group of them sneaked around Lucian's estate. Volf had scouted the grounds to find a guard with a sapphire ring. Now the group crept up behind the man, hidden by Volf's shadow-form.

Yet in all that time, Caerwyn couldn't stop thinking about Jais.

More and more, bit by bit, every day, she was feeling better about who she was and what she'd gone through. She was coming to terms with her once-vow to 'protect the world' and accepting that she just couldn't do that. She was finding more confidence in herself, in what she could do, while recognizing that she wasn't perfect and couldn't do everything. It was a slow process, but in that sense, she was feeling far better than she had even just a week ago. And yet, at the same time, her emotions around Jais were confused and spiraling out of control.

He'd said he loved her.

That had surprised her, and yet, the more she thought about it, perhaps it shouldn't have.

If there was one thing that she'd observed about the man's behavior, it was that he seemed a font of passion, always overflowing with his need to find someone special. There had been Alnia, then Elria, but with their deaths, he'd turned to her now.

She was flattered, but wondered if his emotions were true, or just his drive to find someone, and she was the only someone to find. She just couldn't be certain.

Yet she didn't know how to talk to him and find out what he truly felt, after she'd lied to him and been so brutal and callous. Their 'relationship' might not be recoverable.

At the very least, Jais was a good friend. He hadn't been with her near as long as Barami had, but still, he was someone she could count on. She'd forgotten that in the few months since the wizard in the north. She'd dismissed him—and Volf —as a bit frivolous. But she knew that wasn't true. They were loyal and dedicated. She may not be able to turn to them as she had to Barami, but that didn't lessen their friendship and contribution. And she felt like she'd lost some part of that now.

She should tell him how she felt, what he meant to her... but first she'd have to be able to put it into words herself. She honestly wasn't sure how she felt. Donallo seemed to think she had some lingering thoughts about Jais. But she couldn't pin them down, couldn't make her mind or soul sit still long enough to determine anything when it came to that brash, brawny young man. And right now, they had so many other things to worry about.

Find a sapphire stone. Steal it. Free Astria and Andrei. Flee from this place without bringing Lucian and all his minions down on them. Easy to say, but each of those steps would be a significant challenge.

And they were about to enact the first part of that plan,

she needed to pay attention. She focused on the task at hand, drawing a long breath and letting it out slowly.

Their small group was ready to pounce on the guard they'd found, but there were two problems. The first was, the second person walking beside the one they wished to assault. Luckily, that second person didn't also have a ring, but they'd need to be subdued just as quickly so as not to raise an alarm. The second problem was finding a place to attack these two where others wouldn't notice if they suddenly vanished, being drawn into Volf's shadow-form.

The pair rounded a corner of the estate and for a moment at least, no one else was in sight.

"Now!" Caerwyn hissed and rushed forward with Jais and Donallo, as Volf extended his shadow-form around the two guards. Caerwyn would take the one with the ring, while her two allies would tackle the other man.

The man with the ring spun and lifted his hand, probably to blast wind at her, but she was too close. One swift chop removed that hand and the ring with it. The man shrieked, or would have—mouth wide and face contorted in pain—but Volf had shielded them from all sound as soon as Caerwyn had given the command to attack. A flick of her wrist and her blade slid along the man's well exposed throat as his head tilted back from his cry of agony. He was dead before he hit the ground.

She looked at her allies, who had easily subdued the other man, pinned on the ground, under Jais. He was alive, but a punch to his temple from Jais and he stopped moving. Jais plucked the man up as if he were no more than a rag-doll as Donallo placed a simple illusion over the scene. It was more a trick of thought to ignore this area; don't look here. After he did it, Caerwyn kept having to force herself to look back, her mind and her gaze otherwise just wanting to look elsewhere.

The guard who was still alive was bound and gagged, though Caerwyn was sure he wouldn't wake any time soon.

Caerwyn removed the ring from the severed hand, then the five of them were off, Volf using his shadow-walk to move them quickly around the estates to the kitchens. With Volf's ability to mask sound and Donallo's 'don't-look-here,' they managed to open the door and sneak through the kitchens without anyone noticing the door, which would have seemed to open and close itself.

Then they were down the stairs and into the cellar.

So far, so good.

Volf had mentioned Lucian might know they were around, probably because of some ability or gift from Davul, so they had to move fast.

Yet, as they opened, then moved through the secret door into Lucian's storage area, Caerwyn felt a faint moisture cover her. It was like moving through a brief shower of mist.

Almost instantly a shout erupted from the darkness beyond, "They're at the door! Take them!"

And any surprise or hope of getting out of this without a fight vanished.

Gouts of fire erupted from dark corners, illuminating a room filled with men and women, all ready for them and attacking with various elements.

Mirala and Donallo were graceful and quick, ducking back into the kitchen storeroom with ease. Volf was similarly out of the way of the attacks with alacrity. Caerwyn seemed stuck, slow to move, compared to the others. Then Jais was in front of her, grabbing her and moving her to the side and safety, even as several of those blasts of fire hit his back.

He didn't even scream, just gritted his teeth.

Caerwyn wanted to ask if he was well, once they were behind cover, but Volf still had his silence up. She tapped the slender northerner and pointed to her mouth when he looked. A moment later she could speak.

"Jais? Are you well?" she asked turning back to the man. The pain on his face was gone.

"I've healed it. Don't worry about me."

And yet, she did.

The five of them huddled to one side of the door as various attacks blasted through the portal: flashes of fire, whips of water, blasts of air, and flying stones.

"What can we do?" Mirala's voice quavered with fear.

It was Donallo who answered, taking control of the situation. "Caerwyn, you have the ring and can fight well. Go with Volf, hidden, to get Astria. The rest of us will create an opening and a diversion for you."

"Oh?" Jais asked, sounding unsure. "How?"

Donallo turned to Mirala. "They will probably be advancing on that door soon. I'll hide us, suggesting they look elsewhere, while Mirala creates a sense of urgency to look upstairs. Hopefully, they'll follow that lead and keep looking elsewhere in the estate for us. Jais, you'll stay with us in case they don't fall for the ruse. We'll stay here and guard the exit while Volf hides Caerwyn and goes down to the dungeons to get Astria."

That was a decent plan, except for one thing. Caerwyn grabbed Jais' hand and slid the ring into it. "No, send Jais with Volf. No offence Jais, but I'm still the better warrior and I'll have a better chance against all these minions if this goes wrong. Also, I can negate Lucian's attacks if he shows up." Though could she? She hadn't been able to negate the attacks from his minions. Doubt clouded her thoughts, but she couldn't afford to be uncertain now. She hoped what she'd said would be true with Lucian. She was immune to drahksani powers, perhaps his minions were different since they weren't truly drahksan? She had to hope that was the case.

Donallo shrugged. "Done. Are we ready? I can sense them drawing close to the door."

The attacks at the door had abated for a moment, and in the silence that followed soft, tentative footfalls could be heard from the far side.

"Let's go!" Donallo hissed.

Volf and Jais vanished.

Two people came through the doorway, looking around cautiously, ready. Then, in unison, their heads turned toward the stairs.

"I think they've fled up into the estate," one said.

The other nodded then turned to those behind him saying, "Follow us!"

A line of men and women filed out of the other room, probably twenty or more. Once the doorway was empty, Caerwyn hoped Volf and Jais were already moving through.

The line of enemies ascended the stairs, all intent on what lay ahead... until the second to last man. He paused, and the woman behind him bumped into him.

"What...?" she asked, as the man turned slowly. His gaze sweeping over the cellars.

"Holn!" Donallo whispered harshly as the man peered closer at where the three of them hid.

"Go! Into the next room!" Caerwyn hissed. She'd had a sling-stone readied, just in case and with a quick whip of the leather thong, sent it flying to a spot between the man's eyes.

The woman who'd been behind the man screamed.

A second sling-stone silenced the woman quickly enough, but all pretense was gone. The enemy knew they were behind them.

Caerwyn followed Donallo and Mirala into the other

room, Lucian's private cellar, closing the secret door behind her. That wouldn't hold them for long, but it was something. She said as much to the other two then added, "Once they open the door, we'll have them bottle-necked at least. We can fight them here for as long as the others need to get Astria and get out." Caerwyn started throwing crates and items in front of the door. It wouldn't do much, but anything that would slow the enemy down would help.

"The only way out now is up through Lucian's study, though," Mirala said.

Donallo shrugged. "It's not an ideal exit, but..." he trailed off, his head turning toward the stairs up to Lucian's rooms.

It occurred to Caerwyn only then, that she was no longer masked by Volf's Shadow-form, which meant Lucian would know where they were; and she could sense him too. The powerful essence was descending the stairs, heading straight for them. That must be what had caught Donallo's attention.

"Lucian!" Mirala hissed.

Damn. They'd be trapped between him and his minions. Perhaps coming in here hadn't been the best idea, but it was too late now. They'd make their stand here.

Or... better yet.

"I don't suppose either of you have been down into the dungeons?" she asked. They both shook their heads.

"No, why?" Donallo asked.

"If you had, and there was an alternate exit from there, then perhaps we could just join the others, but if there isn't any way out, we'd all be trapped even farther from the exit, with all of the enemy between us and it."

Donallo grimaced. "Let's not do that if we can avoid it."

Caerwyn nodded. "Anything you can do to slow Lucian down?"

"I'll try an emotional push, but I don't know how effective it will be," Mirala said.

"The others are coming!" Donallo hissed, as the door began to open. Caerwyn pushed one last large and heavy crate in front of the portal, then quickly dodged out of the way of a blast of fire which came through. She ducked to one side, huddling with Donallo and Mirala.

"I have an idea," she said with a bit of a wild grin. "You two do everything you can to keep those others from getting close to that door. Your powers are hopefully going to be more effective on them. I'll handle Lucian." They nodded, and Caerwyn headed for the stairs. She ensured her immunity to drahksani powers was active then charged up to attack Lucian.

She hoped it would be the last thing he'd expect.

A gout of fire hit her but did no damage. Thank all the gods, she was immune to his magic. She charged through the flames to stab him—attacking blind. She got him in the shoulder, the blade sinking deep. He fell back, off the blade, with a clipped cry and tried to push wind at her. It did nothing.

He rolled out of the way of her next attack then scrambled up the stairs a little. "Who are you!" he shouted. "Why can't I affect you?"

"I'll tell you when you're dead," she said grimly, following him. He drew a dagger from a sheath at his hip, then he motioned with one hand. Suddenly a cloud of dust and tiny stones pelted her. She had to step back, blinking the debris away, even as she called for, "Davlas!" and—commanding it with her mind—sent the spear in the direction Lucian had been. She heard another cry but didn't know if it was from surprise or pain.

But that cloud of miniscule debris continued assaulting her. This moment seemed all too familiar. She was reminded of her fight with the wind-powered-woman in the forest. Just like she had then, she closed her eyes against the dust being blown at her and used her echolocation once more.

Yet she needed more noise to 'see' what was around her. She called out, a wordless shout and felt the echoes return to her. It wasn't a clear picture, but she managed to find Lucian backing away up the stairs.

She mentally commanded Davlas to strike at him once again.

His reflexes were quick, and he batted the spear away with his dagger, though she still believed she cut his upper arm.

"How can you—?" He tried to grab for the spear, but she pulled it away. He waved a hand in front of him, she didn't know what he was doing, but when she stabbed with the spear once again. It hit some form of barrier—like what that wind-witch had used—and veered off to one side. So that's what he'd done.

Davlas might be affected, but she wouldn't be. She sheathed her sword, it would be pushed away by his storm-shield, but her fists would do just fine.

She charged up at him. He stood there, probably thinking she'd bounce off his shield. She didn't.

Hitting him hard mid-torso, she knocked him back onto the stairs and began punching him. Yet her sound-vision was erratic now with all the noise and movement and she found it hard to find him. That, and he had a dagger. She felt his blade plunge into her arm, high, near the shoulder. That, however, would be his only strike. She spun and at the same time grabbed his hand, wrenching it off the dagger. Then she pulled the weapon out and tossed it away.

Now she had him.

She rained blows down on him, and started to wonder if

she just might be victorious. If she could defeat him here, it would end all the madness.

But he let out a roar and she heard something from farther up the stairwell. Her sound-vision didn't catch the object soon enough, it had been hurled at her with amazing speed. It caught her forehead and tore her off Lucian, sending her pitching backwards down the stairs. She rolled over the wooden steps and bounced off stone walls.

She landed, groaning, in a heap at the bottom, aware enough to know her head was bleeding, blood was flowing over her one—still clenched-shut—eye.

Lucian wasn't moving. He'd remained where he was farther up the stairs.

Caerwyn rose slowly to a sitting position. Her body ached all over, but other than her head wound, and where the dagger had cut her shoulder, she didn't think she was badly hurt, just beaten and bruised.

She wiped blood, sweat, and grit from her eyes, and tried to look around her. Once again, her vision was blurry.

Yet she could see well enough to notice Mirala running toward her. At first Caerwyn thought this was to see if she was well, but Mirala shouted, "They're coming, we need to move!" Then Mirala was helping her up.

Donallo was by the door, sword out and ready, and attacked one of the ring-bearers as they came through the opening. That person lost their hand.

"Go!" Mirala urged. There were tears in the woman's eyes. "He's going to keep them here for as long as he can."

No, Caerwyn would do a better job at that. "Davlas," she said, and summoned her spear, sending it flying into the next man who tried to come through the doorway.

"Donallo!" she shouted at the man. "I can keep them at bay for a moment. Come on!"

He hesitated, then bolted for them.

Caerwyn, helped along by Mirala, moved slowly, walking backwards, keeping Davlas in the doorway to keep the attackers at bay. Gouts of fire tried to burn it, but they didn't know it had been forged in dragon-fire. Wind tried to blow it back, but that also didn't work. Then hands of stone rose up and clenched around the spear, holding it firm.

Blazing shadows of Holn!

"We're at the stairs," Mirala whispered. Caerwyn glanced behind her, calling Davlas back.

But that moment, brief as it was, cost so very much.

When she looked back, two men had darted through the doorway, even as Donallo reached her and Mirala. Caerwyn sent Davlas to skewer one of them, but the other got off an attack, a barrage of small to moderate stones, hurled with amazing speed.

One caught her in the shoulder, half turning her, sending her stumbling back into Mirala. The majority caught Donallo in the back, pitching him forward.

Caerwyn caught him, even as she took several unsteady steps down the stairs. He was limp in her arms.

"Oh, gods, no!" she whispered. She scooped Donallo up and together with Mirala ran down the stairs, but she was already certain the man in her arms was dead.

JAIS WAS CONCENTRATING HARD, TRYING TO CONTROL AIR.

He and Volf had descended into the bowels of Lucian's estate. Volf had guided them to the odd iron-clad room and unlocked it. There they'd found Astria and Andrei. Gods, but his brother was big... and beaten all to Holn.

Ever since then, he'd been trying to free the two prisoners with little luck. It seemed this ring didn't have the power needed to overcome Lucian's storm-hold.

But Astria had come up with an idea. If Jais could get the ring to her, she might be able to use it along with her own wind and storm powers to overcome Lucian's air-binding. The trouble was, getting the ring to her.

Jais was using a combination of his ring's power and his own stubborn strength to push through the swirling barrier of air to get the ring to one of Astria's hands, but by all the gods, it wasn't easy or quick. His arm was trembling with the effort of simply trying to remain straight and not being blown away. He was inches away from the girl's hand, so close!

"It's been too long!" Volf urged. "We need to hurry!"

That wasn't helping.

"Someone is fighting Lucian!"

"What?" That distracted Jais just a little too much and his arm was blown free of the barrier around Astria. "Shades and shadows!" he cursed. "Stop distracting me!"

"Sorry," Volf said from somewhere behind him as Jais tried once again to push his fist into the barrier around Astria.

He let out a roar of frustration and put everything he had behind thrusting his hand forward, like one long slow punch. Finally, he broke through and dropped the ring into Astria's hand.

His arm was blown out once again, but a moment later, Astria was falling to the floor, landing lightly.

She took the ring from her palm and put it on a finger, then ran over to Andrei. "Jais, please catch him!" she called and Jais followed her.

When the invisible hold on the man went away, he fell into Jais' waiting arms. Jais was driven to his knees by the dead weight of his brother. It didn't help that he'd used up a lot of his strength just trying to get to Astria.

"They're coming!" Volf said.

"Who is?" Jais asked.

"Caerwyn, Donallo, and Mirala, I think? But I can only sense two of them."

"Yes, it's my mother and Caerwyn, Astria verified. I don't know about Uncle Donallo."

"Why are they heading for us?" Jais asked, hefting himself to his feet—still holding Andrei—and turning to face Volf. The other man shrugged.

"I'm guessing things aren't going well up there. We may need to find another way out of here."

"I don't think there is one," Astria said. Jais turned to her. She had closed her eyes and seemed to be concentrating. After a brief moment she shook her head. "No, there isn't. We're trapped."

"What did you do?" Jais asked.

"The tunnels down here are all dug out from the earth. I can sense through the earth to see where they go."

"Ah."

Rushing footfalls out in the corridor alerted Jais to the arrival of the others. A moment later Mirala ran into the room and Caerwyn followed close behind her, looking bedraggled and well wounded, and carrying a limp and lifeless Donallo.

Volf swung the door shut.

"We need to see if there is another way out of—"

"There isn't." Jais interrupted Caerwyn. "We've already checked."

Caerwyn sagged to the floor, in a controlled collapse, where she set Donallo down, kneeling over him. "Then we're all doomed."

"At least Lucian wasn't following after you," Volf said, trying to sound hopeful. "Are you certain we can't face the others?"

No one responded quickly.

Jais went to Caerwyn. He still didn't know what he thought of her. He just knew he was hurt from what she'd said and done, but that was no reason to deny her healing. He set Andrei down and laid a hand on her arm.

She looked at him, then nodded as he began his healing. Other than a nasty wound to her arm, a heavy gash to her forehead, and a fractured rib, most of the other wounds were superficial. He healed the major ones, conserving his energy in case it would be needed to fight their way out.

"Thank you," Caerwyn breathed. He opened his eyes and she was still gazing at him. There was something in that look

—as they lingered for a moment watching each other—which Jais couldn't place.

Would he ever understand her? He highly doubted it.

"Any time," Jais said softly. Whatever he thought, whatever she'd done, he was a healer and wouldn't avoid someone in need.

A loud clanging noise drew his attention from Caerwyn. The heavy iron plates from several places on the walls were tearing themselves away and flying over to the door. Astria seemed to be directing them. Once over the door, they heated up and fused together, forming a rather solid barrier over the portal. It would take a serious effort to break through that.

Yet Astria said, "A powerful earth-ring could push through that fairly quickly. I've only stalled them a little." Her voice was tremulous. She sounded scared.

The enemy would be stalled. What could Jais, or any of them, do with that time?

Jais looked around, desperate for some inspiration. Yet he'd never been much of a planner, no great mastermind. He went with his gut, ran on instinct. Volf seemed to be doing the same as Jais, looking around, as if the bare, iron-clad room might give him any sudden thoughts for escape. Mirala was winded and crying, kneeling over Donallo. Caerwyn was on the other side of the same man, looking down at him with a shake of her head, seeming deflated.

Jais turned to Astria. "You said you have powers over earth, can you… create a tunnel out of here?"

Astria's brows rose as she cocked her head to one side, seeming to consider this. "Yes," she said after a moment. "But my father will know where we're going."

"I think Lucian is mostly out of the fight for now. I beat him fairly solidly," Caerwyn said, still distracted.

Astria went to the wall opposite the door and began her

work. Some other iron tiles ripped away, to fly over and rein-force the door. Then stone was scooped out and it too went to building a pile of heavy debris in front of the entrance way.

Pounding on the other side of the door began, but it seemed distant for the moment.

With that underway, Jais turned Caerwyn. "I assume…"

"Yes, he's gone."

He put a hand to Donallo's forehead to be certain. There was no life in the man.

"He sacrificed himself," Caerwyn said. "He was going to stay behind and hold up the others."

"I'm sorry." Whatever Jais had thought of the man—and his relationship with Caerwyn—it couldn't be denied that Donallo had been a good man.

Caerwyn looked up at him with that strange look once again. "Thank you," she said softly. "When this is all over, we… need to talk."

Jais found his eyes widening, brows raised. Those words were not what he'd been expecting from Caerwyn in this moment. He didn't know what to say to that, other than, "As you wish." Though he didn't really know what they'd speak about. He'd thought she'd made her mind fairly clear already.

She looked away with a heavy sigh. "I think there will be a long way to go before then."

Jais nodded to that. Turning to Mirala he asked, "Do you need healing?"

"No." She shook her head.

But there was someone else here who did.

Andrei lay unmoving next to him. Touching the man's forehead, Jais began—what would be a long process—to heal him. There were so many injuries. Jais could feel a weak force within the body so very slowly healing the wounds. He real-ized quickly that he wouldn't be able to use the other man's energy to cure the wounds, he'd have to use his own, and completely healing the man would drain him. He would have to be careful not to use too much energy yet still do what he could to mend the more serious injuries and try to infuse a little energy into the other man to aid in Andrei's own sluggish healing process.

He was tired and winded when he finished... and Andrei still wasn't conscious.

"She really is quite amazing."

Jais looked up at Volf standing nearby, gaze fixed elsewhere. He followed the other man's stare to see the whirlwind that was Astria. She seemed to have found some rhythm to her work. Stone and dirt were gouged out from the wall, while strong winds whipped it away from her to the doorway, around which there was a rather heaping pile of earth. Jais couldn't see how much of a tunnel she'd dug, not with the constant stream of dirt and stone whirling around the girl, but he guessed it was getting fairly deep.

There was still a pounding on the door, but it seemed ever more distant.

Jais looked around at the others.

Everyone was watching Astria. Mirala appeared the most stunned, which seemed odd. Jais would have thought she'd know her daughter's capabilities, but it seemed even she was amazed by what the girl could do.

So Jais joined them simply watching the miracle that was Astria at work.

YOU INSIST ON DEFYING ME? DAVUL HAD BEEN TRYING TO distract her from her work for some time. Astria had only been able to ignore the god to a point.

Why must you be so cruel and demand death? If you didn't do that, I wouldn't have to defy you. She took a deep breath and redoubled her efforts with the tunnel. She knew she was getting close to the surface and had two choices now. The tunnel was angled slightly upward, to reach the surface faster while still being easy to traverse. Where it was at the moment, she could either continue that same path or head directly upward. If she went up, she'd reach the surface quicker, but it would be harder to get out. Yet she could put divots into the wall to help people climb. If she kept the tunnel as it was, she'd have to dig through three times as much material, and most of it—beyond where she was now—was stone. She decided to go straight up.

"I'm nearly done!" she called to the others.

Through her emotional sense, she felt their amazement. Above them all was her mother's astounded pride. That warmed Astria the most.

And what of those in this world who are cruelest, meanest? Do they not deserve to die?

No. Not even them. Perhaps they deserve to be locked up in dark places, but not death.

Ah, I see. So, death is the line you will not cross?

Yes. People deserve life and a second chance and some love.

Love? Truly? the voice laughed, mocking. When it stopped it asked her, *And your father? He has been most cruel to you. What would you have done to him?*

He is cruel because you made him that way. Before you found him, he sought power, yes, but he wasn't nearly so cruel. He didn't demand death and sacrifices.

You are correct. If we stopped with those rituals, would you consider following me then?

No. Just because you stop those things, doesn't mean you don't want them. She was a little afraid to ask the questions troubling her mind: why was he so intent on her? What did he want with her?

We shall see if you feel that way, in time, Davul said ominously. Then his presence was gone from her mind.

I will, she thought. Then her digging finally broke through to the surface, and her winds cleared the last of the rubble away. "We can go now!" she said turning to the others. Despite dazed and amazed looks, they were quick to react and soon everyone was moving. Jais carried Andrei, Caerwyn carried Uncle Donallo. Astria knew he was dead, she could sense nothing from the spirit-link, but she couldn't think about that now. Mostly she couldn't and didn't want to think about how he'd died coming to save her.

She led the way down the tunnel. Strands of fine dirt fell trickling from the ceiling in places as the weight of the ground above threatened to cave in the tunnel. She was keeping that at bay with her powers at the moment, but she was beginning to grow quite weary.

From somewhere far behind them came a loud blast.

Her father's minions had used a mixture of wind, fire, and earth to blow away the pile of dirt around the doorway. They'd be following along soon enough.

But Astria was already at the end of the tunnel and showing everyone where the divots were to climb up as she did so herself. She reached the top and looked back toward the estate—the house she'd grown up in.

It was still only midday. The sun, high above, shone brightly on the marble walls of the building. The other reason she'd chosen to come up here, was because it was just beyond the walls of the estate.

The others were up quick enough, and Astria then stopped holding the tunnel up; in fact, she encouraged the earth to cave in.

It did so quite willingly. It would take those within some time to dig through that.

"We must go, quickly!" she said to the others. They were still far too close to her father and his allies. "I can do something to get us away quickly, but it will be far from pleasant and I'll be done with my powers afterward," she said. She wasn't going to tell them the details unless someone insisted.

"I don't much care," Jais said, "Whatever gets us away quickest." The others seemed to agree.

Her mother knelt next to her. "Are you sure about this, my child? You've already done so much."

Astria could see how tired and dismayed the others were. No one seemed able to make a hard choice. Well, then she would. "We need to get away from here before Father gets better." Astria tried to be stern. It seemed to work.

Mirala nodded. "Yes, you're right." She embraced Astria

tightly for a brief moment. "Sometimes I wonder when you got so grown up and willful." Releasing her, Mirala said, "Do what you must."

"Prepare yourselves," Astria said by way of warning. Then swirling winds began to whip around them. A moment later they were sucked up into the air. After that, once lifted, even stronger winds pushed them hard, throwing their bodies over the hills around Rodathia, sending them all tumbling. The others were screaming, afraid. Astria didn't blame them, this was highly unnerving. It wasn't true flight, since it was only barely controlled and highly unsettling, but it succeeded in throwing them some distance over the hills to the west. It went on for as long as she could maintain it, then—leaving only a sliver of her power left—she dropped them from the sky.

More screaming.

But she'd saved enough energy to create a buffeting cushion of air where they would land, to slow them, easing them to the ground.

At which point Astria collapsed.

Volf was sick, retching. None of the others looked well. But they were far away from Rodathia now.

Astria finally allowed the built-up tension with her to ease. Her emotions were frayed and tattered and her head foggy with exhaustion. She laid back and fell into an exhausted slumber.

VOLF KEPT THEM ALL MOVING. HIS SHADOW-WALK MEANT EACH of their tired and staggering steps took them much farther than normal, but he was growing ever more tired... and Lucian was gaining.

They had travelled like this for half a day, before collapsing to make a tentative camp. They'd hoped they'd have the time to rest and regain some strength.

But they hadn't been given the chance.

Volf had sensed it, as had the others—all but Jais. Lucian was coming for them, and he was moving at amazing speeds.

Soon after that, a storm had moved in, rains drenching them, lightning flashing all around them. Mirala had said that this was Lucian's power in full fury. So, they had risen and staggered onward.

That had brought them here, to a scrub-brush plain of rolling hills. It was late into the night. Volf kept them hidden and moving fast, but he wasn't sure how much longer he could do so. He'd been doing this far too long with far too many people. He would soon falter and fail.

He stumbled and fell to his knees. For a moment he lost concentration and they flashed out of his shadow-walk then were back in it. That would have given Lucian a glimpse of where they were.

A hand, heavy, calloused and warm, was set on Volf's neck as he drew in ragged breaths trying to rise. Suddenly energy was flowing into him. "Have a little more, friend." Jais stood over him, having set Andrei down for a moment. "I don't need it as much as you do right now."

It wasn't much energy. Jais must have been close to exhaustion as well, and who could blame him, having to carry that massive man for so long. Before he rose, Volf surveyed the rest of them. Mirala was carrying Astria, who still slept soundly. Caerwyn refused to leave Donallo's body, so she still carried him with them as well. Volf was the only one not carrying someone but then, he was the one keeping them hidden and moving.

Everyone looked to be at the end of their energy, slumped and bleary of eye.

Lightning flashed around them, hitting far too close for Volf's liking, splitting a tree nearby.

"We need to move. Lucian will know where we are," Caerwyn said. With that they were all up and ready, if not moving fast, once again. Volf kept his shadow-walk going, at least for a short while, to get them away from where Lucian would have sensed them.

Yet that storm was still moving up fast all around them, soaking them with rain, fraying their nerves with blasts of lightning and cracks of thunder.

I can't keep this up. We can't keep this up. He didn't want to say it out loud. He was certain the rest of them knew it. But they all kept stumbling onward anyway.

Finally, Volf stopped his shadow-walk. Even with Jais' extra energy, he couldn't keep it up as well as his shadow-form, and remaining hidden would be far more valuable right now. Which meant their pace dwindled to a crawl.

At first, Volf thought the storm might pass them by, Lucian was certainly moving far faster than they were. Mirala said he was flying, riding the winds. And yet, somehow the man seemed to know they had slowed. Always the storm was close, harrying them, searching and nearly finding them.

"We need to stop." Surprisingly, it was Jais saying this, perhaps the strongest of them.

"We can't," Caerwyn said. "That storm seems to know roughly where we are, even with Volf hiding us. If we stay in one place, some lucky strike of lightning will find us soon enough."

"But we're all exhausted, we can't go on."

Mirala gave a fatigued moan of agreement to this.

Volf could feel, even more than the physical toll these last few days had had on him, the emotional exhaustion as well. Already one of them had given everything for this cause, and what were they fighting for, really? All they wished to do was get away from Lucian, that was it, but such a goal seemed impossible.

"Wouldn't Lucian be getting tired as well?" Volf asked. Surely, the energy needed to keep up such a storm would wear him out eventually.

"He is a master of his element," Mirala said, voice hoarse, rough. "Not to mention a fourth generation pure-blooded drahksan, nearly a thousand years old, and stronger than all of us. I have seen him stretch himself to his limits. It takes some time for him to do so, and he is feeding off rage at the moment. I doubt he will give up before we do."

"Then what can we do?" Jais asked.

"I can surge my strength," Caerwyn said. There was a note of vehemence in her voice. She seemed to be taking Donallo's death even harder than the man's sister was. "I will stand against Lucian and let you all get farther away.

"Like Holn you will!" Jais was suddenly full of fire. "I will not lose you today! If anyone is going to stand against that madman, it's me."

"Jais, this is no time for—"

"For what? Stupid heroics? I'm only proposing to do what you'd already suggested you yourself do. I'm just not willing to see you die over this!"

"So, you'll die instead?"

"I don't' know, but I'm not going to let you die. I love you!"

CAERWYN WAS STUNNED TO STILLNESS.

She was exhausted and soaked through from the storm. She could see the others were at their limits of endurance as well. She knew, with a surge of her strength, she'd be able to fight for a short while. She didn't know if Jais could do the same or not.

Yet, apparently, they were going to have it out, here and now. Well she'd driven him away, when he'd tried to talk to her before, so she only had herself to blame for this awkward and dangerous situation.

And it seemed Jais hadn't given up on his feelings for her. Though the shock on his own face after he'd shouted those words made it clear to her that they'd stunned him as much as her.

She knelt, setting down Donallo.

"We're stopping, now?" Volf asked, fatigue mixed with sarcastic incredulity in his voice. After a moment he went on. "Apparently we are. Gods! This is insane!"

Caerwyn looked up to see Jais kneeling to set down Andrei as well. The large, unconscious man stirred but didn't wake as he settled on the wet ground. Jais looked at her then. There was that pain in his eyes again, the same as when she'd driven him away. Yet his exhaustion must have weakened his will to remain silent.

"I don't care what you say, Caerwyn, I love you, and I think I will always love you." He shook his head and his expression turned sour. Though she suspected that look wasn't for her and his next words confirmed it. "I know I haven't always shown it. I... loved Alnia, and Elria too. I don't know how or why my heart seems to leap into such things, but it does. Yet all the while, I knew that I shared... a connection with you. That much I've known ever since I first saw you. And no matter how you feel about me, I... just need you to know that."

And she did.

If she'd been uncertain before, she wasn't now.

She looked down at Donallo, sweeping sodden hair off his too-pale brow. He'd known it too.

She shook her head. She'd made a mess of all of this.

Jais spoke again, before she could form a reply. "Caerwyn, I... I don't care that you—" his voice broke.

She looked. It was hard to tell with the rain, but she suspected he was weeping.

He steeled himself and went on. "Look, if you are having his child then... then I'm well with that. I'll help raise it, if that's what you want, and if not..." He swallowed and it seemed a difficult thing.

Oh, Jais.

"His child?" Mirala was kneeling using the upraised knee to help cradle Astria. She looked at Caerwyn now, confused and a bit accusatory.

Caerwyn shook her head. "No, I am not carrying his child." Then to Jais. "We didn't... do anything together. I just said that to push you away, because I didn't know how I felt when you came to me the last time. I didn't know how I felt... about you."

"Me?" Jais blinked.

Caerwyn rose, steady, firm, resolute, a heavy breath escaping her. "I do now," she whispered. Something had solidified inside her as she'd listened to Jais. It occurred to her how hard it was for her to speak her emotions. If it was equally as hard for him, then none of what he'd said could have been easy. And if he could be that firm and forward, so could she.

With that, she was ready.

"Yes," she said with certainty in her voice. She looked down at Donallo. "I can't let anyone else die." Then she raised her gaze to Jais'. "I can't let someone I care for die. I can't let you die. So, I will remain here and face Lucian. The rest of you need to go, now."

"Care for..." Jais repeated, a strange new light in his eyes.

"Yes, now go, please!"

Andrei groaned and broke the moment. The man coughed and Jais turned to him. It seemed the large man was waking up. He still didn't look good, but his wounds had been slowly healing throughout the time Jais had been carrying him.

Jais knelt next to the man as Andrei's eyes opened. Andrei raised an arm to keep the constant rains from his face. Caerwyn and the others joined Jais.

"We don't have time for this," she hissed. "You need to go!"

But they weren't paying attention to her anymore.

"Mirala?" Andrei said, his eyes catching on her. "Who is...? Where am I?" He sat up, grunting as he did. He was still in pain, that much was clear. "I remember..." Then his voice turned hard. "Lucian. I'll kill that man! I don't care if he raised me. He's a monster!" It seemed like many thoughts were rushing back to the man at once. Then he started, seeing the prone form of Astria. "Astria! Is she safe?"

Mirala knelt next to the man and laid a hand on the thick rolling muscle of Andrei's shoulder. "There is too much to discuss now. Lucian is pursuing us. We need to move on. Know that Astria is well, but…" She swallowed hard. "Donallo died when we came to rescue you both. These others here are Volf, Caerwyn, and this is Jais—he's your brother."

Andrei had been looking at each of them as they'd been introduced, and his eyes widened as he came to Jais in time for the last of Mirala's words.

For a long moment the two of them simply stared into each other's faces. Caerwyn wondered what it must be like to see a face so much like your own… but not. There wouldn't be any reason for Andrei to doubt Mirala's words, and the emotions she saw playing over the man's face told her he was accepting it, if in far too harsh and jolting a manner.

"Hi," Jais said sounding far too tired.

"Brother?" Andrei said slowly.

Lightning blasted the ground not more than twenty feet away. The crash of thunder was deafening, and the force of the impact threw everyone to one side. Dirt and sod were blown over them. Then a series of three more strikes, far too close, overwhelmed Caerwyn's senses with noise and light.

"We need to move!" It was a shout, but Caerwyn barely heard it over the ringing in her ears. She staggered to her feet, as another flash of lightning sent her stumbling. Someone caught her arm, helping her move.

"This way!" She couldn't discern who had said it.

It took a moment for Caerwyn to right herself and return to her senses, blinking spots from her vision. Jais was holding her, supporting her.

"Thank you," she said softly. Perhaps his ears were as deaf-ened as hers, for he didn't seem to notice nor respond.

They only managed a few staggering steps before a wall of earth shot up in front of them, twenty feet high.

Andrei, who had been in the lead, bounced off it and stag-gered back a few steps.

"I know you're there!" came a voice like thunder, crashing down from above.

Lucian had found them.

VOLF LET HIS SHADOW-FORM DROP. IT SEEMED IT WAS USELESS now, and he was too far gone into exhaustion to have kept it up much longer. Even as he released the ability, he stumbled and collapsed to his hands and knees. He was close to the earthen wall and, rolling himself over, he simply sat against it.

He'd done what he could; it would be up to the others now.

He watched them draw weapons and ready themselves as the storm seemed to quiet just a little. The heavy clouds billowed back to reveal not only Lucian, but four of his disci-ples, all touching down on the ground from where they had been hovering amidst the storm.

"And now you will all die!" Lucian's voice, once again like thunder, rolled over them. Spittle flew from the man's mouth, his face contorted in rage. Yet Volf could see the telltale signs of fatigue in Lucian's swaying gate, stumbling forward. His face was also well mottled from bruising, from his previous encounter with Caerwyn the day before.

The question would be: who was more tired? And how long could each side last?

Elements were thrown at Volf's allies. They scattered and

ran to engage the enemy, all but Mirala and Astria, the first crouching over the prone form of the second. Donallo's corpse lay close by as well. That left three of them: Caerwyn, Jais, and Andrei against Lucian and probably his four most powerful minions. Volf didn't hold out much hope.

And yet...

Suddenly Caerwyn was sprinting with incredible speed, a war cry on her lips. She blew past Lucian, scoring a hit on his arm, deep. It happened so fast Volf didn't even see it. Apparently neither did Lucian, who cried out in pain, his other hand rising to clasp his shoulder. Blood poured out from between his fingers.

Caerwyn wasn't done. She reached one of the minions still at a full sprint. A gout of fire was blown at her. She dove and rolled under it, then came up, cutting one of the man's legs from under him. Yet even before he fell, she'd risen and—now behind him—slashed back with a heavy swing which took the man's head from his shoulders. All of this within the span of a few seconds.

Volf's heart surged, perhaps—

A horizontal column of fire caught Caerwyn as she paused for a heartbeat. The firestorm, borne on a vortex of whipping winds seemed to strike her with the force of a charging horse. She was thrown a dozen feet and landed hard, smoldering.

Jais screamed and lunged in to attack the one who had sent that devastating strike.

Andrei faced Lucian. The large young man had no weapon, only his open hands, but he seemed little daunted.

Even as lightning flashed down upon him, he leapt and tackled Lucian, or would have, had the man not been protected by some swirling shield, which threw Andrei off to one side. Still, the impact of the large man sent Lucian staggering a few steps.

Andrei was up quickly. Fearless, he strode in and began a brutal series of blows on Lucian's shield.

Volf wasn't sure, but he suspected with Andrei that close, Lucian wouldn't want to summon lightning, and indeed none was forthcoming.

Volf's attentions shifted as two things seemed to happen at once. Jais was thrown back by a similar strike to what had hit Caerwyn, a swirling cone of wind-borne fire. Yet in the same instant the woman who'd sent the attack staggered to one side, clutching her shoulder, where Davlas had just taken a chunk out of her. She collapsed to her knees.

He looked to see Caerwyn, propped on an arm, badly burned, smoke still rising from her as the spear returned to her. She used it to help her rise.

Jais seemed to be having just as much trouble rising, even as one of the minions—tearing up a chunk of earth to throw at Jais—drew near.

Jais only just managed to get to his feet as the massive hunk of earth and stone was hurled at him.

This started a chain reaction of events.

Jais caught the enormous lump of earth and redirected it slightly, shouting: "Andrei, down!"

The earth careened into Lucian, smashing and disintegrating against his shield, but also seemingly weakening it, as dirt and small stones were caught up in the swirling winds and battered Lucian as they were thrown both inward and out with great force.

Lucian had to drop his shield and when he did, Andrei swung a leg under the man, knocking his legs forward so he fell on his back, hard. Lucian screamed and a flicker in the clouds above him was the only warning.

Caerwyn tackled Andrei, knocking him out of the way of the lightning blast, which took her full in the back.

It was Jais' turn to scream, even as he raised his father's sword and a beam of light blew a sizable whole through the earth-hurling minion.

But in the next instant, Jais was frozen in place as the last of the minions fully joined the fight.

Volf!

His attention was drawn away by the voice in his mind. He looked over at Astria, who had eyes open and looking at him. *Next to you. Get my mother and get away!*

He glanced to his side to see a hole had been formed in the unnatural earthen wall.

He nodded to Astria. *I'll get you too*, he said, not certain if she'd be able to hear his return thought or not. He rose, unsteady and swaying on his feet. With some last vestige of energy—gained perhaps by his short period resting—he brought forth his shadow-form and shadow-walked to Mirala and Astria. Yet even as he touched Mirala to bring her into his shadow-form, a blast of lightning hurled them both to the ground.

His mind spun, his body weakening. He was able to rise only because Mirala was helping him. They were leaning on each other. He felt his mind wander and kept having to drag it back to the present moment.

He tried to look for the others, but the field was a mass of lightning, some torrid expression of Lucian's fury. It was too dangerous here. And when he looked to where Astria had been, she was gone.

Go! the girl's voice shouted into his mind and with it came a compulsion to flee this place. He had no strength to resist.

"Astria!" Mirala cried out, but she must have been affected by the girl's mental push as well, as they both fled—in a stumbling run—as fast as they could away from that place.

Perhaps it was some effect of Astria's mental command or

his own delirium, but Volf began to lose himself. He knew he was moving, shambling along with Mirala, but he wasn't seeing what was before him, nor hearing much of anything either. His mind was a blur, blank, reeling, and slowly a swirling, torrent of fevered disorientation gripped him.

Then he knew no more.

23

"Jais! No!" Caerwyn screamed as she burst from darkness to bright light stabbing her eyes.

She sat up, then immediately groaned in pain. Her body was on fire, aching and searing in turns. What had—oh yes… The fight. Lightning. Jais!

Which begged the question: how was she alive at all? Also, where was she, and what had happened since?

"Lie down. You're seriously hurt, and I healed you enough so you wouldn't die, but I couldn't do much more." The voice was achingly familiar.

"Oh, Jais, I'm so glad you're—" When she turned to where the voice was coming from, it took her a long moment to reconcile what she saw. "—not Jais." Andrei was sitting with his back to a wall of trees. Astria was resting next to him. Donallo's body wasn't far away.

Caerwyn looked around, searching for the others, but no one else was here. They were in some odd bower of trees, which seemed to have grown together into a sort-of wall.

"Jais?" she said again softly, slowly laying herself back down again. "What happened?"

She lay there, looking up at a small roughly circular patch of sky above her in the center of the interlaced branches of the trees. She knew there was little she could do at the moment. Not only was she utterly exhausted—that surge of her strength and speed in the fight had taken all her reserves, and still not been enough—but in so much pain as well. She tried to still her breathing and rest as Andrei spoke.

"After you saved me from that lightning—thank you for that—things got a little messy. Lucian was going a little mad and using up all his power to rain down as much lightning as he could."

Caerwyn rolled her head to the side to see the man as he spoke. He raised a badly burned arm. "I got too close to one when I went for Astria. But I'm telling things out of order now. You got hit and I pulled you away from Lucian. Jais—" Andrei shook his head slowly. "My brother had been trapped in ice by the last of Lucian's minions, a woman by the name of Nika. I couldn't get to him. Astria had been thrown by a blast of lightning close to where Donallo lay. I picked you up and went to get them. Astria said she could hide us from the spirit-link. I don't know how, but Lucian hasn't followed us here, so I assume it's working. I don't know what happened to Mirala and Volf, but... Jais." The man's shoulders fell. "I'm sorry I couldn't... didn't save Jais. I fear he is either dead, or worse, captured by Lucian."

Caerwyn nodded slowly. She looked away, rolling her head back to look up at that patch of sky. Clouds were sliding by, quickly, but there was no great storm about. Lucian, or his storm effects at least, was gone.

In some macabre way it seemed only right that, after she'd finally said how she felt, this would happen. It seemed their luck—both hers and Jais'—with relationships, was truly horrible. For some unknown reason that thought made her laugh, a single, harsh thing with no mirth in it.

"What?" Andrei asked.

"Nothing."

He grunted his acceptance of that. After a moment he sighed.

It was Caerwyn's turn to ask. "What?"

It took him a long moment to respond. "I've trained my entire life to fight. My father made sure I had the best instructors in all disciplines. I am a master of a score of weapons, even fighting with just my bare hands... and yet... with all that skill and training, I still couldn't defeat him. I failed... twice."

What had Mirala said? Something about Lucian being a fourth generation drahksan and pure-blooded? Essentially... "He's old and powerful." Caerwyn hadn't really believed it. Her fight with him on the stairs had gone... well perhaps not well, but she'd thought she'd bested him, slowed him, won that battle. And she might have, but the war was apparently far from over. "I fought him, alone, not long ago." She wasn't sure how much time had passed. "I thought him beaten, and yet he still had enough strength to summon that storm and follow after us. Don't blame yourself too much. I underestimated him too."

"But that's just it. I know how powerful he is. I've grown up with him. I... he... what he did, in that dungeon..." The man's voice was soft, trembling. But after a moment he cleared his throat and drew a long breath. "I know he's no master warrior. I should have been able to finish him once his shields were down, but—"

"And he knew it too."

"Sorry?"

Caerwyn rolled her head to look at the man again. "He

knew you had him, that's why he risked blasting himself with lightning to get you."

Andrei blinked. "I hadn't thought…"

"You're recovering from… some nasty stuff. Don't worry if you miss a thing or two."

He gave a harsh laugh at that. "True enough."

After a long moment of silence, Caerwyn closed her eyes. She needed rest to recover. She knew she needed time. As much as it pained her to be here doing nothing, when she wanted so badly to be out there fighting Lucian and saving Jais. By all the gods she hoped Jais was still alive. So, she willed herself to rest, to sleep. She'd recover quickly enough. Then she'd find Jais and make Lucian pay!

"Jais!"

It was the second time Caerwyn had awoken, jerking up to sit—still in pain—with Jais' name on her lips. Her dreams were far from comforting.

She groaned.

It was dark. Night had fallen. She had no clue how much time had passed since she'd last been awake. It could have been a half a day, or many days. Yet she still felt rough, which suggested not so much time had passed.

"Bad dreams?" Andrei's voiced drifted to her. He had kept his voice low, soft.

Yes, but she didn't want to talk about them.

"How long?" she asked instead.

"It's probably close to dawn, the next day. How are you feeling?"

"Better, but still really tired and sore. You?"

"Astria healed my arm. That helped. I didn't know she could do that, take powers from others."

"Can she?" No one had mentioned that to Caerwyn. Odd. It explained a lot though.

"She used my own ability to heal on me. That helped me along a lot. My own healing should have me back to normal before the end of the day. I could give you a little more healing if you like."

"No, save it for now. I ache and my muscles are tight, but beyond that I'm better than I was before. Your initial healing seems to have cured the more serious wounds." Caerwyn laid herself back down for the moment. "And Astria?"

"She seems well, just tired." There was a pause as Andrei took a breath. "She is quite amazing."

With the ability to use another's powers? Certainly. "Yes, quite. Is she still keeping us from the spirit-link? I can sense you and her, but not the others."

"Yes. She said she warded this place. No one outside will sense us, and we can't sense them."

"It would be good to know what happened to Volf and Mirala."

A grunt signaled Andrei's agreement.

Neither spoke for a long time. The sky began to lighten just a bit. Andrei had been right, dawn was coming.

Finally, Andrei spoke. "Did you want me to bury Donallo? I have a little power over earth. I could do it fairly easily."

"Is that their custom? Burying, not burning?"

"I honestly don't know. I never had much time to get to know Donallo... after he told me who I really was."

"We could wait..." she trailed off. She'd been going to say: *until we find Mirala and ask her.* But she knew that might not be something that happened any time soon.

"He'll start attracting scavengers if we wait much longer.

There are coyotes in these lands, savage ones. I could fight one, perhaps two or three, but this time of year, they patrol in families with up to five full-grown pups."

"We seem to be in a protected area." Caerwyn recalled the strange wall of trees around them.

"Yes, I did that. My earth ability; I can help things grow. But there is a way in and out, and when we leave here…"

They couldn't carry Donallo everywhere they went. They should lay him to rest and this man-made glade was peaceful enough. Yes, they should bury him here. But…

"Can we wait, just a little? I have things I need to say to him."

Another grunt from Andrei.

Dawn came slowly. They couldn't see the sun rising in the east. The only indication was the gradual increase of light in the glade. Once she could see well enough, Caerwyn rose, slowly, groaning as her muscles protested the movement.

She knew she'd need another couple of days at least to fully recover on her own. She'd want healing from Andrei if they were going to leave any sooner.

She crawled over to sit next to Donallo. He was starting to smell.

Looking over at Andrei, she asked, "Could you give us a little room?"

Andrei nodded and rose. He moved across the 'room' of trees to the entrance, which seemed to be a short hallway wrapping around the roughly circular area. He took a few steps into that hall and stopped. Caerwyn could still sense him through the spirit-link, but he was far enough away.

She turned back to Donallo.

The man was far too pale now, with mottled darker spots on the underside of his body. She'd seen the effect before as the blood pooled within a dead body. It was just another reminder that he wouldn't be coming back.

Caerwyn had known, nearly the instant it happened, that Donallo was dead, but there had been some part of her hoping for a miracle to bring him back. It wasn't going to happen. She'd only just come to terms with that.

"I'd hoped," she began slowly, whispering. "I'd hoped to have more time with you." Her heart constricted. "I don't think I loved you. Perhaps I don't really know how to love or what love is. I don't know. Certainly, I've never wanted that sort of thing in my life. But you... you were just so willing to help and listen and you never pushed me in any direction. You never asked for anything." Her tone turned bitter. "And yet I got you killed. You, who were so giving and kind." She shook her head.

No, she didn't get him killed. He'd have gone back to save his niece with or without her. Caerwyn had forgotten that this hadn't been her fight at all. But it was now.

"So, you were brave too." She sat there looking into his frozen face for a long moment. "I don't think I've ever known a man like you, Donallo. You were exactly what I needed. Thank you." She laid a hand on the cold skin of his cheek.

With a sigh, she lifted her hand away and turned to look at the wall of trees. Though in truth she wasn't seeing them. She was peering into her mind's eye.

"You also helped me realize so much about myself." She drew in another heavy breath and let it out slowly. "And you may have been as close to a perfect man as any can get, but I see now you weren't necessarily perfect for me. I need someone who'll challenge me, help me grow. I just wasn't willing to see that." Once again, her heart tightened. "Oh, Jais."

She cared for Jais, she knew that now, had said as much to him. Yet... what she'd just said to Donallo was also true. She wasn't sure she knew what love was. A growing part of her was hoping that she might be able to learn... with Jais.

Her gaze fell back to Donallo. "Thank you," she said again. "If not for you, I'm not sure I would have ever found myself again." She shook her head as tears welled in her eyes.

Not long ago, she would have seen tears as a weakness and tried to restrain them. She had a different view now. She needed to be honest with herself, not keep things bottled up inside, as she had done for so very, very long. So, she let the tears fall and the emotions come.

Andrei returned a little while later, "I heard only weeping," he said softly as he sat next to her.

"I am done," Caerwyn said through her tears. "Do what you will with... with the body."

Andrei nodded and moved away.

Caerwyn watched him work. It was like a dance, though heavy of step: low and hunkering close to the ground, involving long sweeping motions of his arms. With his movements large swaths of dirt were dug up from the ground and piled to one side. It wasn't long before he had a trench of several feet deep.

He came and got Donallo, carrying the corpse easily. Caerwyn rose and followed.

Donallo was laid in the pit and Andrei made some motion with his hand over the body.

"What's that?" Caerwyn asked.

"The sign of Suur, for fallen warriors." Andre looked up at her. "My martial training included a lot of theory as well, including rites for the dead. I also know the signs for Lassira and Lansus."

"Is there a sign for Thadros? Those who inspire and heal?

Andrei looked a little befuddled by that. "Ah... well, yes, I think so. I don't know if I can recall it." He took a long moment. "Oh, yes." Andrei made another motion with his hand, it seemed more swirling and softer than the first. That seemed better, knowing what little she did of Donallo.

"Yes, thank you."

Andrei nodded. "Any last words?"

"I've said what I needed to."

"Might I?" They both turned to see Astria standing nearby, looking a little reluctant to draw nearer.

"Of course," Andrei said, sitting back on his haunches.

Astria slowly made her way over and looked down. She knelt beside the grave, hands on her knees as she leaned forward. "I'm so sorry, Uncle. If I hadn't run off…" She shook her head. "I know you would have come for me no matter what. I learned so much from you and a part of you will be with me always. I hold you in my heart and in my mind. I know you loved me like I was your own child. You were the father I wished to have."

Caerwyn found more tears welling in her eyes. Not just for Astria's touching words, but for this girl who'd had such a harsh life and had to grow up so very quickly. That resonated a little too well with Caerwyn who'd had to do the same at around Astria's age.

She couldn't help herself. She knelt next to Astria and put an arm around her.

The girl turned and, pristine silvery-blue eyes, welling with tears, gazed at Caerwyn.

"At least I have my mother," Astria said as if reading Caerwyn's thoughts. Then she put her arms around Caerwyn and wept. This prompted even more tears from Caerwyn.

When Astria finally drew back. She turned back to Donallo and said simply, "Good-bye, Uncle. Save a place for Mother and me in the fields of Erival." Then she rose, seemingly stoic now, her emotions quelled. "I am done, brother, you may proceed."

Brother?

Yes, of course. Astria was Lucian's child and Andrei had been raised as the same, they'd have thought of each other as brother and sister before discovering the truth about Andrei's heritage.

Andrei began moving the earth over the body.

Astria put a hand on Caerwyn's shoulder. With Caerwyn kneeling and Astria standing they were roughly the same height, Astria being slightly taller. "Worry not, he knew how you felt."

Caerwyn looked up at Astria confused at these words. But the girl only gave her a sad, enigmatic smile before turning away.

Caerwyn felt a bit of a chill in that moment. Gods, who was this girl?

24

ASTRIA MEDITATED. IT WAS SOMETHING SHE'D LEARNED FROM Uncle Donallo and seemed appropriate to do now. She needed to find a stillness within her so she could begin to work on the myriad problems around her. Of all the questions in her mind, two were most prevalent. The first: how to deal with her father, ideally without killing him. He may be an evil man but killing was evil as well. There had to be a way to stop him without continuing the cycle of death he'd started. Also, dead, he might become a symbol, a martyr for his minions.

The second question was a bit more personal and niggled at her constantly: what was she?

She was aware of the thoughts and feelings of others through the use of her own powers with soul, and she'd spent enough time around Uncle Donallo to have his abilities with mind as well. Yet these powers only helped to glean from others how... odd and powerful she was.

And that scared her.

She trembled for a moment, before drawing a breath and trying to return to a calm mind. Yet her question persisted: who was she?

She was the daughter of a fourth generation pure-blooded drahksan—as Lucian loved to remind all around him. He was old and powerful, yes. Her mother was also powerful in her own right. Not entirely pure-blooded, but close, and Astria didn't know how many generations of drahksan had come before her mother. Yet the woman's powers were not insignificant: empathy and empathic transmission were two of the most powerful soul abilities and they were just a part of her mother's abilities. So perhaps it was just some combination of her father's and mother's powers which had given her such strange abilities to borrow and maintain the powers of others.

Even Astria herself could see how powerful this was. It meant that all she had to do was spend time around any one drahksan and she'd be able to use their abilities just as they could. Already she felt stronger and with greater fortitude in her small frame from the time she'd spent around Andrei, Caerwyn, and Jais. She would need more time before she could match their abilities, but the fact that it was even possible to get to that point and do what they could do... it meant she could potentially master all the realms of the drahksan, if she just had someone to glean the powers from. That was... far too powerful and far from normal.

Perhaps that was why... Yes, it had to be why Davul wanted her.

Perhaps.

Astria shuddered, shot through with instant apprehension as she realized her mistake of using the being's name. She considered for a moment whether she'd try to break off the connection, but decided this time, she'd speak to the god. She'd just have to be very careful. Her fear was slowly replaced with cautious apprehension.

Will you tell me what you want with me? Can you be that honest and direct? she asked.

I can, yes. But what would that gain me? Would you promise to devote yourself to me if I told you?

Why? Why did he need her devotion? Why her specifically? It seemed likely for the power she possessed, but was there more? *You know it would be silly of me to promise devotion before I know what you plan.* She tried something, being ever so subtle, ever so vigilant, she sent a tendril of thought back along her connection to the being. Perhaps she'd be able to find out the thoughts behind this being's words. Though she didn't know if it would work on a god.

Exactly. Trust, that is the key, the one who called himself Davul said into her mind. *You don't trust me, and I cannot trust you. We are at an impasse. Though I believe I can give you what you want, if you are willing to trust me.*

She felt her thought-probe make contact with... a vastness of a mind. Whatever this was, it was beyond human. That shook her for a long moment before she recalled what it had been saying.

It wanted to give her what she wanted...

What was that? She wouldn't ask. It was far too tempting, and she didn't want to know... not yet at least. Instead, with her mind-link firmly in place she simply asked. *And what do you want?*

'Revenge!' This was the startlingly strong, hidden thought behind what the being said next. *I wish only to build my followers and draw more to the worship of Davul.* With her mind-link in place she could also sense both the truth in the first part of that sentence... and the lie at the end.

She threw up her mental shields, severing the connection with the being, going cold. Tremors shook her body as she shrank in on her thoughts and chaotic emotions. She'd suspected that whatever it was that contacted her and her father wasn't indeed the god Davul... now she knew it wasn't.

She had reacted so suddenly in breaking the link between them that she regretted it in the next moment. She should have asked him who he was and used her mind-link to find the truth. But even asking that question was dangerous now. If that being suspected she knew he wasn't who he said...

Another shuddering of fear surged through her, sinking icy talons into her flesh.

What had she done? What was she doing? She was playing with some semi-divine being, one who had been lying to her and her father for dozens of years. One who, even if it wasn't the god it claimed to be, still had immense power, enough to give Lucian's the ability to empower humans.

Then there was that last, hidden thought... Revenge! Who did the being want revenge against?

It was all a little too much for her.

Her shakes had subsided to a mild trembling. She hugged herself, wanting to cry, but she couldn't. This is what her entire short life had been like. Having to be strong because she knew too much to sit in a corner and weep. She knew too much... yet still she was only a child.

A single tear traced her cheek.

She drew in a shuddering breath. She needed to distract herself. Caerwyn and Andrei were talking quietly nearby. She listened in on their conversation.

"...horrible things my father made me do." Andrei was saying, head hung low, shoulders slumped.

"You were following a man you thought was your father. I can't imagine it's easy to break from that, if it's what you've known your entire life," Caerwyn said softly.

Andrei nodded, looking up. "He was never mean to me... well, not in the way he was to others. His discipline was strict, but once I knew how to follow his rules, I rarely saw it. He was firm, yes, but never inconsistent. But then, as I grew, I

saw what he did to others who didn't do as he wished. Then...
then I was the one meeting out those punishments." Andrei
swallowed hard. "I should have known long before I did, that
he was an evil man." He shuddered. "I think it was easier to
follow his rule, looking the other way when I could, than it
was to look at those rules and challenge them." A sigh and
shake of his head. "After Donallo looked into my mind and
showed me who my true parents were, it was only then that I
began to change my ways. I have a lot to atone for." He
frowned; lips tight.

"And you have already started," Caerwyn said soothingly.
"You helped Donallo and Mirala escape with Astria the first
time, though it cost you greatly. Then you endured horrible
things at the hands of the man who should have shown you
love. That couldn't have been easy."

Andrei couldn't seem to speak. He just shook his head.

Astria sent a light probe over the man's thoughts and feelings. She'd seen some of what her father had done to the man,
keeping him on the brink of death. It had been horrible.
Andrei's own experience of it was a spike of remembered-
pain through the link she'd sent to the man. She withdrew
instantly, leaving him to those private and painful emotions
and thoughts. Her own recent experience with her father,
though much less aggressive, was enough for her to sympa-
thize, recalling her own terror. She didn't want to think on
that anymore and went back to focusing on what the other
two were saying

"And you tried to fight him off when we escaped again.
You've done a lot already, Andrei." Caerwyn spoke with hope
and strength in her voice.

Andrei looked up—obviously miserable and scared, but he
nodded and gave a quick smile. "Thank you."

"And we'll need you in what is to come," she said. "I have to believe Jais is alive and I'm not going to leave him to that same fate, are you?"

Andrei's face hardened. "No." His voice was sure, if still a little heavy with emotion. He drew in a long breath after a moment and straightened. "No," he said again. Then: "Could you tell me a little about him? Jais… my brother?"

Caerwyn nodded. "Certainly. Physically, as you know, he is a lot like you, though he seems to have inherited more 'short and stocky' genes."

"I think that would be from my mother's side. She was a small woman from the bits of memory I have of her now. Father was like me, much taller."

Caerwyn nodded. "And his heart is true. He is a passionate man… in everything he does. He throws himself fully into his fights and relationships."

"That's not like me at all. I tend to be much more reserved, observant." Andrei smiled, gaze distant. "It's good to know we have a few differences."

"You probably have many. I hope you get the chance to find out."

Listening to the two of them wasn't enough of a distraction from the tumbling thoughts and emotions within her. She needed to do something in order to get away from her own fear and dismay. Astria rose and joined them. "Would you like me to find out what I can?"

Caerwyn looked up at her. "What do you mean?"

Astria explained, "If any of us leave this glade, our spirit-link will return, and we should be able to sense the others. But if either of you leave, everyone, including my father, will know where you are instantly. If I leave, using Volf's shadow-form for a while, then I can reveal myself at some distant location. I'll be able to sense the others without giving away the position of this glade."

Andrei was nodding. Caerwyn had that same look in her eyes as she'd had after Astria had told her that Uncle Donallo 'knew how she felt' as they were burying him. It seemed something akin to marvel or awe. Astria didn't think she deserved that. It made her feel awkward and somehow separated from the others.

Caerwyn said, "You're one very intelligent girl."

Astria felt those words sink into her soul, reassuring her. More than the words, the look of appreciation and admiration Caerwyn was giving her, eased Astria's mind and emotions. She smiled. "I just want to help Jais. He helped free me, and I should do the same." The man hardly knew her and yet he'd come to save her. That seemed like it needed to be repaid.

Caerwyn shook her head, still with that same look on her face. "And far stronger than I was at your age." After a moment she added, "Yes, please. Don't endanger yourself, but if you can get a sense for the others, that would be very helpful."

"And when I come back, will you tell me about the dragon in the north?"

Caerwyn's jaw dropped, eyes going wide. This time Astria giggled. She'd known that would be a bit much.

"Dragon?" Andrei asked, also seeming stunned.

"How did you know?" Caerwyn asked, awed.

"I have some of Uncle Donallo's abilities to read minds. When we first met, I wanted to know more about you, so I may have looked in your mind a bit. Sorry."

Caerwyn's expression turned dark. "You really shouldn't do that. You should ask first. That's what your uncle did."

Astria grimaced and nodded. "I know, I'm still just learning to control these powers." That was a bit of a lie. She'd had them for years now and could control them well enough. "And I found you fascinating." That wasn't a lie.

"Me?" Caerwyn seemed abashed. "Well, you fascinate me too, Astria. When all these troubled times are over, we'll sit down and have a long talk, how's that sound?"

"I'd like that, thank you. I'll go now." Astria left the compound, hiding herself in a shadow-form.

Yet what she found, once she did reconnect with the spirit-link, was troubling. She could sense no drahksani at all. This told her two things: first was that Volf might be hiding himself and possibly Mirala and even Jais, but it seemed unlikely that they'd all be with Volf. Because the other thing she realized was that Lucian had to be in one of his 'torture rooms' lined with cold-forged-iron to hide his spirit-link. It was the only way he could be hidden. And if he was in one of those rooms, then he'd have someone with him.

The question really was… who had he captured?

MIRALA WAS GROWING MORE AND MORE WORRIED. VOLF HAD collapsed the previous day after they'd walked, supporting each other, for some time. She'd been nearly ready to do so as well, exhausted and at her wits end, after being separated from Astria.

Yet somehow, even though Volf had fallen into uncon- sciousness, his powers had kept working. The day around them was dimmed slightly, an effect of his shadow-form. She was being hidden and couldn't sense any spirit-links other than Volf's. But he was delirious and feverish, his body far too warm and his dreams seemingly restless. He would thrash about from time to time, muttering incoherently. She didn't know how he was maintaining his powers while so distressed, but he was.

She didn't wish to leave him in this state, but she also wasn't a healer and didn't know what to do to help him. They'd stopped not far from a pond with a small stream burbling into it. She'd gone there several times through the night to soak a rag—a sleeve of her shirt she'd torn away—to help cool him. That was all she could think of.

Jais was a healer, as was Andrei, but she didn't know what had happened to either man. Astria had commanded her to leave; she wouldn't have done so otherwise. Mirala hoped her daughter was safe, but there had been so much lightning and chaos, she hadn't been able to tell much as she and Volf had limped away from the fight.

She'd even tentatively tried to leave Volf and break away from his shadow-form to sense the others, but it seemed to be stuck to her, and she wasn't sure if she wanted out from within Volf's powers either. Then Lucian would be able to sense her as well. And she didn't know if she'd be able to find Volf again afterward.

So, she had little choice but to wait for Volf to recover, except that was not happening quickly.

She went to the stream one more time and came back with the rag, cool and damp, to set on his forehead.

Volf's eyes snapped open and looked about wildly. "Nowhere to hide!" he muttered.

"Volf?"

But he didn't look at her; his gaze seemed to slip off her. Whatever he was seeing it was something else, probably still trapped within a waking nightmare.

She grabbed his shoulders and shook him a little. "Volf!"

But his eyes slid shut a moment later and he began to tremble.

Gods, this was not going well.

She put her hand to his cheek. There was one thing she could do. She sent her soul-sense into him and felt roiling emotions. She calmed them, soothed him, and slowly he settled, the trembling abating.

His breathing evened out, and he seemed at rest.

She'd done that a few times for him as well, though it never seemed to last for long.

She'd grown more and more concerned over the course of the new day. So, she decided to try something. It was an ability she rarely used. She could send herself into the dreams of others if she and they were both asleep. She could speak to anyone she knew, no matter the distance between them. In the years since she and Donallo had fled Bulovas, she'd used this power a few times to try to reach old friends. Yet in all that time, she'd found no one.

She lay down next to Volf and closed her eyes, relaxing into a semi-sleep. She kept his hand clutched in hers. The contact wasn't necessary, but it reassured her.

Then she sent herself into his mind, into his dreams.

She found herself amidst an unstable landscape of ashen hues, greys and blacks. Above and around her swirled a great storm, angry red flashes within heavy, dark clouds. She could see little but barren ground below her, seemingly shifting beneath her feet.

"Volf!" she called out. Saying the name should bring him to her, or her to him, in dreams it was the same thing.

He appeared next to her. She knew it was him, the hair and eyes were the same, but he was a child, terrified and shaking.

She knelt and took his hands in hers. "It's well, Volf. I'm here."

"I'm so scared!" he said, his voice carrying the high timbre of youth. "The shadows are everywhere!"

"Shadows?"

He nodded, looking around.

Why would he be afraid of shadows? He could control them. But when she followed his gaze, she could see vague monstrous shapes within the storm swirling around them, no more than mere shadows or silhouettes with glowing red eyes.

Odd.

Did he see his powers as living things? Did he fear what he could do? She shook her head. No, that was too literal. Dreams were rarely as they seemed at first. They could be direct and literal translations of the waking world, but often they were more metaphorical, one thing representing another. So, what did these monsters represent?

The trouble was, she could soothe emotions, even here in his dreams, and she could manipulate them a little, but mostly it would be Volf himself who had the power to change what he was seeing. Yet, it was rare for most people to take such control in their dreams.

She sent soothing warmth into boy-Volf through his hands still held by hers. He seemed to calm a little, and the storm withdrew from them.

Interesting.

If she extrapolated correctly from that... it meant the storm was his own emotions, or perhaps thoughts related to his feelings. Which would make sense, as he probably had a lot of troubling thoughts and things to worry about, given the last few days. She knew his feelings for her were mixed in to this dark confusion, yet she felt a lot of other emotions as well, fear and uncertainty chief among them.

She'd have to help him deal with this, if she wanted to find her daughter.

"Volf?" The boy looked at her, clear, blue eyes wide. "What do you fear the most?"

Screams echoed throughout the dreamscape, horrible things, the sounds of the dying. She looked around to see those he knew: Caerwyn, Jais, Donallo, and others she didn't recognize as well. They were all dying.

The boy huddled in closer to her. He didn't want to look. She couldn't blame him, this was horrible. Through his emotions, she sensed a primary fear: being alone. Not just alone—he'd been alone for most of his life and been fine—but losing those who were like kin to him, his closest friends, those he considered his family. He feared to lose them and be the only one, the last of his kind. Now that he knew what he was, he wished more than anything to keep those connections with other drahksan. She saw that clearly now.

She held the boy close, curled into her. He seemed to relax a little and the visions of the dying vanished. But then...

Over his head, behind him, she saw herself. She was... well she didn't think she looked that good even on her best days. It was how he saw her, she realized, some ideal version of her. It was quite flattering. But what truly stunned her were the three small children in a chain, all holding hands, with the eldest holding her hand.

"Is this your desire Volf? A family?"

The child in her arms nodded.

"Ah, yes, I see. You want even more of your kind, and more of an actual family. As great as your fear of losing everyone is, you have an equally strong desire to... create more of us." She felt like she understood him in that moment, a deep part of him.

She put a note of stern command in her voice. It was her 'behave child' voice that she'd used often enough as a mother. "Volf, if you want that, if you want to get out of this place, you need to be strong. Can you do that?"

The child squirmed a little out of her grip and looked up at her, those piercing blue eyes so large and bright she almost lost herself in them. "For you I can."

She kept her hard tone. "No, Volf. Don't do it for me. Do it for you. I know you love me, but I'm not here to fix you. If you want me in your life, you need to be strong enough to take care of yourself. Do you understand me?"

Those eyes stared at her for several moments longer, before the child nodded.

Then there was no child there, but the Volf she knew. She rose from her crouch to stand next to him. "Good. You're starting to take control of yourself and your dream."

He nodded. "Thank you." He looked off to one side. She followed the gaze. He was looking at those shadow-monsters locked in the storm-wall.

"What are they?" she asked.

"I… don't know. But they scare me. They want to hurt me? No, that's not it. They are seeking something. They—" He shook his head.

"Keep going Volf, you can do this. What are they?"

"I…" he shook his head again grimacing. "I'm terrified of them."

He seemed to be saying the same thing in different ways. She tried to help. "Could they be things you fear? What are you afraid of?"

He trembled and once again came the mournful and grating sounds of people dying, in pain. He shook his head and the sounds vanished. His lips were pressed tight. Finally, he drew a breath and answered. "Perhaps. I think you might be right. They are all the things I fear: losing my friends, being alone in this world, drahksan with more power than myself." He sighed heavily, looking down, deflating. "I'm no warrior."

She wasn't sure where that had come from. "You may not be a fighter like Jais or Caerwyn, but in this place, you hold all the power, if you are willing to claim it."

He looked up at her then, doubt in his eyes. "I… I can't fight…"

Was that it? "Volf this sort of battle isn't one you win with swords and shields. Battling your fear—" Something occurred to her. "Do you think Jais and Caerwyn have no fears and that's what makes them warriors?"

"Uh..." He didn't want to say it, but she could see the answer on his face.

"Volf, that's not it at all."

"No?"

"No. For one, they're afraid too. Every time they run into battle, some part of them fears for themselves and their friends. More than that, there are many other things which scare them as well."

"Truly?"

Mirala nodded. She'd know. "Secondly, as I said, in this place, you don't need to be a warrior to fight your fears, you just need to take control. That much I know you can do."

He looked skeptically at the red-eyed-shadows. A frown creased his face. "But... there's more to these things. I... can't fight them. They're too powerful."

"Your fears?"

"No, well yes, but..." A sigh and grimace. "I sense that there is something more behind these fears, something giving them power beyond what they should have."

"Whatever that is, it is still only something within you. And if it's a part of you, you can control it."

"But I can't..." He seemed to be struggling, having trouble expressing what he was feeling.

She blew out a calming breath and started fresh. "So, there is more than just your fears here, yes?"

"Yes."

"Can you name it? That extra something?"

He was peering into the whirling winds of the storm. It took him a long moment before he cocked his head to one side. "This storm."

"What about it?"

He held out a hand to her. "Can you please... calm my emotions?"

She took the hand and did as asked, curious where he was going with this. The storm drifted a little farther back, but didn't dissipate. Volf stood a little taller, surer. The beginnings of a wry grin—one which seemed to suggest he'd figured something out—crept onto his face.

"What is it?" she asked.

"The storm isn't my emotions nor my fears, it's something else, and my fears are locked within it." The grin vanished in an intense, thoughtful pressing of his lips. "They are feeding it... no!" He turned to her and smiled fully this time. "No, it's feeding them!" Even with your help, my fears still lurk at the edges of my mind. Something is fueling them, and I think it's the storm itself." He turned back. "So, then, what is the storm?" He was excited now, eagerly trying to claim this dream-realm back from whatever force had taken control of it.

Something clicked in her mind then. She wasn't sure if it was related, but a sneaking suspicion told her she needed to tell Volf. "Your powers, they're still manifesting in the real world, even while you're sleeping."

"My powers?" He didn't seem like he'd fully heard her. "Really?" He turned to her, then back to the storm. "I—" Then suddenly, his eyes lit with understanding. "Yes! My powers, of course!" He turned to her and embraced her. "That's it, thank you!"

"What's it?" She wasn't sure how this all connected yet.

"Something's wrong with my powers." He drew back holding her at arm's length. He was a little too ebullient given what he'd just said. "I didn't set them before I... I just collapsed." His smile was gone replaced by a thoughtful look. "Yes. I collapsed. I was exhausted. If they're still working then... They're doing so all by themselves. They're not under my control." Eyes widened again. "That's it! They're not under my control, they are in control, and they're draining me and affecting me, even here in my dreams!"

That sounded like it could make sense. She was about to ask what he could do about it, when he simply smiled. "Now I know what to do."

And she was shunted out of his dreams.

She woke with a long inhalation of breath then sat up.

Volf remained still next to her for a long moment, then he groaned. The dimness around her flickered then faded away, revealing the bright morning light. Then Volf stirred with another groan and opened his eyes.

He tried to rise but couldn't, falling back down. With another groan, he put a hand to his head. "The real world is a lot brighter and more painful than my dreams. Gods, I'm exhausted." Then he rolled his head to one side to look up at her. A slight smile, still pained, but with a hint of gratitude reached his lips. "Thank you."

"And thank you," she said smiling down at him. "Now, I can hopefully find my daughter."

26

VOLF FELT ENTIRELY WRUNG OUT, TWISTED LIKE A WET RAG, ALL his energy gone. He lay there, eyes closed to the bright light above him as Mirala sought for Astria.

Yet, he could sense no other drahksan at all.

That was quite disconcerting.

Shading his eyes, he squinted them open to look at Mirala. She stood next to him, long dark hair blowing in the stiff, warm breeze which rolled over these grassy plains.

Then, for a moment, he sensed two drahksani to the south, then only one. From the level of power off that one, it was most likely Lucian. The other one…

"Oh, no!" Mirala whispered. She'd come to the same conclusion he had. Lucian had those special dungeons for drahksan, to keep them from being sensed by others.

"I don't think that was Astria," Volf said, trying to reassure her.

"No," she said softly. "It was Jais."

Sometimes he forgot she was a lot more practiced with her abilities than he was; truly a marvel.

Mirala had come into his dreams and saved him… from

himself. He could still recall the 'dream-child' version of himself being held close to her, warm and safe and comforting. She seemed all too aware of how that interaction had drawn them closer. She didn't seem ready to talk about it yet, though, so he didn't. But one vision from that dream did stick with him: her with a string of children—some with her dark hair, some with his pale blond. It had been a beautiful sight. And until he'd seen it, he hadn't known just how much the idea of a family, his own family, had meant to him.

"Astria must still have access to your powers and be using them to hide herself and hopefully the rest of the others," she said. Her tone was uncertain, she was trying to reassure herself.

"I'm sure that's it," he said to help.

Mirala hadn't turned to him. She gazed off over the plains.

The fact that Astria had somehow borrowed and could still use his powers seemed somewhat crazy to Volf. But then, sometimes the world was crazy. Sometimes you had to fight madmen who were allied with gods for the sake of people you barely knew... crazy.

"Do you want me to hide us again?" he asked. He doubted he could, but felt compelled to ask, now that they could sense Lucian to the south. That meant he could sense them too.

She shook her head. "No, save your strength and rest. We'll know if Lucian is heading back this way and you can hide us if that occurs." She turned back to him then. One sleeve of her shirt was missing. It left a slender arm exposed. His shirt would be a little big for her, but he wanted to give her something. She'd done so much for him.

An idea came to him. "My far-sight."

"Far-sight? What is that?"

"I can see to distant places. Usually places I've been before."

"How will that help us find Astria?"

"Astria?" That hadn't been what he'd been thinking. "Ah, I don't know, perhaps there is a way. I was thinking it would allow me to spy on Lucian and find out if he has anyone else prisoner down there."

Mirala nodded. "That would be a start." She sat next to him once again. "Is there anything you need?"

"No. Just keep an eye out, as I'll lose my senses here." He closed his eyes, hoping this would work. His far-sight didn't take as much energy as his shadow powers, but still… "I don't know how long I'll be gone. Shake me if anything happens here."

"I will," she said next to him.

Volf threw his senses back into Lucian's estate. He was now familiar with the dungeons, having been there twice recently. His senses came alert in the hallway off which Astria had been imprisoned. He could see the damage and debris around the one doorway. Inside, the room was empty. There were two other doors, however, both closed, along the hall.

He had been inside those rooms when he'd been exploring the dungeons the first time, so it shouldn't be too hard to push his senses past the portal. He just hoped that whatever it was that kept the spirit-link from penetrating into these rooms, didn't stop his abilities as well.

He tried to push his far-sight past the first door, it wasn't easy. Yet he was able to get a glimpse inside the first room. It was empty.

Already growing fatigued, he tried the second door. It seemed to take a colossal effort to push his awareness into the room, and once again it was only for a moment before he was pushed out, but he saw enough. Jais hung suspended in the air, held—most likely—by Lucian's invisible wind-grasp. The man didn't look good, well bruised and beaten, blood dripping into a pool below him, each drop echoing around the chamber.

There were no other rooms off that hall. So Jais was the only prisoner.

Poor man.

Volf returned to himself and drew in a long breath, opening his eyes to stabbing light. Some impulse caused him to try to sit up, but that only caused his head to spin, and he fell back the few inches he'd managed to rise. Gods, he was tired.

"Jais is the only one there, and he's still alive. My guess is Lucian will use him to lure us back." He put a palm to his forehead to stop a slight pounding which had begun there. "And I need some rest."

"Then rest," Mirala said laying a hand on his shoulder. "If anyone comes out of hiding, or if Lucian starts heading this way, I'll wake you. I'll need you at full strength for what is to come."

Volf's headache eased a little once his eyes were closed. "You mean to go after Jais?"

She sighed. "My first concern is my daughter. But assuming she's safe, then yes. He risked everything to help Astria. I will repay that bravery." There was steel in her voice.

MIRALA WATCHED VOLF SETTLE. SHE SENT A SLIVER OF HER powers to him, helping him to relax and find sleep, and he was unconscious a moment later.

She should rest as well but was a little too unsettled to find peace. As much as it was good to know that Lucian didn't have Astria, she was still worried for her daughter. Jais was the only one captured, but that left two options for the others.

Either Astria was with Andrei and Caerwyn, hiding them with Volf's powers or… they might all be dead. As long as Mirala had that uncertainty, she knew she wouldn't be able to rest.

And Jais had been captured helping her and her family. She hardly knew the man, which made his sacrifice that much greater; like Andrei's had been that first time. The two brothers shared that much.

She sat and tried to work through her own thoughts and emotions to find some sense of peace.

Her first concern was how to get Jais out, assuming Astria kept hiding herself and remained—hopefully—safe.

With only her and Volf, it would not be easy to get Jais out. She'd learned to defend herself well enough, studying a little weapons-work. She was passable with a bow, better with a crossbow, and wouldn't hurt herself if she wielded a sword. That was far from what she'd need to go up against Lucian and his minions. Her empathic transmission would work on some of them, but it wasn't a guarantee.

Then there was Volf. She'd seen him fight a little. He was passable with a sword, but she got the impression it was the only weapon he'd studied. He was more a scout, able to hide and determine an enemy's true position. That would be useful. They could avoid people and potentially get to Jais, but Lucian would know the instant they opened the door to Jais' room and come for them. She didn't know how, but some-how, he'd found them even when they'd been hidden by Volf's shadow-form when fleeing with Astria. Which meant… they had little hope of pulling off any sort of escape with Jais.

She shook her head, discarding that line of thinking. Instead she decided to focus on something else: Volf himself. She looked at him. Unbidden, a memory came to her: Erith, her late husband, lying next to her as she sat in bed, only they'd both been naked. He'd been dozing after a particularly passionate session of lovemaking.

Mirala gave a breath of a laugh, harsh and mirthless. Erith had been many things... but he couldn't be a father. Many drahksan were blessed with rather incredible fertility. It must have been a genetic trait, to keep the race going. Yet Erith had been one of the few who could sire no children at all. She'd wanted children, but not been able to have any with him. She had a daughter now, though she didn't care at all for the girl's father.

She did want more of a family.

As did Volf... with her.

That made her smile for a moment, remembering his rather idealized version of her. She knew he had strong feelings for her. So... how did she feel for him?

He was a good man, with a good heart, kind and dedicated. True, he didn't really know where he fit into this world yet, but then... neither did she, truly. Drahksan in general were a fading species. She didn't know what had happened to those who had lived in Bulovas, but she suspected most, if not all, were dead.

If she did want a family with another drahksan, then her options were limited. Lucian wasn't on the list at all. Jais... well if they managed to get him out and if Caerwyn was still alive, Mirala suspected something would grow between those two. Andrei... Perhaps he was a good man, but she'd seen just a little too much of him as a brute to feel fully comfortable around him, not yet anyway.

But Volf...

She sighed. Such thoughts were for later, after this whole mess was done. She had to put an end to things here first. Though how she'd do that without the others...

She felt her brow furrow as a thought came to her. She

couldn't sense them using the spirit-link, but perhaps there was another way.

She closed her eyes. True, she'd not be able to see any danger coming, but what she was about to do would hopefully help her locate every living being for miles around her. That should also work to sense any predatory animals at least.

With a slow, deep breath, she reached out with her emotional awareness. At first, all she felt was Volf, close and at peace. She stretched it farther, expanding in all directions. There were many beings of limited emotions in the pond nearby, as well as in the forests to the north and west, even a few out on the plains to the east. She reached farther still. She'd never tried to sense this far with her emotional awareness before, she'd never had any need to. It was fascinating all the beings she could sense. Animals, though not sentient, still had primal emotions: fear, desire—whether to hunt or mate— and a few other basic feelings.

Then she felt something. Just on the edge of her awareness to the east. She retracted her senses from other directions and pushed her senses farther east.

Yes.

People.

A group of three. They mourned and felt a certain restless desperation. She tapped into one of them deeper and formed an emotional connection.

Astria?

Mother? Alarm and joy filled the being. Yes, this was her daughter. Mirala almost lost the connection with her elation and excitement.

I know where you are now. I assume you are with Caerwyn and Andrei, yes?

Yes. And... A pause, and an odd sensation, as if someone were walking along the connection between her and Astria, like a spider on a single strand of webbing. Then: *I know where you are too!* Somehow Astria had just figured out how to use the same ability and used it to trace the connection back to Mirala's location. The girl never ceased to amaze.

That's great, Astria. Can you bring the others here? Volf is resting and I don't want to wake him if I don't have to.

Yes, Mother, I will do that. Another pause, regret and sorrow filled Astria. *We buried Uncle Donallo.* A spark of sadness-tinged-wonder. *But it's in the most beautiful glade, Mother. You need to see this place... sometime.*

I will. Astria. She sent reassurance and warmth. *How is everyone?*

Sad, and angry, and worried about you and the others. Is only Volf with you?

Yes, Jais is with... your father.

That's not good. A child's capacity for understatement was astonishing.

No, it's not. Bring the others here and we can discuss what to do.

I will, Mother. See you soon!

Mirala broke the connection and retracted her awareness. Opening her eyes, the sun was suddenly a little too bright. That had taken a lot out of her. She couldn't rest yet though. She'd do as Volf had asked and keep watch.

Looking down at the prone man she whispered, "Just don't die on me. Then, perhaps we can have a talk about that family you want, once Lucian is dealt with."

He was still well slumbering and hadn't heard.

That was probably for the best.

27

JAIS HAD WITHDRAWN DEEP WITHIN HIMSELF. IT HAD BEEN THE only way to survive, to stay sane through the pain. The sensations of his body were a distant thing... most of the time. Occasionally pain would lance through him, causing him to scream and recall where he was and the fullness of his horrid situation.

Lucian had been... thorough in his first few torture sessions. He'd used lightning to burn and stones to break Jais' flesh and bones. At first, Jais had tried to heal himself, to keep up with the rate of injury inflicted on him. He'd thought he'd needed to in order to survive, but he realized now, that's what Lucian had wanted. The man was careful and devious. He needed to keep Jais alive if he were to lure the others back here. But he also couldn't have Jais surging his healing to be ready when they arrived. So, the wounds were to fatigue his body and his powers as much as they were a way for the evil man to inflict pain, which he seemed to enjoy.

So Jais had begun conserving his power. After his first bout of trying to heal himself, he'd let only his body's natural quick healing take place, slowly, ever-so-painstakingly-carefully preserving some of his power within him. It was hard to live with the pain and know he could diminish it, but he believed this would serve him in the end. He just had to keep hope that the others were coming soon.

Soon.

And hopefully they wouldn't bring Astria with them. It seemed she was the focus of Lucian's ire. Jais didn't really know why or what the man wanted with her, but he rambled on about his daughter and her betrayal when he was down here inflicting pain.

Luckily, Lucian wasn't there at the moment. Jais would have a short time of peace, if still in horrendous pain. But the pain was distant, he told himself. He was a being of mind and spirit now, bundled in on himself, waiting.

Sleep was hard to find, but occasionally he'd have livid dreams only to wake up in a sweat and not know when or how he'd fallen asleep. These fever dreams and delirium were a constant companion now. And when another vision pushed its way into his mind, he had little strength to resist it. He fell into darkness, only to wake wailing and crying... only it wasn't him as he was now. He was an infant, held in loving arms. That was a pleasant sensation, and yet, he was terribly sad and angry. Words slipped along the edges of his consciousness...

I'll take good care of him, Liria, as if he were my own. Aunt Sarelle's voice. He was in her arms, he could feel the vibrations of her voice through her chest as she held him close, softly bouncing and swaying to get him to stop crying.

I... yes, please do. Oh, gods Deklon, are we doing the right thing? He's our son! Jais didn't know this voice and yet, he did. A voice he'd never known he'd heard, and yet it was a part of him.

Mother.

Now he knew why he was weeping. His parents were leaving him.

Somehow, he'd kept this memory from his early childhood and was only recalling it now. Yet as much pain as it held for him, he wasn't able to escape it. He was bound here, in this moment, forced to relive it.

Eyes, blurry with tears, opened and he looked up at the three towering figures around him. Sarelle he recognized, the other two...

There were tears in his mother's eyes, her cheeks were wet. She was short and slight of build, with a slender, angular face framed by waves of soft brown hair. She leaned over him, close. Her brown eyes so large and caring. And yet, she was leaving him. How could anyone who cared that much leave him?

Some distant part of him knew the answer: that it had been to protect him... but in this moment that wasn't enough. In this faded memory, as a babe in arms, he didn't understand. Why did they have to go? Why couldn't they do as aunt Sarelle was doing and settle, live quietly. If they had, they wouldn't have died and left their other son to be raised by a tyrant. It was a horrible decision. It made no sense.

We have to keep him safe. His father's voice. This he knew well enough now. The man leaned in close, putting an arm around his wife to gaze down at Jais.

As much as Jais knew the voice, the face was new to him, and yet... he'd seen it before, or parts of it, in his own reflection—and in Andrei's features. That strong brow ridge, those clear blue eyes, the square jaw and full face. His father's hair was darker than his, near to black, more like Andrei's. Jais apparently had his mother's hair and was closer to her height.

Just the sight of them, together, over him, leaving him... nearly broke Jais.

Why?

So many questions beginning with that same word tumbled through him.

I know you're right, my love, but... I just... More tears from his mother. The pain on her face made no sense. If she didn't want to leave him, then why would she?

A finger reached down to trace his cheek. His mother's touch, soft, tender. It calmed him for just a moment, his wailing abated. Perhaps...

Then the finger lifted away and with even more tears she said, *Goodbye Jaistheric, I love you. I'll be back for you. I promise.*

It's time now, dear. This from his father, tight lipped, restraining his emotions.

They turned away.

More pain within, more wailing from him.

No, you won't return! You broke your promise! How could you leave me! I hate you!

The vision broke, but the pain from it remained, sinking vicious claws into Jais' heart, deep and rending. He was weeping, he was aware of that. And he'd been screaming. Had there been words or just incomprehensible noise?

"Mother?" Lucian's scathing laughter cut clean through his hazy awareness. The man was back. "I'm fairly certain I killed your mother." More laughter. "I didn't really see who you were until I noticed your sword. Or should I say, your father's sword. It had been hanging on my wall for years before mysteriously vanishing. Apparently, it went to you. I'd recognize that blade anywhere. Then, of course, there is your resemblance to Andrei, uncanny. So yes, I can say with much certainty that I killed your mother... and I quite enjoyed it. I took my time with them. I rent their flesh and broke their bones as I'm doing with you. They were begging for their deaths by the time I sacrificed them to Davul; your mother particularly. Oh, should I tell you of all the things she offered to do for me, just so I would end the pain and kill her?"

Lucian had drawn close. His voice was very near.

Jais opened his eyes—well one eye, the other was swollen shut—and saw the man's sneering face.

"Oh yes, she was quite creative in her offerings. It's a good thing I'm a pious man and wouldn't take her up on any of her salacious offers." Another laugh. The man was lying, pushing on a sore spot for Jais. He had to be. Jais didn't doubt the man had killed his parents, but everything else…

He daren't say anything or let the man know how much his words stung. It would only prompt more pain for Jais and more Joy for Lucian.

Lucian reached out a long finger to Jais' cheek. "Is it a mother's comforting touch you seek?" Where the finger touched, scorching, crackling light erupted and Jais felt shocks shudder through his head. He clamped his eye shut once again, trying to retreat from the pain—the mockery of the soft touch he'd felt and seen in his recent vision.

He screamed. He couldn't help it.

The finger lifted away, the pain ceasing for a moment. "It seems you are far weaker than your brother. He held out for days and it seems you've already used up your powers and are quite broken within as well. It's sad really." The voice drifted away, Lucian was no longer standing so close. "I'll have to be careful not to kill you."

Then something hard and heavy slammed into Jais' stomach, tearing flesh and crushing organs.

Lucian was using stones again.

Another crunched into Jais' ribs. It wouldn't have broken any ribs normally, but most of Jais' ribs were already fractured or broken as it was. So, this only crushed them further.

Then one more into his head, sending Jais spiraling into darkness.

But even the darkness wasn't an escape.

Searing pain from strikes of targeted lightning drew him back to his body, over, and over, and over again.

And only when it ended could he safely retreat into himself once more.

Then came even more dark dreams and visions.

Some distant part of his mind called out to his friends even knowing they couldn't hear him.

Hurry! Please!

ASTRIA KNEW SHE WAS DREAMING.

She hadn't been born with her mother's ability to dream-walk, but enough time around Mirala and she'd picked it up. She had never sought out others, but with the ability came a certainty, a knowing of what was dream and what wasn't.

The sky roiled with clouds. Her feet crunched on loose dirt and stones down a narrow path toward... a mountain. Somewhere down there was a cave, a cave with answers.

Then she stopped, suddenly certain that she was not alone. She looked around, frantic, but saw no one.

Her heart skipped a beat when a booming voice issued from all around her. "No, you cannot see me here." Davul's voice, and with such puissance she stumbled and fell, scrambling back, stones cutting her palms, though she didn't know in truth what was 'away' from him and what wasn't. "Dreams were always my realm." He chuckled, malevolence thick in the sound. "Well... nightmares in truth."

She tried to wake herself. Usually she'd be able to, lucid as her dreams were, but not this time. Her heart hammered, sweat soaking her. Terror gripped her chest, breaths coming hard.

"Don't leave just yet," the voice spoke with false kindness, "I have something I wish to say to you first."

Astria tried to find words, but couldn't. She hoped this ended quickly.

Another laugh from the being, the sound grating on her, all around her. "Not as cocky here as you are when I speak into your mind, are you? No. And you've done quite well at keeping me out of your mind of late. Well, this is my realm, and you shall hear what I have to say!" The voice rose to a thunderous crescendo, frightening her even more with its vehemence. Yet, when it spoke again, it was composed, softer. "I have a way for both of us to get what we want. I have a way for you to deal with your father without killing him."

She waited, but so did the voice.

After a long moment it went on. "That is what you want, is it not? Speak up, girl!"

"Yes," she cried out, mouth dry, terror nearly choking her.

"Good, that wasn't so hard was it? Now, as I was saying, I have a way for you to make your father harmless. It's rather ingenious actually."

Astria let the being gloat, hoping that would speed up this encounter.

He went on soon enough. "You've always been able to borrow the powers of others. That is something no drahksan can do. That... that is of me."

What did he mean, her power was 'of him'? That made no sense.

"I am chaos, child. And that ability is... well quite chaotic." The way he said 'Chaos' made it sound like a name. "In truth I don't know why it took me so long to come up with a solution, though I supposed I was forced into it by your stubborn refusal to simply kill your father. So, with that not being an option, I found another. Your ability to take powers, it can do more than just borrow them, it can strip them from a drahksan...permanently."

The being of chaos was silent for a long moment as his words slowly sank in for Astria.

She could... permanently...?

Her eyes widened, but that meant...

"Yes, you can drain your father's powers. He will be nothing more than a mere human, powerless. You will not need to fear him any longer, and he'll live. Is this not what you want?"

It was, so very much, and yet...

Astria's voice was tremulous when she spoke, barely getting out her words through her quivering lips. "And... what will you get? What do you want?"

Chaos laughed, a grating, booming sound, which filled her with terror once more. "Why child, chaos has always been my desire. And with Lucian's powers gone, his city will fall to anarchy. That is all I want."

"How..." she stammered, not able to get out more words, but Chaos seemed to understand.

"You cannot simply be near your father. You'll have to physically touch him. Then concentrate on simply pulling his power from him into you."

And then...

"And I'll be done with you?" she asked, finding an edge of confidence.

"If that is what you wish, yes."

In that moment, terrified and alone in a dreamscape she no longer controlled, with the full essence of a divinity bearing down on her, she would say anything to get away.

"Yes, I'll do it!"

More laughter, fading, then she felt her dream slip away.

Astria woke with a start.

"What is it?" Mirala asked, a hand coming down to stroke her hair. She'd had her head in her mother's lap. In that instant, she recalled where she was in the real world. She'd led Caerwyn and Andrei to where her mother and Volf were. From there, the group of them had hidden themselves within another peaceful glade of a nearby forest, although Andrei hadn't grown the wall of trees this time. He was conserving energy for the fight to come. Astria had been so glad to see her mother again and felt far more at peace than she had in a long time. That had allowed her to fall asleep. But then...

She sat up quickly, looking at her hands. The cuts and pain she'd felt in the dream were no longer there. Her heart was still pounding in dread, but the dream was over. She took several long and deep breaths to try to calm herself.

Mirala asked again, "Astria? What's wrong? Bad dream?"

The worst.

And yet...

"I... I... think I know how to deal with Father."

"Oh?" Mirala raised a brow. "All that from a nap?"

Slowly the terror of the dream was fading, and in its place Astria felt a growing curiosity. Had the god truly given her a way to defeat her father. It... it made sense. Yet there would be no way for her to test it. Perhaps the god was sending her into a trap. Yet, with everything she'd felt from the being during the dream, she'd sense a certain honesty behind his words. The being wanted her father dealt with. She didn't know why, and for now she didn't want to question it. She had a way... finally, a way to defeat Lucian.

"Yes." Astria slowly nodded, at first more for herself, but then turning to her mother, she continued the action. "We should tell the others." She began to rise.

A light, restraining hand caught her arm. "They are all resting. Let them. It's nearly evening and if we're going to do anything, it will be tomorrow at the earliest. I know Jais is probably in grave danger and great pain, but we will need to be at our best to free him."

Astria nodded and sat again, though she couldn't stop fidgeting. She was anxious to move. She had a course now and though it could prove her doom, she somehow suspected the god had not been lying, at least about her powers. She was starting to feel more and more like she could do as it had suggested and drain her father's powers. She just wanted all of this to be over.

"What is this idea you had, for your father?" Mirala asked.

"Less of an idea, more of a… realization of… something I can do." The lie came a little too easily, but she didn't want to worry her mother.

A faint sigh and a weary smile. "More new powers?" Her mother was trying to put on a brave face, but she was concerned and scared. Astria's passive emotional sense could pick that up easily enough.

"Don't worry, Mother, I'll be well. And no, not a new power in truth, just an extension of something I can already do. I can… borrow powers, but now I believe I can drain them permanently as well. I can make Father… harmless."

Mirala was doing a poor job of hiding her astonishment. Even if Astria's passive emotional sense hadn't felt the woman's bewilderment, the expression of awe and surprise on her mother's face was clear as day.

"How…?" Astria could sense her mother's unsaid words: *how can you do all this?* Yet her mother never asked. After a moment of pursed lips and concerned looks, she simply slid over to embrace Astria. "I'm so sorry you've had to endure all this. It can't have been easy for you." Despite her mother's own fears, Mirala was sending soothing waves into Astria. Even in her own state of shock, she was tending to Astria's worn emotions.

Astria leaned into the embrace and found tears in her eyes. The apprehension and uncertainty lingering from the dream finally eased. A mother's unconditional love could do that. "Thank you for not yelling or getting too upset. I don't know how or why I can do what I can. Sometimes it frightens me too."

Her mother held her all the tighter.

They stayed that way for some time. When Astria was finally starting to feel... normal again, Mirala released her. The expression on her mother's face was one of grudging acceptance. "Whatever you can do, if it will end this peacefully. I think... I think that is the best way."

Astria smiled, tears on her cheeks. "Thank you, Mother." It felt so good to hear those words of affirmation.

Mirala let out a heavy breath in a huff and her expression cleared. She tried to smile, though it was a sad thing. Astria could feel the turmoil within her mother. She wanted to accept her child, but also feared what Astria could do.

So did Astria.

Perhaps Mirala felt the welling of fear once again within her daughter, as she leaned in once more to embrace Astria. "I love you, my dear, no matter what. You are a gift, so... very special." Her mother held her all the tighter.

Astria wasn't sure if her mother heard her next words— soft as they were and muffled by Astria's head resting on her mother's breast: "I don't know if I want to be special anymore."

～

VOLF SAT WITH THE OTHERS AROUND A SMALL FIRE. THEY HAD all rested well and eaten a solid meal. Caerwyn had caught them several small forest animals with only her sling, and what little remained of the meal was drying out and sizzling over the dying fire. They would rest again soon, sleep for the night before going to help Jais in the morning, but first, they needed to plan.

Astria had told them of her ability to 'drain' a drahksan. None of them had been too pleased to hear it. The girl had been eerie before, but now, the thought of her being able to pull the power from any one of them if she got too upset… was downright frightening. Yet Mirala had eased their concerns. It was clear now, this was the only way, scary as it might be.

"We'll have the same problem we had last time," Caerwyn said. After an afternoon of rest, the woman looked a lot better than she had when the three of them had found him and Mirala. Before, Caerwyn's face had still held scabs and scars, faded bruising and faint wheals. Nearly all of that was gone now. She was back to her old self—the woman who had found him in Cold River, thoughtful and powerful, commanding and direct. "Lucian alone we might be able to defeat, but he'll have his minions and be ready for us. They are what tip the balance in his favor."

Though, Volf was starting to wonder if Astria was tipping the scales significantly for them as well. It was hard to ignore everything the girl could do. And yet in this moment she seemed so innocent, sitting quietly with those large, silvery-blue eyes.

"I can ignore most of Lucian's powers, but the power of his minions is different. My drahksani immunity doesn't work on them." Caerwyn shrugged.

"It's their rings," Andrei said, though it was something they all knew. "Without them they're just normal people."

Which suddenly gave Volf an idea. "I could try to steal their rings."

Everyone looked at him.

"Could you do that? Take the ring right off someone's finger?" Mirala asked. There was hope in her voice.

"I honestly don't know. I've never tried it before. I get the feeling some would be easier than others. Certainly, they would probably know I was doing it after a moment. But if I got the ring off before they could react, then they would have no way to retaliate, well they would have mundane ways, but I think I can evade those. It would be the ones with thick fingers, where the rings are stuck on, who would be the biggest problem." He shrugged. "It might be worth a try. Though also, after the first few, they would probably start to warn each other. I don't know how many I'd be able to get, but if I could disarm a few of them, that might be worth it."

"It would, yes," Caerwyn said, considering. She turned to Andrei. "Is there a way to tell the more powerful rings from the less powerful ones?"

Andrei blew out a breath. "I honestly never paid much attention to them. I don't know if the stone in them is bigger or what."

"It is," Astria said softly. "The stones in the four primary rings are larger than those in the lesser rings. It's not much, but if Volf were to look around for a bit, he'd probably be able to determine at least a few of the more powerful rings." Silence hung as everyone took that in. "Also," Astria continued, "I would advise against using the rings. There is power there, yes, but a dark power, one that is connected to Lucian... and this other being. Destroy the rings if you can. Don't use them."

"Understood," Volf said.

"Well, that's part of a plan, then. But we still need a way in. I don't think we'll have as much luck going in through the kitchens as we did last time." Caerwyn looked around expectant, waiting for ideas.

"Do you want me to dig another tunnel?" Astria asked.

Mirala cut in. "No, dear, you save your power for... what you need to do." Even the girl's mother had trouble speaking the words. "And also, while I'm thinking of it. I want to keep you as safe as we can." Mirala looked over at Andrei. "Would you mind staying by her side when we go in?"

The large man nodded.

"Then it's settled." Mirala clearly didn't like the idea of Astria going back with them, but she knew it had to happen if they were going to do this without any killing—or with as few deaths as possible at least.

"Instead of tunneling," Caerwyn said, picking up where they'd left off, "Astria, do you think you could 'throw' us through the air like you did before, only just a short distance—and hopefully with more control—to get us up to Lucian's study? If we all go at him there, with Volf getting as many rings as he can beforehand, then perhaps we can end this. If he's powerless, perhaps the others will cease to follow him."

"The common villagers will. But the others, those of any rank within his cult, I highly doubt they'll stop even if he's dead," Andrei said. "Those with rings are the elite of his followers, fanatics, most of them will probably die before betraying him, whether they still have their rings or not. If he's alive, they'll try to save him."

Caerwyn grimaced. "Then it will mean their deaths, sadly." A heavy sigh. "But they will have brought it on themselves."

"What if Lucian isn't in his study?" Volf asked. Even now

he couldn't sense the man, which meant he had to be down... with Jais.

Caerwyn sighed. "We'll try to catch him there if we can. It will allow all of us to support Astria. Also, you said his study had direct access to the dungeons. So, it will be easy to go free Jais. If he's not there, then Andrei and Astria will go after him, while we free Jais. If he's with Jais..."

And Volf could tell from the looks of the others, this was the outcome they all feared. It would mean Lucian had a bargaining chip. If he was with Jais and had his powers long enough to kill the man, they would have to rethink their entire plan. "Well, hopefully he isn't."

"But what if he is?" Volf insisted. "He isn't a stupid man. If he knows we're coming he might consider that his best defense!"

Caerwyn's jaw tensed. Her eyes were hard. She shook her head. "If he's with Jais... then the plan's the same. Astria and Andrei go for him, the rest of us try to free Jais and keep Lucian from hurting him." The next words seemed incredibly hard for her to say, but she did. They came out slowly, torn from her. "If Jais dies... If Lucian kills Jais to defend himself, then... that will be a terrible outcome, but if it's what must happen to defeat this tyrant, then so be it."

Volf raised a single brow. He couldn't believe Caerwyn had said that.

"But," Caerwyn said with a hard, vicious expression. "If Lucian kills Jais... then I'll kill the man myself." Her tone was grim.

No one said anything to that.

Andrei nodded slowly.

Astria looked away, tight-lipped. "I'll try to make sure he can't hurt Jais," the girl said, after a long moment of silence. "Or anyone else, ever again."

THE NEXT MORNING, AFTER THEY HAD ALL RESTED, VOLF shadow-walked them all back to the walled glade where Donallo was buried.

Mirala wanted to give her last respects.

The others gave her some space as she went to the area of new grasses, which barely looked disturbed—Andrei was quite skilled in his earth-based abilities—and knelt there. She ran a hand over the short-cropped lawn.

"Hello, brother." For a long moment words escaped her, and she continued to caress the grasses over the grave. "When everything else in my life fell apart, after Erith…" She pressed her lips together. It had been some time but recalling the death of her first husband still bore pain for her. He'd been a valiant man and had tried to defend their city. He'd died, overwhelmed by a swarm of angry men and women—humans who'd hated the drahksani and had come to destroy them. She'd been some distance away, but had watched, horrified as the line of defenders was overrun. Then his spirit-link had winked out, and he was gone. "You were always there for me. I don't know what I'm going to do without you. You always said I was the strongest of us, the best of us." She shook her head. She didn't believe it. Finding a tear in her eyes, she wiped it away and drew in a long breath. "But you were the single fixed point in my life." She released a shuddering sigh. "And with Astria..." *being so powerful!* She loved her daughter unconditionally, but there was a part of her which feared the girl as well. "I could use you now more than ever." She steeled herself. "But I shall have to do without. I'll have to become as strong as you thought me to be." She gave a faint soft laugh then. "And here I told Volf he needs to figure himself out. I'm just as much a mess inside, now that I think about it. Perhaps we're all a mess inside and some of us just hide it better."

She brought her hand up from moving over the grasses. "You were my last tie to the past. And in this you are still helping me learn. I need to look to the future now, to my family and how to protect them. To... this new family." She glanced behind her at the others. "Odd as it may be. We are all drahksani, and that unites us."

She looked back at the grave as she began to rise. "Good-bye, Don. I love you. May this everlasting slumber bring you peace." Certainly, she'd have no peace until she'd finished dealing with Lucian.

She returned to the others. There were things which needed to be said to the living as well. "Volf, might I have a word with you, in private, before we leave?"

The others stepped outside the glade and Volf joined her.

She collected his hands and held them cupped in hers, staring at that joining for a long moment. He remained silent, waiting.

"I know how you feel," she began softly. "I was in your dream. I know what you want, the family you desire... with me."

He was tense. She didn't blame him. Her words could be

leading to a rejection, but they weren't. "I wanted you to know, before we went in to face Lucian—before we do this crazy thing which might get me or you or all of us killed—I wanted you to know how I felt."

She looked up to meet his eyes. She could tell he was holding his breath.

She couldn't help just a little bit of impish mischief in making him wait a little longer as she said, "Gods, I don't know how the rest of you do it, not knowing how others feel?"

He was turning a little blue, eyes slightly wide.

She laughed a little. "I wanted to tell you, that I want the same thing as you, a family."

His breath hissed out and his eyes went wider still. "Truly? With me?"

"That is my hope, yes."

He quirked a brow, confused by this.

She smiled, trying to reassure him. "I still hardly know you, and you me, but if we do survive what is to come, and if we find we do connect as we both seem to hope, then yes I would like to start a family with you… eventually."

He smiled, and it lit up his face. "I'd be the luckiest man in the world."

"Yes, you would be," she chided, and he laughed. Yet her tone turned somber quickly. "If… anything should happen to me, I want to make sure someone will look after Astria. I know she seems capable and strong, but she is still just a child. Would you—"

"Of course, I'd be honored. And nothing's going to happen to you, if I have any say over it."

She gave a faint grin, but it vanished quickly. "Seriously, Volf. She might be a handful. I don't know about this other being and how it affects her, but she'll need someone to love her, no matter what. Someone to show her what it is to be a good person in this world, so she can always see what's right. Can you do that?"

He nodded, somber, matching her temperament. "Yes, I can and I will."

Mirala looked away for a moment. "I'm worried about her."

One of his hands slipped from her grasp and came to her upper arm, rubbing it softly. "We can all see the toll this takes on you and on her. Whatever you need, whatever she needs, we'll provide it. We're all here for each other now."

That had been what she'd needed and wanted to hear. Mirala always worried just how much of Lucian was in the girl, even though she seemed to show no sign of such cruel or evil behavior.

She released Volf's hand and stepped in to embrace him. It wasn't lingering, a simple show of affection. As she pulled away, she kissed his cheek and whispered, "For luck, and thank you."

If anything, he seemed even more stunned.

"Shall we join the others and get this over with?" she asked putting out a hand for him to take. He did, his warm, long-fingered hand taking hers.

"Yes. Let's get this done."

He seemed confident, glowing.

She sent him a little more confidence, not enough to make him arrogant in his abilities, but enough to keep him sure of what he could do. He would have the first and hardest part of this mission.

CAERWYN SAT, MEDITATING, OR TRYING TO, AS THEY WAITED FOR

Volf to do his pilfering of rings. The slender young man had moved them to Rodathia quickly with his shadow-walk. They'd arrived just after midday. Now they had to wait.

Caerwyn had never been much good at waiting.

Yet she wanted to be ready for the fight to come, and that meant, settling her mind. Far too much had happened in the last few days. How long had it been since they'd met Donallo and Mirala on the road to Laskovic? It seemed like half a lifetime, but it had been less than two weeks.

What she'd forced herself to say the night before—if Jais died as part of their defeat of Lucian—hadn't been easy, but she was glad Volf had forced it out of her. She'd said the words, acknowledged that death—for Jais, or any of them really—was an option. Certainly, she'd work to prevent that, but she was clear now. She couldn't protect everyone all the time. She'd do her best, but sometimes, even with one's best, people died.

As she sat there meditating, she went back through those she'd lost. Her mother and father had been killed by a dragon hunter. That, in truth, was what had begun her on the path to where she was. She'd never truly come to terms with their death. It had been nearly impossible as the girl she had been at the time. It had festered within her. She'd been able to ignore it for a time, with the new family she'd found in Afgen, but it had still skewed her perceptions of life and family, turning her hard. She'd built a wall within her to keep out close connections. If she didn't get close, she wouldn't lose someone she loved again.

She'd had the chance—not even more than a year ago, in the Festorium before she, Jais, and Barami had faced the krolloc—to speak to her long dead parents. She'd thought that had brought her all the peace she'd needed, but she'd been wrong. It did, however, allow her to bring to mind their faces now as she imagined herself back at the small home in the woods where she'd spent her early childhood.

You died, she said to the images she held within her. *I couldn't protect you, and you couldn't protect me, except to send me running away. I remember hating you for that, for so long. You should have been there for me, protected me, and you weren't. I loved you, and yet I hated you. I hated you for being weak and not being able to survive the dragon hunter. I hated you for leaving me alone in the wilderness. There was a time when I even hated you just for bringing me into this world, when I thought I'd be better off dead. Death certainly seemed preferable to the cold and hunger and desperation of living on my own for those years.*

Her lips were tight, and she was trembling. She could feel moisture beneath her closed eyelids. She drew in a long breath. *But I see now, you did what you could. As we all must in this world. Sometimes you win, sometimes... you die. You didn't want to leave me. You were trying to protect me, save me, and you did.* She released a heavy sigh. *You did your best, and now I will do mine.*

The image of her smiling parents in her mind's eye wavered then was gone.

She opened her eyes and tears fell as she blinked the moisture away.

"Mirala said you might want some company?" Andrei said setting himself down next to her. "She said you were going through something?"

"I was... I am, yes." She looked over at Andrei. A thought occurred to her. "You, me, and Jais, we're all orphans, even Volf. Our parents died protecting us or trying to make the world safer for us."

He nodded.

He didn't ask what had happened to her parents. For that she was thankful.

"I think we all have our scars because of that," she said after a moment of silence. "You were raised by a foster father who taught you to be a brute. Jais was raised to avoid conflict and stay safe and anonymous. I... well I kind of raised myself, but I learned some things which stuck with me and made me try to protect everyone and save everyone."

"We all have our scars," he repeated her words, nodding. "It's how we live with them that matters."

She raised a single brow at that. "Wise words," she said.

He gave a short laugh. "I've read a lot of philosophy. Most of it was philosophy of warcraft, but some wasn't." He grew more somber. "I've got things I'll carry with me, regrets and pains that may never go away. Up until a few days ago, I was choosing to have those things make me hard." He shrugged. "Now I'm choosing differently."

"That easy?"

He shook his head slowly. "No. Every day is a trial."

"That's how I feel."

"I think," he said softly. "I think we just need to keep working through those days and those trials until they're easier, less burdensome."

"What would your philosophy say?" she asked with an impish grin.

"Actually, there was one man, a great warrior from the far south-east named Shendik Umal, who eventually sought only peace. He said, 'the scars a warrior carries, both within and without, may fade over time, but they never truly vanish. But, if a warrior chooses to use those lessons to make themselves better, instead of sour and angry, then they can still live a life of joy and peace.'"

"Sounds wise."

Andrei nodded. "We just need to give ourselves time, for wounds to heal and scars to dissipate."

Caerwyn drew in a long breath. "Thank you, Andrei, you've been very helpful." She rose, and he followed suit.

He was only slightly taken aback when she drew her sword and summoned Davlas. She rolled her shoulders, loosening up. "I need to get out some energy. I was going to practice some forms, but we could spar if you like." It was only then she realized he had no weapon. "I... we could try to find you a sword?"

"I don't need one. I've got yours." He gave a half-grin.

Her heart clenched at how much that grin reminded her of Jais. But another memory came to her as well, even as she said, "Mine?" She nearly laughed. His words had been the same—or close enough—to what she'd told Jais when training him, testing him, that day in Klasten's Green, before they'd gone hunting krolls.

She was about to ask if he was truly that good, when he went on to say, "I've studied several forms of weaponless combat. I think that's what I'm most comfortable with now." He looked away for a long moment. "I've hurt a lot of people and some of it was... far too easy. I think, from now on, if I'm going to hurt anyone, I need to feel it myself. That will remind me I don't really want to be doing this at all."

"You don't want to fight?"

He looked back at her. "No, not anymore. I'll fight to free Jais, but after that... I think I'd like to see what true peace is like, try to follow the path of Shendik Umal."

Caerwyn nodded. She could see the appeal of a peaceful life, but she wasn't going to give up her weapons any time soon.

Volf looked down at the five rings in his hand. This was taking too long, and he was certain he still hadn't found any of the leaders of the cult, those with the largest stones in their rings.

He'd only been scouting around the estate so far. He hadn't gone inside. He was just a little scared of heading into the house. Lucian had the help of a god, and could sense Volf even when hidden. Yet time was running out. Some of those from whom he'd stolen rings would already be on their way to warn Lucian and the others. He needed to act fast.

He shadow-walked swiftly up to the estate. He'd been climbing buildings all his life and could leap exceptional distances. He jumped up to a second-floor balcony and easily sailed over the railing, one hand on the thick marble, to land quietly. There were voices within, through an open door. Volf crept closer.

Lucian was with several of his minions, making plans. Volf could see the rings on the fingers of the nine others in the room with Lucian, all large.

Here Volf hesitated, watching Lucian. The man made no

indication he knew Volf was here. Volf waited just a little longer, trying to be as certain as he could that Lucian wasn't aware of him... but then his hand was forced, he had to act.

Five of those in the room were dismissed. Volf surged into his shadow-walk once more and made it to the door as the first one reached it. He slid through, shrinking himself slightly as the first man passed by, then he looked at the man's hand: two rings!

Now came the careful part. His shadow-walk allowed him to move faster than any normal person, but generally only in a walking motion: forward movement. Yet, he'd been practicing other movements. He reached out, a blur of movement, though he could see himself well enough, and slid the rings from the man's hand. It happened so quickly the man didn't even notice, except to reach over and idly scratch his hand.

The next two who passed him, only had one ring each. Volf was able to get one, but the other had pudgy fingers and Volf didn't think he'd be able to get the ring off. He knew he could shrink their fingers just a touch to help, but he hadn't yet figured out how to do that while using the 'fast-grab'-shadow-walk, so he let that one go. The second to last person had two rings. He slid one off, but even as he did the woman glanced at her hand and cried out in alarm!

Double-blasted-shadow-spawned luck!

Volf shadow-walked back through the closing door, having to shrink himself once again to fit through the small gap in the last seconds before the door closed.

Then he locked it, sliding a bolt into place on the inside of the door. He'd made sure to silence the area around the lock to make sure no one in the room heard it.

Time to see how many rings he could get off those in here, then get out as fast as he could.

Even as he sped himself over to the others, the door to the office shook. Then there was pounding on the other side.

"What in all the shades?" Lucian cursed, rising to look at the door. He was upset, good, hopefully that would distract him for a moment. The others were also distracted by the noise at the door.

Volf surveyed the four minions in the room. One of them had two rings, the rest had only one. This wasn't going to be easy. Best to just do what he could as fast as he could, then bolt from this place.

He did the easy one first, the woman with only one ring. Yet even as he moved onto the next the woman cried out in alarm. Using both his hands, he managed to get a ring off the next man, and one ring off another, but by that point they knew what was happening. He ran, using this shadow-walk to move him even faster—out onto the balcony, then leapt far away. He landed as lightning crashed down not twenty feet behind him. He stumbled forward, deafened for a moment, then fell. He caught himself quickly enough to roll and come up moving. He'd done what he could. Now to get back to the others and destroy these rings.

He'd collected seven more rings from what he believed were the most powerful minions. Hopefully he'd done enough.

But one thing was certain: Lucian would know they were coming.

Volf materialized before the others and threw the rings down. "I did what I could," he said, breath coming in huffs and heaves.

Caerwyn shared a glance with Andrei. They nodded in

unison. Earlier that day—before Volf had gone in—they'd snuck into a smithy and stolen a few hammers. Now the two of them went to work destroying the rings.

Astria's agitated voice reached through the clanging and crunching of metal. "Father is upset, I can feel it from here. He knows where the rings are, but he's not coming for them. He'll be ready for us.

Caerwyn swore under her breath as she worked, destroying one ring after another. Even as she slammed the hammer down on the last ring, seeing it shatter and the stone break, she felt a cold feeling in her gut.

"Astria, drop your shadow-form," Caerwyn said as she rose, tossing the hammer away. The girl had been keeping them hidden while Volf had been away.

"But Lucian will know—" Mirala began.

"I know!" Caerwyn cut the other woman off. "Astria, please?"

Caerwyn felt her connection with those beyond return. She felt Lucian through the spirit-link, but she could also feel Jais! Then both of them vanished.

She clenched her jaw, restraining the string of curses she wished to say. So, it had come to this. Her worst fears were coming to pass.

"We need to act fast," she said. No one objected; they'd all felt that too. They knew what Lucian was doing. "Volf, get us there, quickly!" she said, cold and stern. With a nod, he wrapped them all in his shadow-form, then they were moving, each step carrying them hundreds of feet.

She only hoped they'd make it there in time to save Jais.

LUCIAN CLOSED THE DOOR TO THE DUNGEON CHAMBER BEHIND him and rested his back against the sheets of iron. By all the gods, how had he missed that!

Why did you not tell me the shadow-wielder was among us! he asked his god, but Davul was silent. *Davul! Answer me! What is going on?*

Still nothing.

"Davul!" he cried out so vehemently all those in the room with him flinched and shuddered.

They all then murmured among themselves:

"Yes, Davul will save us."

"He will come. He will deliver us. He has never forsaken us!"

"We still possess his power. Davul be with us!"

Lucian shouted over them. "Shut your mouths, all of you. I need to think!"

He'd done what he could with what he still had. Three of his top disciples were in here with him, Syasha, Jurid, and Kalia. He'd also left a force out in the hall—all the remaining struvrti and piati he'd been able to round up from the estate, twenty in all—led by Viktor, the next most senior in rank who still possessed his rings. He hoped that would slow down those coming. Though, only then did he recall that they had tunneled out from their prison last time. They could do the same to enter this place. Perhaps he should have more forces in here?

No, the room was already feeling a bit crowded with the four of them, plus his prisoner.

Lucian sent a blast of lightning from one hand into the young man, holding the attack for a sustained moment as his victim screamed. That helped him vent some of his frustrations and would hopefully ensure the young man wouldn't be a factor in the fight to come.

Davul, talk to me. Where have you gone?

Yet Lucian feared he knew already. The god was more interested in Astria than it was in him. There was something about his daughter the god wanted.

Have you sided with her against me?

And why shouldn't I? The god had finally responded, but not as Lucian had hoped. *She will be far more powerful than you ever were. She was born from you while you held my powers within you. They are a part of her. Though I can increase them if I wish, I cannot fully take them from her, not yet. And...* Laughter. *There is more, but I think perhaps I will not tell you. You have served your purpose Lucian, but your time is done. If I must choose between you and her, as she has made me, then I choose her.*

Lucian was stunned by that: *'as she has made me'*. By all the gods, what power did his daughter possess to sway a god in such a way?

Also, since I believe you'll be dead soon anyway. I see no reason to continue my charade. I am not Davul, Lucian. That Kytien was a hedonistic, self-absorbed ass. It disgusted me to pretend to be him for so long. My name is... well, you are not worthy of such an honor.

And so, this was how it ended. Idly, Lucian wondered if the powers within the rings of his followers would still work if the god left him.

Oh yes, my power remains with them, even with you. I will revel in the slaughter and chaos today shall bring. For whichever side wins, all will die for my cause! And each death makes me more powerful!

More powerful? Was that why the god had demanded death sacrifices?

Lucian couldn't fathom what was truly going on here. Some grand scheme of a higher being was swirling around him and he knew now he was only a pawn, despite all his allusions to power.

Yet something in what had been said gave Lucian an idea.

"Be ready for anything," he said to those in the room with him. "Our enemies might come from any side, including through a wall, though I will seek to dissuade them from that."

He opened the door behind him and kept it open. He couldn't sense the spirit-link of his foes. They were hiding themselves once again. But perhaps they would come out from those shadows before they drew too near. If they did, they might be lured to him by his spirit-link. That would hopefully mean they'd come through the estate and down the hall filled with his minions. He was fairly certain his followers would die in that attack, but perhaps his enemies would be injured or made wearier by the attempt.

Let them come, let them grind through his followers. He'd be ready for them. He'd show that bastard god how powerful he could be!

To be safe, he drew his prisoner closer to him. Better to have the man nearby in case he needed to use him as a shield or bargaining chip.

Then, to reassert his power, and make himself feel better,

he laid a hand on the young man's face and sent lightning through the connection, feeling the skin under his hand shrivel and burn away as the prisoner screamed.

He kept that up until the man screamed no more. He was still alive; his spirit-link was weak, but present. Good. Let his enemies come. Let them see Lucian's full power. Perhaps he'd make one more sacrifice of this man before he left this world.

One thing was certain, he'd be blasted to the deepest shadows of Holn before he let others take what was his!

JAIS? THE VOICE WAS DISTANT IN THE DARKNESS THAT WAS HIS mind. He thought it Lucian at first, but no, it sounded more concerned... more feminine. Yet he couldn't think of who might be calling to him. He shrank away from the physical, his mind whirling in a delirious, dream-like state once more. The pain on his face had been excruciating. He could still feel the mark of Lucian's hand on his cheek. One of his eyes was blind now from that attack. He didn't want to think of what had happened to it, to him.

So, he stayed in his dark and secret place and bided his time and his energy. He had enough now, he knew, to heal himself fully. He may not be able to do much more than that, but he'd be whole once more for when the others arrived.

He'd spent a lot of time in this dark and secret place within his soul. At least, it seemed like it had been an eternity. He didn't know how long it had been in truth. In this place where dreams and visions met soul and spirit, time was a vague thing.

And that meant, he'd had a lot of time to connect with himself on a level he'd never known before. And he'd not been idle as he'd roamed through this abyss. Through the visions of his life, and snippets of memories, he'd begun to form something he called his 'core.'

For so long he'd sought to know who he was, wished for someone to tell him. Yet his father had suggested he already knew. That had prompted this deeper soul-searching.

Before he'd been captured, he'd figured out at least one thing about himself: he was a passionate, all-in lover. He gave his heart fully and completely to friends, causes... and women. Alnia had been the first. Then, after her death, he'd been ready to throw in with Caerwyn. But she'd not wanted or needed a man. So, he'd turned to Elria. After her death, he'd been adrift, until he'd realized he still had strong feelings for Caerwyn.

He'd had time to think about these women and what they'd meant to him. For a while—after he'd had that vision of his parents leaving him and seeing his mother for the first time—he'd wondered if he'd been attaching himself so strongly to these women as some sort of surrogate for his mother and the love he'd lost. He found perhaps some truth in that, but there was a deeper knowing he'd found through that line of questioning. It wasn't so much that he was seeking his lost mother, he was seeking lost love. He'd felt a deep and abiding need for love, kinship, closeness. His aunt had kept him so distant from everyone else in his village growing up, and he'd begun to feel... separate, alone, forsaken. These women had been filling a need within him for deeper companionship, and he'd latched onto it vehemently wherever he'd found it. It was upon knowing this, that he began to understand more and more of himself.

Oh Jais... He recoiled from the distant voice once again, sinking ever deeper within himself.

He thought back on his relationship with Alnia and Elria and tried to figure out what might have happened if they hadn't both passed onto the next life. He knew now, he would have taken everything they could give to fill the void within him. He honestly didn't know how that would have affected them. He suspected it would have eventually broken Alnia. He was fairly certain Elria would have pushed him away, unable to provide what he wanted. And he could see how his latching onto Caerwyn had only hindered and hurt her when she'd been most vulnerable. She'd been suffering, and he'd been asking for more and more from her.

Gods, he was a fool.

He had been a fool.

He wouldn't be any longer... if he lived through this. He would make sure that if he was going to be with Caerwyn it was on even footing, giving and taking—hopefully more giving than taking. He didn't need her love to fill that abyss within him anymore. He'd managed to fill it himself. That self-love had come through other revelations.

He'd been using all the visions and memories floating around him to get a clearer picture of his life, of his patterns, of who he was at 'his core,' and it was an interesting mix.

He'd seen himself as a boy with his uncle, hunting. The training he'd received on how to stalk prey, and know which animals to take, and which to leave to keep the balance within the forest. The use of a bow, so many days practicing shooting, growing stronger and more accurate. How to skin and prepare hides or smoke and salt the meats. All of that made him a hunter.

But he'd also watched his aunt with her medicines, fascinated, enthralled. When he later learned he possessed healing powers of his own, he'd felt a certain sense of completeness. Of all the times in his life when he'd felt most useful, most alive, most helpful, it had been when he'd been restoring life and energy to others. He knew now, he was a healer.

Like your aunt... The voice seemed somehow closer now, though Jais was deep within himself. He dismissed it yet again, far too much was on his mind to consider.

As much as he mended allies, he'd battled foes, and he could do so with great abandon. He was a practiced warrior who could use his swords to good advantage. But he wasn't just a murderer, a man who killed without reason or slew the innocent. He fought to protect others. He battled not only monsters—krolls and a krolloc—but villains and tyrants, like that wizard in the north and Lucian. This had been reinforced when he'd learned about the Palassi from his father and Donallo. They stood up for those who couldn't stand for themselves. They defended the weak and upheld justice and truth. He was, as his parents had been before him, a protector and defender.

Like your father, yes... Oh Jais, you're so close I can feel you now!

Close? No, he was distant, far from the outside world. He was within his core, where he saw himself truly. He could see his patterns of loyalty to friends and family, his kindness and bravery, and also his stubbornness, which on far too many occasions had gotten him into trouble. Yet it had been that same stubbornness which refused to let him give in to pain and torture. It was how he'd survived and why he'd created this safe place within him.

For so long, he'd been trying to find the one thing that personified him and made him who he was. He realized now, that there was no single thing. He was: a healer, a hunter, a defender, an all-in-lover, a brave and loyal man, who could be kind, or incredibly stubborn. That's who he was at his core. And that's what had been keeping him sane through the pain and torture.

And in the darkness within him there flared to life a brilliant light. It was from that light, that a voice issued forth, the woman's voice he'd been hearing. "Jais, I am so sorry you had to endure all of this to find yourself, but you've done it and finally freed me!"

"Freed?" He didn't know how he was speaking, he had no mouth in this place, though some essence and image of himself seemed to manifest within the darkness, a shadowy arm raised to block out that light. Though the light was dimming, and within he could see the form of a woman.

"Who are you?" he asked, still not certain how he was doing so.

"Jais." The woman, her radiance now fast fading, stepped toward him in the nothingness. He lowered his arm to get a better look at her and even as she spoke, he knew the truth of her words. "I'm your mother."

She was a match to the woman he'd seen in his vision from when he'd been a babe, and she smiled at him as she drew closer, standing before him in the darkness of his own soul.

"How..." He didn't know what to say.

The smile on her face slipped, faltered, lips going tight, tears welling in her eyes. "I'm sorry, Jais. I... I didn't mean to... You were the only one I could find."

"Find?" None of this made any sense. Why was he seeing his mother again? Was this yet another episode of delirium? It must be.

She approached, reaching out and touching... his face. She must be seeing him in this place just as he was seeing her, as real as any person. She drew in a long breath to speak, steady if still somber. "I... died..." she said, the words not easy for her to say. He couldn't blame her for that. "I died, but before I did, I... I sent your father's spirit into his sword. I sense you've reconnected with him. I'm glad for that." She smiled, though it was tinged with sadness. "And when, finally… my spirit left my body." She gave a grim grin. "I was always strong with spirit and I knew what was happening, so I… sought another body. Alas I was drawn only to those I was close to, family. Andrei was too young, not ready, not able to take me. But I felt a pull from farther away still. So, I flew, faster than any bird, to… you. Your spirit was so like mine Jais, powerful and… in need. You desperately wanted your parents back. You'd been seeking for me with all your spirit." Her hand fell away from his face.

This was all just a little too much to believe. He had nothing to say. If this was some fever dream, it wasn't a completely unpleasant one.

"I was selfish, Jais, I'm sorry. I didn't want to die and…" She turned her face away from his, clearly ashamed.

"Mother?" He faltered. Too much emotion and confusion were mixed in with the word. His aunt Sarelle had been his mother, the one who raised him. This woman had left him…

She sniffed back tears. "I… damaged you Jais. When I came to you, when our spirits merged, it overwhelmed you. You were only a few years old. You weren't ready." She swallowed hard, drawing in a long breath, before facing him again. "I'm sorry. I shouldn't have done that. I should have allowed myself to die… fully."

"Mother, no." He didn't know this woman at all, but he knew she was his mother and the thought of some part of her still being alive within him was more than he could bear. Tears welled and fell, though he couldn't feel his own face. He knew that's what she'd see. "Don't leave me."

A sad smile. "It's my time, Jais. I need to move on. Now that you've freed me from the mess I made of our two spirits. I was trapped there for years and could only be freed once you found some sense of your true self. You have that now, and I need to let you be your own man. I need to give you back your spirit."

"My spirit?" He blinked.

"Though, I will leave you with some of my powers. We've been entwined long enough for me to do that. So at least, I know some part of me will remain."

"No, you can stay!" He blurted, even as he knew it wouldn't be possible. So many things were falling into place. His uncertainty about himself had come from having no real connection to his own spirit. Even now he could feel that spirit returning to him and with it—bundled with what he'd discovered about himself on his own—there came a fierce sense of self-worth and personal power. He also knew now, why he'd never been able to feel the spirit-link to others. His mother's spirit had overwhelmed that connection when she'd joined with him, burning it out for a time. It was returning now and with it came an amazing awareness. Not only could he feel Lucian near him, but his friends nearby, drawing closer. Yet more than that, he felt... others.

His mother spoke, helping to explain what he was feeling, perhaps seeing the realization and confusion on his face. "Spirit is what connects all things. Other drahksani can sense each other, for they are powerful beings, but you should now be able to sense all living beings. The powers I give to you will help you connect with them, call to them, inspire or subdue them. This is the legacy I pass on to you."

Indeed, he could feel every person in the hallway around him, even out beyond the immediate area, in the estate above and down the hills into the city. "There's so many!" he whispered in awe.

"Use it wisely." His mother's voice grew soft. He drew his awareness back within him to the image of the woman there. She was slowly fading away.

"Mother! No, I only just met you. Don't leave!" Raw, unbridled anguish tore through him.

A sad smile. "I must. It is the way of all things. But there is enough of me within you now, you'll never truly be without me. Let your spirit guide you. The more you connect with others, the more you'll be connecting with me." The smile turned from sad to soft and peaceful. "I go to Erival now Jais, but I will always be with you."

He knew the truth of her words, even as she faded away entirely. He couldn't see her in this odd place of spirit and soul, but... he could feel her still, through some odd residual spirit-link from the time they'd been so deeply connected.

"Good-bye," he whispered.

Yet even as a melancholy took him at the second death of his mother... hope surged within him as well. He had his spirit-link now. And as much as Lucian was a near-to-blinding presence next to him, he sensed his friends, his drahksan family, coming for him.

They would soon be here... and when they arrived... he would be ready.

"Is it a trap?" Mirala asked. The kitchens were silent, the staff gone. Yet the fires had not been put out: food burned and water boiled over. Everything had been left in great haste.

Astria didn't like how eerie and silent the house was. She sensed out with her emotions. There were people in the estate, but the prevailing feelings were fear and uncertainty. They were hiding or fleeing. Below them, deep in the cellars, she felt a different group. They were excited and fearful, determined and wary.

They hadn't seen anyone around and Volf had lowered his shadow-form once they were in the house. As such, they'd sensed both Lucian and Jais far below them. It had been that, which had prompted Mirala's comment from a moment before.

"Surely, it must be. He knows we're coming. Why wouldn't he be prepared." Andrei was gruff. Astria could sense the wound-up tension within the man. He was ready for a fight. So was she, though she hoped to avoid bloodshed. Yet a nagging uncertainty filled her. She was afraid 'that god'— the being of chaos—had betrayed her. If she couldn't take her father's abilities...

"I agree. I don't think we can assume we have any sort of upper hand here," Caerwyn said. She too was tense, but for a different reason. Astria felt her fear and concern, her affection for a dear friend in trouble.

"What's our best way in then?" Mirala asked.

Caerwyn didn't respond immediately, the look on her face one of intense concentration. Astria switched to her mind-powers, but even as she did Caerwyn voiced her thoughts. "I think if Lucian is revealing himself to us, that means he knows we're coming, yet it may also mean he's smart and being tactical about his defense. If he's in the doorway to that room and has his remaining forces on either side of him, then no matter which way we go at him, we'll have to fight them first, which just gives him time to retreat either into the room or into the hall."

Astria didn't much like this talk of fighting. She still hoped to avoid it, but knew that Caerwyn was too far-gone into concern for Jais to worry overmuch about the lives of Lucian's minions.

"Do we split ourselves and come at him from two directions then?" Volf asked.

Even Astria knew that was a bad idea.

"No, we're better together, where we can aid each other with our wide variety of skills and abilities." That comment from Andrei got a nod from Caerwyn.

She added, "We stay together."

Astria could tell the woman wanted to hurry, yet her words belied this. "We need to approach with caution. Let's move carefully from here. We don't know where Lucian might have placed minions."

Astria had been about to say that she knew, but Mirala

got there first. "I sense no emotions from anyone except those far below us. Our route is clear until we get to the dungeons."

"Can people not hide their emotions? What if they aren't feeling anything?"

Mirala smiled knowingly. "The only way to hide emotions is by being dead. The living always feel something."

And right now, Astria was terrified. She reached out and took her mother's hand. Mirala was startled, but then smiled down at her, squeezing her fingers, whispering, "Stay with me." That helped... a little.

Caerwyn nodded. "Then everyone behind me!" She moved ahead at a fast walk, which was a near run for Astria with her shorter legs. They weren't hiding themselves. There would be little point now. Lucian knew they were here. Both sides would know the location of the other. In that, at least, they were on even footing.

Except you have me.

Astria cringed at the voice of the being within her mind. *I still don't trust you,* was her reply.

And I wouldn't expect you to, not until you see that I haven't betrayed you, that you can do what I have said.

Yet she couldn't shake the remembrance of that dream, and the control he'd had over her. He'd felt so powerful. She'd been terrified. *But that dream... You...*

It was the only way to reach you after you'd blocked me from your mind. And aren't you glad I did? Now you have a way to defeat your father without death. Isn't that what you wanted?

It was, but she still questioned this being's motives. *And all you want is chaos?* She didn't much like that, but chaos could be... controlled. They could all help to ease the citizens after this was done. She wasn't too worried about that.

Yes.

Astria grew suddenly bold. *And will you tell me who you really are? I know you're not Davul!*

The being laughed. *I see you are far more intelligent than your father. I'm glad, I don't have to pretend with you. It's one of the reasons I like you, my daughter.*

I'm not your daughter!

Ah, but you are my daughter, at least in part. A part of me, some of my power, was within Lucian when he sired you, and that flowed into you as well. There is a part of me in you, for good or ill. That is what gave you the power to learn new drahksan abilities and to... take them away. My power makes you everything that you are, the daughter of a god!

Astria gasped and stopped. They were mid-way down a set of stairs and her mother called out as she too had to stop behind Astria. Astria didn't really see the others stop and look. Her mind was churning. She'd sent another tiny tendril of mind-link through to the being during her conversation with it. She'd sensed the truth of its last statement. It may not have been Davul, but it was a god, some god, which made her exactly what it had said she was.

A god?

Oh, yes, my dear. And the most powerful god there is. Her mind-link sensed a duality in this. He was both telling the truth and lying. She couldn't quite figure that out. She sensed that there was some riddle to what the god had said, that somehow, even though she felt he wasn't that powerful, he was still perhaps more puissant than the other gods.

"We need to stop," she said to the others. This changed everything. "We can't... I can't..."

"What is it?" Caerwyn asked, nearly at the same time as Mirala said something similar.

"I just... don't know if I can do this anymore."

Oh? Why not?

Shut up!

Laughter.

It was that laughter, that constant sense of arrogance and superiority, that grated on her. Astria suddenly felt the depths of her ignorance. There was so much she didn't know. She felt the full force of her youth and inexperience in that moment. She was trying to match wits with a god and for a time she'd thought she could, but now she knew she'd been wrong. What had she been thinking?

And yet, what choice did she have? They had to get rid of her father and using her powers was the only way of doing that with the fewest people getting hurt. Yes, the god would get what it wanted, it would get chaos, but that didn't change the fact that this way was the only way to do what must be done. In fact, the god would get what it wanted either way. If Lucian was killed, or just left powerless, this entire area would be left unstable. So... if it would get what it wanted no matter what, then she might as well do this her way, with the fewest deaths possible.

"Astria?" her mother asked. "What is it, are you well?"

Was she?

"Yes, I... I'm well, I just had a moment of doubt, but I'm... better now. We should go."

The others shared a dubious look but in truth, their choices were limited too.

And so, onward they went.

And a god's laughter followed Astria, as she descended the stairs to meet her father.

"DAVLAS!" CAERWYN HISSED AS SHE REACHED THE BOTTOM OF the steps. The spear appeared hovering next to her head, pointed forwards.

Torches lit the stairwell behind her and the hall before her. Normal people needed light to see. And there were several 'normal' people between her and Lucian.

She tried to keep her emotions in check upon seeing Jais floating there beside the tyrant. Jais looked awful, burned, bloody, and bruised, a mess. There was a weeping red wound on the one side of his head in the shape of a hand print. The young man looked to be unconscious at the moment. Yet she knew he was alive from the feel of his spirit-link. That's all that kept her in check as Lucian shouted past his minions at her.

"Come any closer and I'll kill him. I'm sure you can see my handiwork. You know I'm capable. Just ask Andrei there."

Caerwyn paused. She'd play along for a moment. See what it was the man wanted. "And?"

"And hand over my daughter. Once I have her, I'll let your man here go. You can leave with him, and I won't bother you."

"I'll never give you my daughter!" Mirala hissed from somewhere behind Caerwyn.

Lucian seemed almost gleeful as he said, "We may have to kill the girl's mother so she doesn't get in the way. You know how possessive mothers can be." He quickly followed up with, "But you would have your man back, Andrei's brother, which I see is no news to anyone. The remaining four of you could be on your way." Lucian shrugged.

It was a perfectly reasonable exchange, if Caerwyn cared only for herself and nothing for others. Any reasonable person would see it as madness though.

"No, wait. Mother, I will go to him!" Astria said.

Caerwyn had to restrain a smile. Of course, Astria would go to him, that was their entire plan. Lucian didn't know that. This just might work, but she'd have to look like she didn't want it to happen. "No, Astria you can't. We can't sacrifice you to save our friend."

"Maybe... it's the only way?" Andrei said from next to her, sounding confused and disheartened. Good man for following along.

"No, I won't let it happen!" Mirala said, and Caerwyn couldn't tell if Mirala was also playing along or being truly protective.

"Mother, I can't let you or anyone else get hurt. I'll go."

"No, Astria, you can't!"

"Mother, please."

Caerwyn listened to this, never once taking her eyes of Lucian and Jais. Which was why she saw one of Jais' eyes open ever so slightly. He hadn't moved otherwise. Caerwyn kept her gaze on him, trying to figure out his condition. It was the eye on the side of his head facing away from Lucian and after a moment it opened fully and Caerwyn was sure it was looking directly at her. Then... he winked.

Gods! What was he trying to tell her? It seemed he had his own schemes in place. For the moment, she'd just have to trust him. He made no other move, other than to close his eye once again. Though, somehow, he seemed perhaps more relaxed in his cocoon of air.

Well, that was good to know.

"Goodbye, Mother," Astria said, sorrowful, and a moment later the girl was inching past Caerwyn. Astria looked up at her and said, "I'll get your friend back."

Lucian was laughing from the far side of his mass of minions. "Yes, girl, come to me! I'm your father after all. Together, you and I will be unstoppable. You'll be a queen, an empress!" The man was raving.

The minions parted for Astria to pass. Caerwyn felt a slight wave of ease and serenity flow over her.

Mirala must have moved up behind her, for the woman was close when she whispered. "Astria is calming them, making them less willing to fight." Then after a moment, she spoke again, this time her voice heavy with fear and concern. "Gods, I hope this is the right thing to do."

Caerwyn desperately hoped the same thing.

For a long moment they waited as Astria, playing the part perfectly, moved slowly, one shuffling foot after the other, through the crowd, toward her father.

Caerwyn was a little glad that the girl's wave of peace had affected her as well, otherwise she would have been so extremely tense at the moment. Just standing here, waiting, would have been agony.

Astria finally reached the far side of the group of men and women between them and Lucian. Lucian reached out and made a grasping motion, Astria waved her hand before her and Lucian balked. "You dare to defy me, girl?"

Caerwyn didn't know what had happened, or not

happened. She guessed the man had tried to use his storm-hold on her and she'd somehow dismissed it.

"I am coming willingly, Father. There is no need to hold me." Astria reached out a hand. "I only wish to hold your hand, Father."

It was Lucian's turn to bat away the child's outstretched hand. "None of that, girl. Just stand there, where I can see you." He pointed to a spot not far from him.

"Will you give them back their friend now?" Astria asked.

Lucian laughed. "And why would I do that now that I have what I want?"

As Caerwyn had suspected.

Lucian called out to them. "Here's the new deal," he shouted, laughing as he did. "Leave this place and never return and if you do, I won't kill your friend or harm the girl!"

"You fiend!" Mirala shouted. There was genuine hatred and vehemence in her voice.

Caerwyn, however, was watching Astria, who nodded, then with another wave of her hand she dispelled the storm-hold around Jais, who fell limp to the ground with a grunt of air.

"What?" Lucian spun to look at Jais, then back to Astria. "You can't... you've never been able to dispel my storm-hold before!"

Astria turned to her father and said, "I've never been able to do this before either." Then she reached up quickly and grasped one of his fingers.

Lucian's head was thrown back in a vicious scream as his body went tense, seemingly paralyzed.

That was their signal.

Caerwyn surged forward, sending Davlas into the first of the minions before her, then easily slicing through the rest of their front line. They were still stunned by their master's agonized shriek. Two more rows fell to her blade and spear before they finally started reacting. But when they did, their reactions were slow, muted, sluggish. Astria's emotional effect had worked well. Another row was down even as they began their assault. That left a little more than half, perhaps two thirds remaining.

Then Caerwyn felt the oddest sensation, as if a ghost or some spirit moved past her, and suddenly half those before her grew wide-eyed with terror and turned to run. There was enough chaos from that for her to clear away a few more before any significant attacks came her way.

She blocked a blast of fire with her shield, then felt air hit her, trying to push her back. But these minions must not have been as powerful as those she had faced before, as the attacks didn't seem nearly as strong. Caerwyn hunkered behind her shield and closed her eyes, trying to use her echo-location to get a sense for the enemy. There was certainly enough noise to give her a good feel for their position. She sent Davlas into them.

Fire blasted at her. She made sure to keep her head clear of it, behind her shield, but that left much of her lower torso and legs exposed. She'd survive a few burns. Chunks of stone slammed into her legs. She'd have bruises, cuts, but not much worse. These attacks weren't as bad as before. So, she continued onward, sending Davlas repeatedly among them and cutting down any she got close to.

Then, there were no more.

She risked a glance, then quickly ducked behind her shield once again.

Having been right in front of the open door to the dungeon chamber, Caerwyn spun away as attacks came from within. Her quick glance had spotted several enemies, but the most concerning one was that first woman Caerwyn had fought in the forest. She'd had only wind powers then. Later when Lucian had come after them, that same woman had possessed strange wind and fire abilities. Caerwyn had hit her a glancing blow in her shoulder with Davlas and that arm was still in a sling. The woman's expression was one of ire and vengeance.

As Caerwyn drew back from the door way, a tornado of fire blew through the portal. It was hot enough that, beside the door as she was, Caerwyn still felt the heat, her clothes smoldering.

Yet that didn't concern her as much as the other thing she'd seen in her brief peak over her shield. Astria still seemed to be occupying Lucian, but the man's free hand was stiffly jerking around, blasting lightning in all directions. Jais was up and seemed fully healed, but even as she'd looked, he'd been hit by one of those random blasts of lightning. He'd fallen prone from the lightning attack, and that had been all Caerwyn had seen before fire had come at her.

Then she felt darkness surround her as a hand touched her shoulder.

"Heal her!" Volf's voice was insistent.

Andrei was there next to her a moment later, laying a hand on her arm. She flinched from the pain of the touch, as there wasn't much of her that wasn't bruised, broken, or burned. But then a moment later, her skin was mending, her aches easing as Andrei poured his power into her.

Once that was done, the four of them—Mirala was also hidden within Volf's shadow-form—took a moment to size up the scene before them.

The woman who blasted fire was out of the room now and had taken a long moment to look down the hall. She stood only a few mere feet away from the four of them but couldn't see them. Then she turned and raised a hand toward Astria.

As she did, two more came out of the room, a woman and man, both looking for trouble.

"Take the rest, she's mine!" Caerwyn said, jumping forward to attack the fire-woman. She sent Davlas ahead of her. But the woman must have sensed something and shifted to one side. Davlas caught her side and spun her, but did little damage.

Caerwyn spared a glance for Jais as she attacked. He was getting up, slowly, looking rough. His burn wasn't healing quickly, and he was having to fend off chunks of earth thrown at him from the man who'd come from the room, blocking them with his arms.

She wanted so much to help him, but first, she needed to protect Astria and make sure Lucian lost his powers.

She screamed as she struck, stabbing the woman in the back as fire blasted from the woman's hand, aimed at Astria. Luckily the woman arched back when hit and the fire blasted the wall and ceiling instead. But this sent chunks of rock and debris raining down over Astria who cried out, flinching away.

The girl's contact with Lucian was broken.

And even as the woman died on Caerwyn's sword, Lucian —still shrieking—spun and attacked.

JAIS STAGGERED BACK AS YET ANOTHER CLUMP OF STONE slammed into him. He collapsed to his knees and only just managed to avoid another piece, which would have cracked off his head.

He'd used nearly all the energy he'd saved up in healing himself once he'd been free of Lucian's wind-borne prison. He was too exhausted to do much of anything to the earth-wielder who stalked steadily toward him, relentless. The floor and walls were pitted with heavy divots from the stone the man was ripping up to be hurled at his target.

Jais didn't have the strength to charge the man, and wasn't sure what other powers he might have to stop the earth-wielder. And yet, what had his mother said: *inspire or cow them*? Perhaps there was something he could do with his spirit?

He pushed at the man's spirit, shouting as he did, "Stop this! Obey me!"

The man did stop, eyes wide, stunned. He seemed frozen, which was enough of a hesitation for Andrei to catch the man unawares, from behind, with a bare-handed strike to the back of the neck.

The man collapsed in a heap.

Jais didn't even have the energy to smile, that exertion had left him huffing hard, not even able to get up.

Andrei was at his side a moment later and Jais felt an outpouring of healing energy into him.

He gave a shuddering sigh of gratitude. "Thank you, brother."

"That still sounds odd to hear from you."

Jais had to agree. It was odd to say. He looked up to take in the rest of the fight.

Things had not progressed well.

He didn't know what the others had planned or why they had given over Astria. The girl was ducking and stumbling away from bits of the tunnel raining down on her. Lucian, in that moment, spun and attacked Caerwyn.

"No!" he shouted, reaching out, but he was too far away to do anything. He thought to push spirit once again, but before he did, he saw Caerwyn slip out of the way of the blast. But then the bolt hit... something. Volf appeared in that spot. The man's eyes rolled up and he collapsed next to Caerwyn.

Oh gods, Volf. "We need to get to him!" Jais urged Andrei.

"I'll go, you help Caerwyn with Lucian."

Jais liked that idea... a lot. He had some issues to work out on his once torturer. His knuckles cracked as he stretched his hands. Then he lumped them into fists. "Agreed."

They launched themselves back into the battle.

Caerwyn had also thrown herself at Lucian, but had been halted, having to hold up her shield to defend herself from the last of the minions, a woman throwing shards of ice.

This allowed Lucian another shot at her. Jais dove at the man, knocking Lucian's feet out from under him as the man fired his bolt. It put Lucian off balance and the lightning went wide, into the ceiling. More chunks of stone fell.

Lucian fell atop Jais, but was quick and escaped Jais' grasp, rolling away to one side of the hall.

The ice-woman turned her attacks on him, and he had no shield. Jais tried to roll away, but still got hit by several of the shards. They didn't cut him deep, he had a tough hide, but still those wounds would start to tell on him quickly enough. Andrei had given him enough healing and energy to sustain him for a while, but even now Jais could feel that draining. He needed to end this fight quickly.

Then Caerwyn was engaging with the ice-woman. Jais knew that fight wouldn't last long. He turned to Lucian, who seemed slightly injured, getting up slowly. Jais too was about to rise and go pummel the man, when a light hand on his shoulder stopped him.

"Please, no. We have a plan. I just need to get close to my father again." Even as Astria said this, Jais felt a little healing flow into him from where that small hand lay.

The girl could heal?

"What do you need me to do?" Jais asked. That small hand fell away.

"Restrain him, nothing more."

It would take some restraint on Jais' part to do only that much, but he'd do what he could.

He launched himself at Lucian, who was just getting to his feet. The man put a hand out to blast Jais with lightning...

Everything around Jais seemed to slow—like it had that day, not so long ago, when he'd been sparring with Caerwyn —and he felt his eyes close. His mind, senses, and body were working in perfect synchronicity. He knew, without seeing, that the blast of lightning wasn't meant for him. The man's hand was positioned slightly to Jais' right, where Astria had been. If she was the key to all of this, then he couldn't let Lucian harm her.

He knew now this was an effect of his spirit mixed with his battle instincts. It gave him a pure awareness of everything around him.

He shifted ever so slightly, surging his healing and strength—using up everything Andrei and Astria had given him—as he would take that blast of lightning full in the chest at close range.

With time still slowed for him, he heard the crackle of the energy as it left Lucian's hand, then felt it impact on him. Pain was a distant thing. With his enhanced healing and fortitude, he took the hit with little harm, even as he moved closer to Lucian. He felt the man's hand impact on his chest and smelled the searing of his own flesh, but again, these were remote things. He'd done what he needed to and survived the blast. Now he was close enough to grab Lucian's hand, and he twisted it, wrenching it back and away while turning it.

Lucian screamed, and the man was thrown forward, forced to a kneeling position. Jais' other arm wrapped around the man's neck as time resumed its normal pace. He was behind Lucian, half-kneeling, with the man firmly held, locked into place by the hold Jais had on him.

"Astria!" he shouted, though it came out more as a gasp. He didn't know what she would do, and didn't have the energy to say much more, but he hoped she'd act now.

She did. She'd been just behind Jais and reached her father, laying a hand on his head.

The man screamed again and Jais felt Lucian's body go tense, taut, frozen.

He didn't know what Astria was doing, but it seemed painful.

Good.

Jais kept his hold on the man, just in case whatever Astria was doing didn't work. He didn't know how long he'd be able to hold him with the little strength he had left, but he'd keep it up for as long as he could.

DAVLAS WAS LITTLE USE AGAINST THE ICE-WIELDING WOMAN Caerwyn fought. The woman had a shield of air around her, which deflected the spear's assault. That meant Caerwyn had to get close. That wasn't easy though, as her opponent was constantly flinging dagger-like shards of ice at her. Again, Caerwyn could protect her head and upper torso with her shield, but her hips and legs were badly torn up and bleeding from numerous cuts.

Finally, she closed distance to the woman. The ice-wielder had retreated back into the iron-clad room, but she'd not escape Caerwyn's wrath now. Caerwyn surged her strength and slashed through that wind-shield. Two swipes of Caerwyn's sword and the woman was down, hollering in pain. Caerwyn ended the woman's suffering with a quick strike to her head. The woman went limp.

Caerwyn breathed in ragged, heavy gulps of air, as her mind flashed back to Lucian's assault on her.

Gods, Volf!

She still couldn't believe he'd been hit by that blast meant for her. She turned back to the fight and hobbled from the room in time to see Jais take a massive hit of lightning straight to his chest, but continue on to restrain Lucian.

Andrei was over Volf, Mirala was leaning against a wall off to one side with a profusely bleeding head-wound.

Astria was then at Lucian once again and resumed her draining attack on him.

Caerwyn staggered over to Andrei. "How is he?"

The large man looked up at her, haggard. "He'll live, but only because I got to him just in time. It took a lot to bring him back. He's resting. I'm exhausted."

"Mirala?" Caerwyn didn't have much strength for extra words right now. She nodded her head in the woman's direction.

Andrei looked. "I see her. I should have enough left to take care of that." He rose and went to her. Caerwyn followed. She arrived as Andrei was helping the woman sit. She was explaining what had happened but seemed shaken.

"The ceiling, it... chunks fell."

Ah. Yes, there had been a lot of that. Caerwyn thought to look up and was a little shocked at what she saw. The stone above her was pitted and cracked. Even as she watched, one hairline fracture slowly grew, dancing forward, like ice about to shear away from a block. It only occurred to her then that the entire weight of the estate sat upon them.

"We might not want to stay here much longer," she said and turned her attention back to Astria. She wondered how much longer the girl would take. This process seemed far longer than Caerwyn had expected. But then she probably should have expected that taking the entirety of a man's power—a man like Lucian—wouldn't be quick.

A small chunk of stone fell from the ceiling, followed by a rain of stone-dust and smaller pieces.

Andrei must have noticed that one as well. "Uh, yeah, we should—"

Lucian's howl reached a new pitch, soaring higher, ear-piercing, then he toppled forward as Astria removed her hand.

Astria staggered back away from the man... then began cackling with wild laughter.

35

ASTRIA KNEW NOW THE BETRAYAL, THE HORROR, THE DEPTHS OF her mistake.

She was laughing, but it wasn't her doing it, it was the god, Chaos or whatever its true name was. It had control of her. Thoughts tumbled upon each other as she realized what had happened. She had drained her father of his powers, but something else had come with them. Some part of the god that had given those powers. And when that joined with the fragment of its power within her... it had been enough... for it to take control of her.

Her consciousness had been shunted to an ineffectual place, with no power over her own body. The god had possession of her. This had been what the god had wanted all along. She couldn't completely sense its thoughts, but she knew that much through the limited connection between them, which they now shared.

She screamed internally, a panicked terror filling her being. She'd fallen into his trap so easily.

Yes, it was easy, wasn't it? You thought you could manipulate

me! Never! I am all powerful and now that I have your form and
power, I will rain chaos down upon this world!

Like Holn, you will!

Astria resisted the god, but her efforts did little. She barely
even slowed it as the god raised a hand to blast wild energy at
those around them.

Laughter mixed with the words: "I don't need you
anymore, fool." And the god blasted Lucian with his own
lightning. The man screamed as he was consumed by crackling light, burned and jolted, a horrible writhing agony until
he moved no more, dead.

"Astria!" Mirala called out. "What are you—" That was as
far as she got before the god turned its fury on that group,
blasting them. Caerwyn and Andrei managed to dive out of
the way, Andrei taking Mirala with him. Fire-wreathed lightning scorched along the wall behind where they had been. It
was clear the walls and ceiling of the dungeons were ready to
buckle, but the god cared little. He'd be able to keep the rock
from crushing him. The others, however, would die.

More laughter issued from her mouth as she turned to
Jais…

But the man was already there, next to her, grabbing hold
of her.

Yes, Jais, stop this madness!

The god had all her powers and Lucian's, but that was it.
She hadn't yet gained the full scope of Andrei or Jais' strength
and the brash young man was able to restrain her.

The god wailed with frustration from her lips.

Jais held her close. "Hang on, Astria. I don't know what's
happening, but I'll have you free soon."

Would he?

She had no clue how to expel the god from her body. She
was simply glad Jais was restraining her. Yet there was some-

thing in the young man's voice, something she'd never heard from him before, a stalwart confidence in his words. She didn't know what he planned, but in that instant, she believed him.

He could help her.

And yet…

Quickly Jais!

For even as he held her, the god was using her adaptive ability to gain his strength. It was only a matter of time until she'd be as strong as Jais.

JAIS FELT THE GIRL WRITHE IN HIS IRON GRIP. YET, HE KNEW IT wasn't solely her. Something else was within her.

With his newly gained enhanced abilities with spirit, he'd felt most of what had been Lucian flow into her. Yet the power within her now was more powerful than Lucian had ever been and there was a different feel to this spirit. Some foreign, and incredibly puissant entity had taken control of Astria and was using her. He'd felt it, as it had happened, but it had taken him a moment to understand what he was feeling. In that moment, Lucian had died, and the others had been attacked. He'd known he needed to do something. So, he'd charged over to grapple her.

Yet she grew stronger with every moment he held her.

He needed to expel this other spirit and do it now.

"Mother, please, help me," he whispered, for he had just come into these powers, an infant playing with a bonfire. Yet he had no time to wait and understand them fully, he had to act now.

He pushed his own spirit into Astria, feeling around for the separation, where the entity stopped and the true Astria began. The girl's spirit huddled, a small fraction of the possessing power within her, and he forced his spirit between them... then pushed, though he didn't truly know how he was doing so.

"Get out of her, you demon!" He heard his own shouted words as distant, echoing somewhere in a physical world far from where he worked.

He felt the being's resistance. It shoved back, but even as it did so, Jais knew its power with spirit could not match his own. It had a massive essence, yes, but it was clear that Jais' ability with spirit far surpassed this entity.

Astria was snarling, shouting, cursing, all in a language Jais couldn't understand. Again, these sensations were distant. He too grunted, expending all the energy he had left, to send this being back to whatever realm it had come from.

Slowly, inch-by-inch, Jais forced the clawing and screaming being out of Astria.

His own spirit waned. He had so precious little energy left, but he'd spend it all if he needed to.

Some part of him, which seemed to inherently know what his mother had known, was certain if he did expend himself fully in this way, he would die, his own spirit burned up. And if he had to, he would do so, to free Astria from this malevolent essence.

Then a hand touched his back, energy flowing into him... Andrei.

Thank you, brother!

And with that he let out a feral cry as he pushed harder still with his spirit to drive the being out of Astria.

One.

Final.

Push!

And it was done. The spirit seemed to dissipate, fleeing into the ether.

Astria stopped struggling in his arms, going limp, and with his own exhaustion, the two of them fell to the floor.

By all the gods! That had cost Jais dearly. He was as weak as a babe. He'd used every ounce of power he had, then more, borrowed from his brother.

"Jais?" Caerwyn was kneeling next to him a hand on his face. He opened eyes he hadn't realized were shut to look up at her. "What happened? What was that?"

Even as she spoke, parts of the ceiling above her crumbled, collapsing in small bits, spraying dust over them.

"I think—" He had to breathe heavily between words. "We need—" Another breath. "To go."

She nodded, helping him up.

Mirala was gathering an unmoving Astria into her arms and it was clear the other three had no clue what had just happened.

He'd have to explain it to them... later, once they were free of this condemned place and he'd rested.

As they hobbled out, the house lost chunks of stone and wood, slowly weakening behind them.

Their group only just made it clear as the entire estate groaned and crumbled, falling in on itself; sending a massive cloud of dust high into the air.

They collapsed onto the lawns, exhausted, weary, watching.

No one spoke.

They'd won, and that was all anyone needed to know.

36

No one had been in the estate when it fell in on itself, thankfully. Astria guessed that the servants inside had felt quivers and shakes and left before the final collapse. She was glad none of them had been hurt. She'd been so far gone to fatigue, that she must have seemed unconscious as her mother had carried her out, but she'd been aware enough to sense that much around her. When her mother had laid her on the soft grasses of the lawns, Astria had known she was safe, and allowed herself to sleep.

She woke to a new dawn.

The others were up as well, though no one seemed truly that active. They were all tired, that was clear. Someone had scavenged some wood and a fire was going.

No one spoke, though she suspected there were many questions—for her and Jais—about what had happened. She didn't look forward to answering hers. She was quite curious what Jais had done to free her. She'd felt it, remotely, through her spirit-link, though she couldn't describe what he'd done, nor even how it had felt exactly, other than uncomfortable, then ultimately liberating.

Caerwyn left, then returned with several plump rabbits. They were skinned and cleaned, then put over the fire. Astria had chased rabbits in these hills as a child—a younger child. At first, she was put off by the slaughter of the animals, but as the meat cooked, her stomach began to rumble in anticipation. She was famished. It seemed necessity would outweigh sentimentality. And when it came time to eat, she took her share without complaint, all such thoughts of innocence gone.

They ate in silence, but once the meal was done, and some energy had been restored, it was Caerwyn who finally asked, "Astria, Jais, care to tell us what in Holn happened in there?" She shuddered. "It was clear you weren't yourself, Astria. Did Lucian somehow..." Caerwyn couldn't finish, she shrugged, lost for words.

"No," Astria said softly, clearly. "No, it was much worse than that." And here it came. She'd hoped she'd never have to tell anyone about that god, but it seemed it would be necessary now, another necessity, more innocence lost, though not on her part. She'd hoped to keep everyone else away from such things, but now...

Jais cut in, bless him. "Some entity had taken control of her. It wasn't Lucian, but far stronger in fact."

"Oh gods, Astria!" Mirala said, sliding over the grasses to her daughter. "That's horrible. What happened?" Her mother put a loving arm around her, pulling her close. "Don't worry, we're here for you. I won't let anything bad happen to you ever again!"

That seemed... unlikely, but Astria appreciated the sentiment, soothed by it.

She drew in a long breath, and began what would be a long explanation. "I..." A sigh. "Father, he was contacted by... something a long time ago."

"The god?" Volf asked.

Astria nodded. "Yes. Though it was not Davul as it claimed to be. That was just to make it easier to manipulate Father and his cult into worshiping it."

"And that's what possessed you?" Jais asked, eyes wide with shock. "It was strong, but…"

Mirala pulled Astria a bit closer still, whispering, "Gods."

Astria almost laughed at the unintentional dual meaning of her mother's expletive.

"I was getting to all that," Astria said. "It seems that somehow, this being, whatever it was, put some of itself into Father, perhaps that's what gave him the extra powers he possessed. I don't know exactly how that worked." A heavy sigh and inhalation. "But…" Here came the part her mother wouldn't like. "It seems that when I was… made, some of that power was put into me as well."

That garnered a wide array of looks. Mirala, as expected, was horrified. Andrei was grim, hard. He looked like he wanted to break something or someone. Astria guessed he was furious with what Lucian had done. Caerwyn and Volf both shared similar looks, part disgust, part surprise. Jais, oddly, seemed the least affected, nodding slowly, face pale, but otherwise showing little emotion. "I have carried that with me my entire life. I… I was even in contact with this being."

A gasp from her mother, the arm around her tightening.

"I could keep it from my mind most of the time after I had… acquired Uncle Donallo's powers." Another squeeze from her mother at this, but probably for a different reason.

There was a lot Astria wasn't going to tell. She skipped over the bit about her ability to borrow and drain the powers of others being from this god. They didn't need to know those details. In the end, it was only the basics that mattered. "When I stole Father's powers, what was in him of that being joined

with what was in me... and it was able to take control of me."
There. Simple.

She drew in a long breath, shuddering, not wanting to
recall what had happened, the helplessness and terror she'd
felt, how she'd almost hurt those she loved. What she'd done
to her father.

Attention turned to Jais. "And how did you manage to
defeat... a god?" Caerwyn asked, eyes showing a mix of
curiosity and awe. There was definitely something new in
how she looked at Jais.

Astria felt tension flow out of her, now that the focus had
shifted. Her mother still held her tight, and she leaned into
that hug, needing it now more than ever, feeling so very small
and weak.

And yet... When the god had gone... her powers had
stayed, both those she'd possessed prior, and those she'd
gained from her father. Somehow Jais had removed the
essence but left its power. Yet this wasn't something she'd tell
anyone. It was clear they assumed that when the god left, it
had taken the "oddness" from her as well. It was clear that was
what they wanted to believe. There was an ease in the way
they all looked at her now. They assumed she was normal. She
didn't want to dissuade them of that notion. But that also
meant she'd have to hide her powers, use them only sparingly,
or when others weren't around. She could live with that. She
didn't much want all these abilities anyway. Right now, what
she wanted most was to be a normal girl.

Yet she wasn't.

She pushed thoughts of her powers away and listened to
Jais. She too was curious in how he'd been able to do what
he did.

"First," Jais said with a great breath which swelled his
already massive chest. His shirt was in tatters and Astria could

see thick muscles tense then release with that breath. "I should say, I can now feel the spirit-link."

"Oh?" Caerwyn said.

"While I was… with Lucian, I retreated deep within myself and…" He actually smiled. "I found myself. I was able to come to terms with who and what I am. It was… liberating." He huffed out a breath and all the tension in him went with it. "And apparently when I did that, I… I was able to free the spirit of my mother trapped within me."

He held up a hand obviously seeing the many questions on the faces of the others. Astria herself had no clue what he could mean by this.

"Let me explain. My mother was strong in spirit and, when she died, that spirit sought me out." He turned to Andrei. "She would have gone to you, you were far closer, but you were too young." Jais raised his brows. "So, she came to me, and when she did, she latched on to something within me, my own powers with spirit. But in doing so, it somehow cut me off from those powers, including the spirit-link. She was trapped by that awkward melding of spirits, and she couldn't be set free until I rediscovered myself and found what I had lost. When I did. She was freed and her spirit was able to pass on to Erival. That freed up my powers with spirit and she'd left me some of hers as well."

"Amazing," Volf breathed, shaking his head.

"That it is," Jais was nodding. "And so, when Astria was taken by this… this god—it sounds odd to say it. I can't believe… anyway. I could sense what happened. I knew there were two spirits within her. So I… I did what I could to push the intruder out." He grimaced. "I'm still not sure exactly how I did it. It came as more instinct than proper planned thought." He shook his head. "A god."

"Well, we thank you for it," Mirala said softly. "So very much."

"Yeah," Andrei added. "I don't know what we would have done against such a foe, especially in Astria's body. We…" He shook his head. He didn't want to say it.

Astria was glad for that. She was fairly certain they wouldn't have had a chance against her. Would they have been able to do what needed to be done? Could she have watched as they were injured or worse? That was just a little too uncomfortable to think about, so she pushed the thoughts away.

"It's done now," she said softly.

"Yes," Mirala said. "Finally, we are free from Lucian and that god and… everything." Astria could feel her mother's relief, not only through her soul-sense, but in the tension releasing from the woman's body as well, close as they were.

Silence hung over them for a time, before Volf finally said, "I don't know about the rest of you, but I could sleep for a week."

There were nods and noises of agreement, generally that deflated the heavy mood and everyone seemed to relax.

"So, what next?" Andrei asked.

Caerwyn laughed, and it felt good to hear such a light and cheery noise from the woman. "I think Volf already said it. "Let's get some rest. Then we can figure out what's next."

They all agreed to that, and despite the early hour of the day, they set themselves around the fire to sleep.

THE CITY NEEDED HEALING, NOT PHYSICALLY, BUT EMOTIONALLY
and spiritually. Rodathia had never known any other leader
but Lucian. He'd built this place and bent these people to his
desires and whims. Andrei had seen those effects firsthand
many times in his short life. Something had to be done, and he
was going to do it.

It had been about a week since Lucian's death. In that time,
he and the others had rounded up any remaining high-level
disciples of Lucian's—those with lower powered rings. There
had been perhaps twenty in all, and most of them had not put
up much of a fight. The only significant incident had taken
place at a villa halfway up the hill to Lucian's estate. Eight of
the remaining followers had been hiding there. Even so, the
fight had been quick. Mirala and Astria had doused them with
laxness and fatigue, making sure they wouldn't respond
quickly to any threat. Volf had sneaked in and taken the rings
from three of those inside, who had actually been sleeping.
Then Andrei, Caerwyn, and Jais had charged in and fairly
quickly subdued the others, taking only minor injuries.

Other than that, the other disciples had either fallen

quickly to a combined attack or surrendered their rings. They had all been told to leave the city. For what would come next, it wouldn't be wise to keep such people close.

Andrei had consulted with the others and they'd decided that they would do very little to help the city, for two reasons. First, they were all drahksani and the city may not want their help—or might shun them entirely if they tried to 'take charge', even if it was to lead the city into a better age. The second reason was a bit selfish. None of them wanted to stay here. They all wished to be gone from this place as soon as they could.

So, a message had gone out, for any interested parties to gather in the city's market square.

A few sturdy crates had been placed side by side to make a platform for Andrei, nothing more.

The market was a large open area, with the river's docks along one side of the rough square, the sea docks on another, a warehouse district on the third, and a slightly higher class merchant's district on the fourth side. As such, a stiff breeze off the sea tousled Andrei's cloak around his broad form as he stood atop the crates. He faced away from the breeze, so the garment hugged his back and rippled around in front of him. His hair would have been blown into his face, had he kept it long, but he'd decided on a new look within the last few days. He'd sheared off most of his locks in favor of a close-cropped cut. He'd also started growing a beard, though at this point it was still patchy and rough, little more than scraping bristles when he ran a hand over his face. Part of the new look was to reflect on the outside, how he hoped to feel on the inside—different, less of a brute, more of a peacemaker. The other was to differentiate himself from Jais. The two would never be mistaken for one-another, with their height being quite different, but still, having such a similar face seemed eerie—

not only to him, but others had said it over the last little while as well.

The crowd had gathered and there were low murmurings and pockets of louder chatter as he waited to begin.

He drew in a long breath, tasting the salty sea air, as well as the tar of freshly mended ships, and the stink of rotting fish.

He called out to the crowd. "Some of you may know me as the son of your late governor, Lucian Malorva. And yes, I can assure you that Lucian is indeed dead. His reign of tyranny has ended." Andrei gave pause there to let that sink in. He wanted to make sure they heard this next bit and weren't still stuck on the last. "I do not wish to follow in his place. I and a few others have disbanded the cult Lucian had built, ensuring those with their rings and powers are no more. They will not seek to lead you."

That sent a shock of murmurs through the crowd. Andrei had hoped that the people would be happy, but most of what he heard sounded concerned.

"Rodathia, you are now a free city. You must figure out how to govern yourself. You can choose any way to do this, but might I suggest that it be a choice made by all the people, not just those with wealth or any perceived power."

Another murmur, this one quieter and—perhaps he was deceiving himself, but it sounded—hopeful?

"I leave you in peace, Rodathia, and wish you only prosperity and joy!" With that he turned, the wind blowing his cloak back behind him, more like a cape, and leapt down off the crates to where Mirala, Astria, and Volf waited.

"How did that sound?" he asked them.

"I thought it sounded good," Volf said, eyeing the platform and the crowd. It was clear the man didn't like large groups, nor the prospect of standing before them.

"I honestly don't know if it will do any good," Mirala said.

"I hope so, and I've subtly been trying to help the crowd be optimistic, but it's hard to instill civic duty with my abilities."

Andrei grunted at this. "You think they'll run to another tyrant?"

She nodded. "People may say they want freedom, but so few are willing to work for it. Most seek the comfort of what they know. Most likely some merchant will rise to prominence here and proclaim himself some form of ruler."

"He could be a benevolent one?" Andrei suggested, but even he didn't quite believe his own words.

"It's possible, but most of those who would be benevolent rulers, aren't the ones who seek out such positions in such times of opportunity."

If Andrei's reading had taught him anything of civic society, Mirala was right. Still he had hope. "Well it's up to them now."

He led the others away.

ASTRIA CLOSED HER EYES AS SHE WALKED. HER MOTHER HELD her hand, and she'd let the woman lead her for now. She had work to do.

Having overheard the conversation between her mother and her brother—or so she still thought of Andrei—she'd decided to do something about it.

Reaching back with both her mental and emotional abilities, she sought out those in the still milling crowd with the strongest desires for leadership. There were a few, and she searched through each of their minds and souls to determine if they were good men. It seemed none of them were truly good. Some had desires for power solely to elevate themselves and serve themselves. Others wished for greater wealth.

There were a few who were less selfish than the others, a scant handful. In these few, she tried to instill a sense of duty, and thoughts of serving people and this community. In everyone else she'd contacted, she implanted thoughts of crowds rioting against their rule, as well as all the things which might go wrong if they were leading the city, and heavily pushed doubt into their souls. She hoped that would help.

Perhaps, over the next few days, before their group left for the north, she'd see if she could slip away a bit and try to find a few more who might make good leaders. She could try to seed the idea of a ruling council, where voices from all aspects of life in the city could be heard. She didn't know much about such things, but it had been what Andrei had been hoping for when he'd spoken to the people, so she thought that proof enough it might be a good direction for the city.

The others may not want to affect things here in Rodathia, but Astria had—in her very short life—seen how greed and power could corrupt people. She didn't want that for the people of this city. She'd do what she could to help them find a better way.

"What are you thinking about?" her mother asked her as they walked.

Astria looked up at the woman. "Just how this city might become better."

"Oh?" Mirala smiled. "And what are your thoughts on such things?"

"I'm still thinking. I might want to speak to you and Andrei about it when we get back to our inn."

"I'd be happy to tell you of where I grew up. It was a wonderful city." Her mother's face grew a little clouded and she frowned as she added, "While it lasted."

Astria knew much of that city already from her mother's

memories, but she'd still let Mirala tell her. She liked when her mother told her stories, mostly because it made Mirala happy to tell them. So Astria would sit and listen and glean what she could.

"I'd like that."

Mirala's smile widened. There was relief in the woman's eyes. Astria's plan to act more childlike had seemed to lift some great weight from her mother's shoulders. She was very happy about that. So, she'd continue with it, hiding her true thoughts and feelings. It would be a bit odd, not to be openly using all her abilities, but she'd accepted it was no longer wise.

So, she gave her mother's hand a light squeeze and saw the corresponding gleam in the woman's eye before they both turned back to the road before them.

38

Jais sat, leaning back, supported by his arms, drinking in the sea breeze. It was hot today, hotter than it had ever been back home in the northlands… and it was late autumn here!

He and Caerwyn had not wanted to be a part of 'giving Rodathia back to the people' as Andrei had called it. So, they had walked well out of the city to a small patch of beach, secluded and private. They'd even gone down to swim in the tepid waters for a while before returning here to rest and dry and relax. Caerwyn lay on a blanket next to him.

He was reveling in his enhanced spirit-link, feeling connected to all life around him, the fish in the sea, the crabs which scuttled along the beach, the animals which scurried about farther inland, and of course, Caerwyn. Her spirit was a beacon and he drank in how it felt, shining brightly so close next to him.

The afternoon was wearing on, the sun falling to the west.

A strong breeze picked up, and Caerwyn seemed to drink it in.

"I remember the Sahajal, back in Afgen." There was a wistfulness to her voice. Her eyes were closed, lost in some nostalgic moment. "Warm winds off the desert. If it was a moist breeze like this, then storms were probably coming. If they were dry winds, then they might bring sandstorms instead."

Neither of those sounded that pleasant, but she was smiling and that's all that mattered.

He looked at her in that moment and lost himself in her beauty. Perhaps other men might say she was too tall, or two well built, or too hard of feature or demeanor, but they were idiots. She may not be like most women, but that's what made her special.

Her hair was dry. It dried quicker than his as it was so short. It stood on her head in haphazard spikes and waves. She was growing it out again, but that would take a while.

"Thank you," she said softly. "For bringing me out here."

In all the hubbub of the last week, they hadn't found time to talk, as both of them wished to. Jais had hoped that coming out here might spark something, but when he'd tried to earlier, she'd shushed him—politely, smiling—and asked if they could just enjoy the day and each other's company for a while.

He'd agreed, liking the sound of that as well. But, the day was wearing on and...

She drew in a long breath. He watched the rise and fall of her chest. It had been rare, in all the time he'd known her, to see her out of her armor during the day. She wore only a light, short-sleeved linen shirt and a pair of short linen pants she'd purchased—made for swimming.

"So..." she said sitting up slowly, letting out her long breath with an equally long sigh. "We should talk, but I'd like to go first, if that's well with you." She pulled her knees up and leaned forward a bit onto them.

"Of course," he said softly. He adjusted his position, sitting up a little, bringing in his knees as well, mirroring her.

His heart was a rampaging bull. He had no clue what she would say and only hoped it would be a reciprocation of how he felt for her. She had said she cared for him—back when they'd been fleeing from Lucian's storm. But what did that mean? Had it just been the heat of the moment?

She hesitated, her mouth opening and closed a few times, false-starts. Finally, she drew in another long breath and turned her head to meet his gaze full on. "I'm not one for flowery words. So, I'll just say this." Then her mouth hung open again for a long moment, lips moving ever so slightly, as if trying to say words before she finally voiced anything.

"What I said when Lucian was chasing us, all if it was true. Donallo and I were never together, and... and I do care about you Jais." Her lips pursed for a long moment.

Jais' heart did cartwheels. And yet... what did 'care for' mean? She hadn't said 'like' or 'love'. Was this something else? He'd wait and find out.

Yet she was shaking her head now, frowning. What was she thinking?

"I just... I don't know how I feel about much of anything these days," she said slowly with a sigh. "I... I think that I may want a man in my life now?" Even she seemed to catch that that had come out as a question. Shaking her head again. "I don't know. I still need some time to figure things out; to figure myself out."

That he could understand. He'd needed to figure himself out as well, and now that he had, he felt like a completely different man.

"But," she said, blowing out a long breath. With that exhalation she seemed to shed much of her heavy mood. She gave a slight smile. "But I know that I like having you around, Jais. I think that, if I was going to have a man in my life… it would be you."

He blinked.

That sounded hopeful.

He had so much he wanted to say, it all bubbled up within him, but he restrained it. Instead he waited. He got an odd sense from Caerwyn that there was still more she wished to say, so he would bide his time and curb his tongue for now.

She laughed. "I thought you'd say something."

He joined her in a laugh. "Oh, I have lots to say, I'm just waiting for you to be done. Are you?"

She gave a short laugh. "You're quite perceptive, aren't you?"

He just smiled.

With a long inhalation, she went on. "I did want a child." A hard break. She looked away. "I do want a child." This was firmer, surer. "And I did… I tried to convince Donallo to give me one." A sour smirk appeared on her lips a she gazed out to sea. "He saw right through that. He knew I didn't really want him either. It would have been easy to dismiss him as the father." She shook her head. "He also said that if I really wanted to do this. I should be talking—" She looked at Jais. "— to you."

Thank you, Donallo.

The man could read thoughts. He must have caught part of Jais' own turmoil over his feelings for Caerwyn.

Caerwyn was silent for so long after that—at least it felt like an eternity as Jais' heart hung in the balance—and he finally spoke.

"And?"

Perhaps it was the tension drawn tight between them, or perhaps she just had too much going on within her, but she let out a loud and awkward laugh then, and for a moment couldn't seem to stop. It was a nervous, jerky laughter, but the sound was still pleasant enough and he found himself joining in with a breathy chuckle himself.

When finally she regained herself, after a long, deep inhalation, she went on. "Like I said, I don't know yet how I want a man in my life; how I might want… you… in my life. I need some time to think about that. But I do want you in my life, somehow." And with that, something inside her seemed to shift and the words flowed out of her. "I've never had a serious relationship with a man before. I've slept with men, a few, not many, and most of those were courtesans my foster-father had requested from a local brothel when I'd grown curious about such things." She had a far away, slightly slack expression as she said, "I learned a lot, but mostly I learned I didn't really need or want a lot of that… messy stuff in my life. I was a woman of action and duty, not one of the pretty maids who fawn over men seeking a husband to take care of them." She looked him directly in the eye in that moment. "And that's not going to change. I don't need a man to take care of me, I can definitely take care of myself. I want to make sure you understand that."

He nodded. He knew it well enough.

"But—" and with that one word he smiled, feeling ever so slightly eased, hopeful. She saw it and smiled as well, her tone becoming softer. "That doesn't mean I don't want a man in my life at all. I do. I… I want you, Jais… But I think what I'm trying to say, with far too many words, is that I may need some time to figure out what that relationship will look like." Her next words succinctly summed up all she'd said: "First I need to figure out me, then… I can figure out us."

"I—" he began, but she raised a hand.

"Please, let me finish. Sorry, there is a bit more."

He nodded. He'd gotten ahead of himself, too excited by

what she'd said. He clamped down on his thoughts and words and listened.

She hesitated then, lips tight, her face going a little dark. He wondered at this. "I know you said... that you... loved me. I..." A swallow. A sigh. "I... I'm really not sure if I feel *that way* about you." She quickly added: "I know I don't want to lose you!"

Well that was something, but he found himself a bit confused now. Hadn't she already said she wanted him in her life? She had, but... but there were many ways a man could be a part of a woman's life, and love wasn't a part of all of them.

Oh.

His heart constricted just a little at that.

Caerwyn said, "I... I don't know if I've ever wanted... that sort of love. I hadn't needed it. I had a loving father, loving friends, but... a *lover*." The way she said the word made it sound like a meal she wasn't looking forward to eating. "I want to be honest with you. I just... don't know about that. Perhaps..." She shrugged, but her expression was one of pity —attempted hopefulness.

He didn't know what to say, and for the moment didn't say anything. She still seemed to have more.

"I care for you, as a friend, a good friend," she said again, then her brow furrowed. "And when Lucian took you and I thought you might be dead, or could die, I was so very afraid of losing you. So, I'm fairly certain that I want more. But I don't know how much more yet, or what that looks like."

He whispered her own words back to her. "You need time to figure us out. I know. I understand."

There was caring and concern in her eyes. "Thank you," she said softly.

Silence hung between them before she finally smiled and gave a breath of a laugh. "You can talk now."

Good.

They were close enough that he reached out and put a hand, lightly, on her shoulder. "Caerwyn, I am here for you, however you wish me to be. You are definitely a good friend." Thinking back over his life, something occurred to him then. "You're really the only true friend I've ever had."

She quirked a brow at that.

"Well, the boys of Klasten's Green were either scared of me or bullied me. Even once I grew up, not much changed. I think they were all slightly scared of me. The girls were usually indifferent. Alnia, well we weren't really friends either. We knew each other and grew close, but that quickly went straight past friendship to... something else."

Caerwyn nodded. She was doing a good job of just listening too.

"I'm glad you're a good friend and... if that's all you want, I'll respect that." And now it was his turn to be honest. "But I do love you." He felt the rightness, the sincerity in those words and all of his being relaxed a little now that it had been said in truth, not in some tense moment of life-or-death. "I love you," he said again. "And I hope that there can be more to our relationship." He drew his hand back then, looking away, gazing out over the sea.

"As I said the other day, I had a lot of time to think when Lucian had me, I needed to take my mind off the pain and... well you don't want to hear the details I'm sure. Suffice to say, my thoughts were my only refuge, so I did a lot of thinking." He laughed then. "I realized that I too have always been a man of action, just as you are. For good or ill, I don't often stop to think that much. I go with my gut and act."

When he looked back at her, there was a knowing smile on Caerwyn's face. She gave him an *'I'm glad you realized that'* sort of nod.

"I think—" He laughed at that word. "I think I'll be thinking more often now. I spent so long trying to figure out who I was by doing, but I just needed to stop and be myself to finally realize it. And I know this was a long way to say it, but one of the things I realized, is that I am all in when it comes to the women I love."

Another nod from her. This one with a more pensive face. She seemed to be remembering and agreeing.

"Alnia and Elria, they were... I was..." He shrugged after searching for words for a moment. There was no other way to say it. "I loved them, passionately. Even if I only knew Elria for a short period. I loved Alnia because I'd known her my entire life. We had the connection of a shared home. With Elria, we had a shared power which bonded us, and I threw myself into that. With you... it's our heritage. We're both drahksani. We're both different from the rest of the world. And we share... a warrior's spirit."

"I was going to say, if you just wanted another drahksani, then Mirala—"

"It's my turn to ask you to let me finish," he said with a playful tone.

She laughed at that, over-emphasizing how she pressed her lips together. That made him laugh too.

"Thank you." But now the words seemed stuck within him. He sat there for a long moment, simply looking at her for inspiration. Finally, he found it.

"I do hope that you decide to have a child." That got a raised brow. Her expression one of 'oh really?' But he could imagine her thoughts. "And no, not because I want to help you make it. If I'm honest then that's a part of it, but a much larger part is... I want a family." He went a step further. "I want a family with you." A nostalgic half-smile came to his face. "I want to be a father." A hard feeling in his gut. "A better father than mine was." He drew in a long breath. "But if that doesn't happen, then I'm well with that. Having children—and the act that goes with that—doesn't matter as much to me as being with you. I don't necessarily need to be your *lover*." He tried to say it as she had and elicited a laugh from her. "I just want to love you, and be near you, and spend my life with you." After a quick moment, he added, "I know you don't need me. I don't need you either. We're both strong and independent—well I wasn't before, not really, but I know I can be now, and I want to be... independent that is—and your independence is one of the things I love about you." He was rambling. He tried to finish strong. "This isn't about need, it's about... well it's about love." He grimaced. That hadn't been as strong as he'd hoped. "I don't know if that made any sense, but it's how I feel."

"It makes sense," she said softly. She laid her head on her arms, which were crossed over her raised knees. It was a very soft and somehow vulnerable thing to do, and it seemed odd for her. She sighed. "Everything you say makes sense in here," she drew back sitting up to tap at her heart. "It may just take some time for it to make sense for me, in here," she tapped the side of her head.

He gave her a wobbly grimace before saying. "I hate to say it, but sometimes love never does quite make sense, in here." He tapped his own head. "But I think I know what you're saying. And I'll give you whatever time you need to figure things out."

She nodded. "Thank you. "

39

VOLF SAT WITH A HUFF OF BREATH. HE AND MIRALA HAD SPENT half the morning hiking up into the hills around Rodathia. Astria had been left in Andrei's care.

Mirala sat close next to him. "I always loved this view," she said with a sigh. She'd been the one to suggest the hike. She'd said that coming up into these higher elevations had been her refuge while she'd been living with Lucian, and she'd wanted to see the sight one last time, with Volf, before they all left heading north. She'd said this high hill, close to the sea was called 'Seaview Ridge'.

Volf could understand the name. From there, one could see for miles out to sea, where the blue line of water met the paler blue line of sky. But there was much more to see than just the waters. To the east stretched a patchwork of farms along the coast, and up the river heading north. The city below seemed distant and quiet. Lucian's estate couldn't be seen from here; it was hidden behind some other hills. One felt detached from the world of men in a place like this, and ever so much closer to nature: strong winds, sturdy earth, and water as far as the eye could see. It was... peaceful.

"I see the appeal," Volf said softly. And in the peace which he drank in from the scene he found his thoughts wandering. He recalled what Mirala had asked him not so long ago: *If you didn't have these powers, who would you be? ... You care deeply. Consider that...*

Who would he be without his drahksan abilities? He'd spend some time thinking on this since they'd defeated the cult. Pondering the past hadn't help, since he'd lived with his powers for so long, stalking the night, watching others. That wasn't really who he wanted to be. No, he needed to consider the future. The real question was... "Who do I want to be?" He hadn't meant to voice the words, but once they were out it was too late to take them back.

Mirala's voice from next to him was light. "This place does tend to bring out such pensive things. It's a good place to ponder... life."

That it was. She seemed to understand his distraction. He felt a hand on his back, rubbing slowly, some general sense of comfort and ease coming through that touch. It helped him to clear his mind and really focus on that question: *who do I want to be?*

Yet no thoughts were immediately forthcoming.

He turned to look at her. "Do you know who you are or who you want to be?" he asked. Before she could answer, he felt compelled to provide context for the question. "You'd told me to think about who I am without my powers. I'm curious, is that how you think about yourself and what you do? Do your powers impact who you are and what you want?"

Her brows rose as she gave a faint smile. "That was a lot of questions." She gave a breath of a laugh, then sighed and looked away for a moment. Her hand on his back was drawn back so she could hug her knees. She tilted her head as she watched the distant sea. "In a way my powers have defined me, yes." She pursed her lips for a long moment before going on. "I want to help people. For me, my powers allow me to do that." A short, pensive laugh. "But I think that even without my powers I'd still want to help people."

"That's all I really want," he said softly. Curious, he asked, "If you didn't have powers, what do you think you'd do? How would you help?"

She looked back to him then with an eager grin. "I was always interested in healing and medicine. Perhaps I'd be an apothecary or a healer of some sort? I did train with an herbalist for a while in my youth and found the work rewarding."

"Could you teach me?"

She laughed. "I don't remember most of it now."

"Oh." He huffed out a breath and looked down, picking at the grasses around him. Would that be what he'd want to do anyway? Probably not. He tried for a moment to think of other ways he might use his powers to be useful. "I could be a hunter? Or perhaps a messenger or scout?" His powers were suited to those types of work.

"Does that appeal to you?" she asked.

"I don't really know." He frowned. "No, I don't think so, not deeply anyway." And he had to stop thinking about his powers. The intent of this exercise was to see if what he wanted had anything to do with his powers or not. So, what did he want?

Like her, he wanted to help, to be of use to people. And yet... "It's odd," he said slowly, still picking at the grasses around his feet. "I want to help people, but I'm not really good with people. Watching Andrei talking to all those people in the market, I remember thinking: I wouldn't want to do that. So many people together in one place made me so nervous!"

"But a few people together are good? You're fine around our group."

That was true. Though... "I'm good with all of you, because you're like me. You know and understand that I'm different. When I try to talk to normal people, I find myself getting tense and anxious." He shook his head and looked up at her then. "How do I help people without being around them?" Maybe being a hunter was the right answer?

He shook his head, looking away again.

Once again, he felt her hand on his back, and a wave of soothing peace flowed into him. His apprehension slowly faded.

"What about children?" Her voice was a bit distant, thoughtful.

He turned back to her, curious. "Children?" Was she asking if he wanted kids? With her? No...

She went on. "You're quite good with Astria. Perhaps you'd like working with children, teaching them?"

A teacher...

He blinked.

He had to think about that. Yes, he felt comfortable around Astria, but was that because she was drahksan? Had he had good interactions with other children?

He smiled as several pleasant memories came to him. There had been several times on the journey south where he'd encountered groups of children playing and his heavy mood had been lifted by watching them. He'd even interacted with a few. He'd been drawn to them over their adult counterparts as he'd thought they'd be easier to talk to... and they were.

He did like children; they had an innocent and simple, yet often profound, view of the world.

"Why would you suggest that?" he asked, though he was

feeling more and more like it would be a great idea. "Was there anything beyond my time with Astria?"

Her smile was kind. "From what you've told me of your life, you've spent most of it away from people. You're an adult, but I sense that you see the world with the innocence of a child. I find that fascinating and refreshing. I thought perhaps you might like working with children."

He was beginning to think that he would.

She was right. His exposure to people was limited. He'd found the last few months since leaving Cold River to be an amazing growth period for him. It was why he felt so close to his friends. He could talk to them, understood them, but other people still made him a little wary. But not children.

He laughed. "Are you saying I'm really a big child?" He was fairly certain that wasn't what she'd been saying but wanted to hear it from her.

"I'm saying, you're still very much a child at heart, Volf. It's one of the things that appeals to me about you."

Well that was well put indeed.

He found himself nodding slowly. "Yes, I think I'd like to be a teacher, or work with children somehow." There were still a lot of questions within him as to exactly what that would look like, but he felt like he'd at least found the right direction to keep looking. His uncertainty about himself and the future were dwindling. He smiled. "And you?"

"I'll continue to help people with their emotions, if they need it. But perhaps I'll dust off my herbalist skills again."

For a moment they shared a long look before she looked away, back out to sea. After that they sat in silence, simply taking in the vista before them. Volf found his mood lifting and he drank in the brisk sea air in long draughts as he found the tension slowly fading from him. Finally, their trials were done, and he had hope for the future.

And he was here, with a beautiful woman who he found it so easy to talk to, and who seemed to want to help him.

His attention was drawn to Mirala when she gave an audible shuddering sigh. She was shivering.

They had worn light cloaks for the journey, but the winds had picked up, cooler. Volf opened his and extended it around Mirala. The gesture had the added bonus of putting his arm around her.

She gave a light laugh. "I appreciate the gesture, but I wasn't shivering from the cold."

"Ah. Memories?"

She nodded.

He wouldn't ask.

After a long moment, though, she elaborated. "I was remembering the first time I came up here. It was after I'd learned I was pregnant with Astria."

He couldn't tell how she must have felt about that? Luckily, she went on after a deep breath.

"I felt... confused: upset and joyful at the same time. I'd always wanted a child, but not..." Another shiver. "Not like this, with a man like that." Her gaze was fixed, straight out, following the coast-line. "I promised myself I would make the child more mine than his. I didn't know how at the time, but I vowed he wouldn't take this from me. That would be my revenge." She frowned. "Gods, it sounds so petty when I use that word. A child shouldn't be anyone's revenge." She shook her head and looked at him then. "I'm just glad Astria turned out as she did."

Since he'd moved closer when he'd put his cloak around her, her face was very near to his, their noses almost touching. Their mutual breath hung between them in Volf's cloak's enclosure.

Gods, but she was beautiful. He found his heart picking up

its pace at their proximity. Wavy strands of her auburn hair, tousled by the breeze, were blown about between them, lightly caressing his face.

She smiled and giggled, then suddenly darted in to steal a kiss from him. Then more giggling.

He was far from upset, but he wasn't sure he understood her mirth. "What's so funny?" Though he too was grinning.

"I…" Her face remained so near, but her gaze on his darted away for a moment. "You make me feel giddy again, like a girl getting her first kiss. We've stolen up to our secret place, away from prying eyes to be together, it feels slightly forbidden."

Volf understood the sentiment. Sneaking through the nights, in the town of Cold River growing up, he'd seen his fair share of couples stealing off into the darkness to be together, hiding, keeping quiet, and often giggling as well.

He found himself joining her now. He felt like one of those young lovers, and he was all the more mirthful because he'd never thought he'd find someone to steal away with.

Mirala's chuckle turned into a full laugh for a moment before she looked back to him, huddling closer still, their noses brushing. When she spoke, her voice was low and full of mischief. "Though, when I did this as a girl, it was my parents I was sneaking away from, now it's my daughter."

They held there, so close and brushing past each other's faces, slowly their heads tilted forward so their foreheads rested together.

"You make me feel young again, Volf."

"Probably because I'm experiencing this for the first time. Surely you can sense that." Before now, he'd been a bit shy about admitting his lack of experience, but he'd said that without hesitation or shame.

"Really? Your first? I…" She blinked. Though from his

perspective—so close—her two eyes seemed like one. "How old are you, Volf?"

"A little over twenty years."

Mirala gave a bit of a gasp, then pressed her lips together, backing off just a little. Enough that he could see the surprise in her eyes. "I just assumed... I thought you were like me." Her head tilted to one side. She seemed to be seeing him with new eyes.

"Like you?" He didn't feel comfortable asking her age.

"Volf, I'm nearly sixty."

He blinked. It was his turn to be surprised. "But... you seem younger than Caerwyn, and she's forty or so."

Mirala gave a bit of a laugh. "And Lucian was over nine hundred years old."

Right...

"Age is reflected differently on drahksani, depending on how much their bloodline has been mixed with humans. Lucian's was pure. Mine isn't, but it's close. I'm guessing Caerwyn's is more mixed still."

"Oh!" He thought about this for a moment. So, she was a fair bit older than he was. That made sense, now that he thought about it. She couldn't be his age; otherwise she'd have had Astria as a child herself.

She wore a questioning smile as she asked. "Does that change how you feel about me?"

He lifted his gaze to meet hers. "Not at all."

She nodded. "It does change how I see you," she said softly. That odd look she was giving him softened though. "Yet, now you seem to make far more sense to me." A bit of a laugh, then a smile. "It doesn't change how I feel, though..." She bit her tongue for a moment looking away, seemingly thinking. When she looked back, her smile was mischievous again. "It is a little odd that Astria's potential father-to-be is only twice as old as she is, which you will be... in two years."

He thought about that, doing the math. She was right. Astria was nine and he twenty, in two years he'd be twice her age. He was closer to her daughter's age than hers.

And yet she'd also said he was a potential 'father-to-be'!

His heart quickened even as he said, "It seems drahksani can have... strange relationships." Then he laughed. "But I don't mind... if you don't."

"I don't," she said softly. Yet with that, she drew away a little more. He wondered at this, until she brought a hand out from under her cloak and touched his face, slowly tracing the lines of his cheeks, lips, and jaw. Her mood seemed to shift from playful to somber, curious. "So, I will be the first woman that you've been with?"

His entire body was tingling with anticipation. Where her fingers touched his face, he felt lines of warmth, both comforting and exciting.

He nodded. "Yes." It was suddenly quite hard to find breath for words.

Her smile returned slowly. "Then no wonder I feel this way, all giddy and light, excited and curious. You're right, I'm channeling how you're feeling."

It was true, that was exactly how he felt. She used her hand on his jaw to pull him closer as she leaned in once again.

This kiss was deeper, longer, lingering. She pulled away, letting out her breath in a shuddering sigh. Then she drew another quick breath and blew it out. "And now I'm feeling something else from you." She closed her eyes and seemed to revel in the sensation. After a long moment of this, she opened her eyes again to regard him. "You know, this connection I'm feeling with you, sensing your emotions without even trying. It's a good thing. It means I'm comfortable with you, that we've made an innate bond." She looked away. "It's how I felt with my first husband." A tilt of her head. "Though that took months to form."

"We have been through a lot together in a short time," he said softly. Then he laughed. "And I was fairly certain I knew how I felt the moment I saw you. That's only deepened as I've gotten to know you."

She looked back at him. "And I you." Another kiss, this one shorter, if still intense. When she drew back she was nodding to herself. "I said before, that I'd need time to know how I felt about you. Now I know." Another kiss as she demonstrated her feelings.

He got the point well enough.

Though even if he hadn't, in the next moment he felt a rush of emotions tumble into him. She separated their lips long enough to say, "This is how I feel." And it was glorious: love and desire, wonder and giddy joy, curiosity and certainty.

So, though he was quite certain she already knew it. He opened his heart to her as well.

Her kiss only became more passionate after that.

40

THEY LEFT RODATHIA BUT DIDN'T GO FAR. MAKING THE TRIP TO the Northlands in winter would be arduous. So, they decided to spend those cooler months in a warmer clime. They made it as far as Laskovic and stayed there for three months.

The days were cool, but not cold. Occasionally, warm breezes swept up from the sea. There were a few days with a bit of snow, but what landed never lasted long.

Once midwinter was well past, they began the preparations for their trip north.

A warm breeze blew in through the open window of the small room Caerwyn shared with Jais. The others were down at the stables.

Caerwyn... lingered.

She stopped packing her saddlebags. She'd been packing and emptying and repacking them for some time. Her thoughts were distant.

These winter months had allowed her the time to adjust to all the changes she'd gone through in the short period leading up to Lucian's defeat. She was still uncertain about many things, but others...

The largest of those changes was with her and Jais. Yes, they shared a room, but slept in separate beds. A couple times, they had even shared a bed, though they had yet to be... intimate, but they were growing so very close. She smiled, thinking of how Jais had been these last few months, so kind and understanding, patient and caring.

She sat on her bed and looked out the small window of their room. The sky over the buildings of the city was a pristine pale blue, a few wispy clouds scudded by. It was a pleasant temperature. Yet somehow, even with this beautiful day, that sky—so much like the one in Afgen—made her pensive.

There was a part of her that wanted to stay here. It was the warmer southern climate that drew her. She'd lived in the blasting heat of the Afgenni southlands for most of her life. The heat was a part of her.

Yet Barami had given all that up for life in the far north.

If he could, she could as well.

It would make Jais happy. And she was finding more and more that she felt a growing warmth within her whenever she saw that grin of his.

She no longer had the driving need to find other drahksan. That had been well and truly quelled. She'd found three now —the wizard and his brute in the north, then Lucian in the south—who had turned out to be quite malevolent. Such men were a curse on society. And it had probably been many like them who had tainted the drahksani name over the centuries. She could better understand now why the dragon hunters had been created. She knew it had been mostly human ignorance and bias that caused the great purge, but she could see her race was not without some blame for that horrible time.

A heavy sigh, as her thoughts shifted.

She'd found several friends through her searching: Jais, Volf, Andrei, Mirala... and Donallo. Not all drahksani were bad, but she'd seen enough now to know, she wished only a quiet life with the friends she did have. She would not seek out more of her kind. From what Mirala told her, there may not be that many more out there. Certainly, none of them could feel any strong pull from their spirit-link in any direction. Hopefully, other drahksani, if they were still out there, would feel a pull north and perhaps join this small crew one day.

There was a knock on the door.

Jais wouldn't have knocked.

She reached out with her spirit-link and sensed Volf. She'd come to know the feeling of her close friends through the drahksani's innate connection.

"Come in."

Volf entered, grinning. "We're just about ready." He looked at the mess of her items still scattered around her bags. "Need more time?"

She shook her head. "No. I'm just stalling."

He quirked a brow. "You want to stay?"

"I like the warmth."

He nodded. "Makes sense. Nothing says you can't find some warmth somewhere else after this trip."

He was right. And yet... "I've been travelling for the better part of two years now. I think I might want a bit of time settled in one place, at least for a while."

Volf nodded.

She drew in a breath, rising from the bed. "But you are right. I can always find warmth later, or just among good company." She said this while stuffing her things haphazardly in to her saddlebags. Once full, she slung the bags over her shoulder. "I'm ready."

He nodded and waved his hand toward the door for her to go first.

He followed her down to the stables. There was quite a crowd there.

Jais held the reigns for her mount and his, both strong and fine steeds. They had claimed several horses from Lucian's stables and no one had disputed it. There had still been a good dozen that had been given to citizens who needed them, dispersed through a lottery.

Volf went over to kiss Mirala. There was something deep blossoming between the two of them. The two had grown quite close over the winter. Mirala seemed quite eager to be going, mounting quickly after Volf's kiss. Astria waited on the bench of the wagon they'd be bringing.

Then there was the last of their party… Andrei.

Of all of them, the events through the fall had changed him the most. Other than his now cropped hair and new beard, he'd lost weight on a strict—self-imposed—diet. With his new vow of peace, he lived more like a monk, a simple life trying to help others. He was focused solely on his abilities to heal. That was the tenant to which he would devote his life.

Caerwyn and Jais had grown close to the man. She'd sat nearby as Jais had told his brother tales from his childhood, which Andrei loved to hear, mostly because Andrei had so few good memories to share. It was clear the two of them—Jais and Andrei—were brothers in truth now. Each was the other's only remaining family, and there was a bond there that had grown stronger over the past three months.

Caerwyn went over to Jais and, following Volf's lead, kissed him. It wasn't as deep or lingering as Volf and Mirala's had been, but still left Jais blinking in joyful surprise.

"Happy to be leaving?" he asked a bit befuddled.

She shook her head. "No. Just happy to be with you."

A silly grin spread on his face. It made him look so young. Sometimes she forgot he was nearly twenty years younger than she was. "Me too." He turned from her to the rest of the group. "Everyone ready?"

There were nods and comments of agreement all around. Andrei joined Astria on the bench of the wagon and, once Caerwyn and Jais mounted, they were set.

They rode out slowly, matching the pace of the slower draft animals pulling the wagon. The vehicle had been a concession. They wanted to move with haste, but with such a large group and such a long trip, they would need more provisions—especially once they were into the northlands were towns and villages were few and far between. Astria and Andrei could both ride well enough, but they seemed happy on the cushioned bench of the wagon. The group would travel a bit slower because of the cart and its slower horses, but they would also need to forage less and in the end they hoped it would even out the time and provide some level of comfort.

Caerwyn turned her face up to the brilliant sun of the day, feeling its warmth on her cheeks. She drew in a long breath. There wasn't really any place in this world she called home anymore, but still, she felt like this was the beginning of a trip home, to a place where she'd be able to rest and be among family and friends.

And that thought comforted and soothed the still rough edges of her mending soul.

THEY CROSSED SOME INVISIBLE BARRIER BETWEEN CLIMATES about two months later, still about a month away from their destination. They'd been climbing higher into the northern hills and as they crested one peak, everything before them was covered in a layer of snow. It wasn't deep, as it was early spring now, but the nights definitely grew colder and none of them wanted to sleep on the ground anymore. They found inns when they could and huddled together in the wagon— which they made into a makeshift tent—when they couldn't.

It was pleasant enough during the days, even with a brisk spring wind, as long as the sun was out. Caerwyn was still bundled in a heavy cloak, but she began to think that perhaps the north wouldn't be so bad.

They stopped for a couple of days in Cold River to rest themselves and their mounts before continuing up to the Dronnegir camp. They even stayed at the Setting Sun Inn, where she and Jais—and Barami—had stayed their first time here.

It was during one quiet evening, after most of the dinner crowd had left, that Caerwyn sat with Jais over steaming mugs of cider at a small table in a corner of the common room. The others had all gone up to bed, but she'd lingered down here and Jais had stayed with her.

A little while ago, he'd asked, "What's on your mind?"

She had yet to answer, but he'd been patient and quiet, waiting.

"I've been thinking," Caerwyn said slowly, "About us, and… children."

Jais raised a brow at that. "Oh?"

She gave him a smile which she hoped said '*yes, I do think about such things*' while at the same time also hopefully told him '*don't get your hopes up just yet*'.

Jais, for his part, said nothing. He maintained a pleasant smile and let her talk when she was ready. Though Caerwyn was certain he must be curious.

"I'm not sure I want a child anymore," she began. She hesitated just a little before going on to gage his reaction to that.

He surprised her, only nodding slowly. He hardly looked disappointed at all. She went on, saying: "At least, not for the same reason as I did before."

That got another brow raise.

It must have been a massive effort on his part not to say anything.

She smiled, hoping that would ease him a little. "When I left Afgen—it seems so long ago now—I wanted a child for the wrong reasons, I think. I wanted another someone like me, another drahksan. I wanted someone to care for, who loved me unconditionally and wouldn't... wouldn't leave me." That last part was still just a little hard to say. She gave a bit of a sour smile and took a long breath. "I can't imagine what made me think a child wouldn't ever leave me. They grow up and do their own thing." She shrugged. "Yet I'd convinced myself that this tiny being wouldn't grow up *that* fast, and that they had to love me, that they'd be something solid in my life for a while."

She reached out across the table and took his hand. "I don't need a child for that anymore. I have you." He grinned that same silly grin. "And Volf and the others." A nod from Jais.

"But, I think I do still want children," she said slowly, looking away for a moment, gathering her thoughts. "Not for any legacy or to continue the drahksan race, nothing like that. I think... I just want more of a family. Our friends are close, like family, and I'm coming to realize what that means, and how much I want that. So, I think I'd want... even more of that." She looked at him then.

The silly grin was gone, replaced by a soft and caring smile, a tender look in his eyes. "And I want that for you too," he said quietly, squeezing her hand.

"Though, I am a bit afraid," she said with hesitation,

though in truth she had no qualms about sharing her fears with Jais. It was more the simple act of voicing them which made her trepidatious. "I have no idea what kind of mother I'll be. I never really had a mother figure in my life, not for very long anyway, and—"

She was interrupted by Jais sliding off his chair and coming to kneel beside her, her hand still in his. "Caerwyn, I have no doubt that you'll be an amazing mother. You're forthright and true. You're strong and strict, and yet you know enough to temper your discipline with kindness when needed. There is a softness in you now that wasn't there before. You've lived a hard life and now realize it doesn't have to be hard, not all the time." She nodded to that. It was true. "You'll love your children, care for them and you'll have myself and the others, an entire village to help you if you falter." His eyes held the truest sincerity, it nearly made her cry.

Instead, she let out a heavy breath. "And this," she said softly. "This is the reason I need you by my side, Jais." She looked away for a long moment. "I was so certain and strong for so long that I never questioned my own judgment. Then my certainty was... taken away. I questioned everything. Now..." She shrugged and looked back at him then. "Now, I am both stubborn in my ways and still questioning so much. Sometimes it's good to have another person around to tell you when you're just... worrying too much."

"You're worrying too much." His look was accepting and also playful.

She laughed. "Thank you. Now get up and take your seat, the barmaids are staring at us."

He gave her hand a squeeze then rose and resumed his seat. "Whatever happens, I'm here for you, however you want or need me to be."

That much he'd proven. He'd asked so little for himself these past few months and yet also somehow had not been overly annoying and attentive. He'd been a reassuring presence.

She was beginning to think he could become more.

She rose slowly, using their connected hands to suggest he do the same. He did.

"Why don't we go to bed?"

He nodded, and she led him away.

When they got to their room, she held his hand a little tighter as he was about to head to his side, his own bed, and prepare for sleep.

"I'd like it if you'd share my bed tonight," she said softly.

He blinked at her for a moment then nodded with a faint smile—not that silly grin he sometimes got—just enough to let her know this had been a pleasant surprise. They hadn't been in the same bed for months. Sleeping huddled together in the wagon didn't count, everyone else was there too. This was private, special.

They prepared themselves and he joined her under the blankets on the simple bed. It wasn't large enough for the two of them, but he kept to one side, making sure she had room.

Then the frame creaked and broke under their combined weight, the ropes under the mattress snapped, one by one, slow enough that they simply, slowly sagged to the floor.

After a moment of shock, they both began laughing, and couldn't stop.

Gods, but that felt so good. Caerwyn laughed until there were tears in her eyes and her bladder was screaming at her. After a trip to the washing room down the hall, she returned to find Jais had taken the mattresses and blankets from both beds and laid them next to each other on the floor.

He looked up from settling the blankets in place and

smiled. "I figured we'd have a much harder time breaking the floor."

She laughed again, closing the door behind her.

And so, they lay together, near but not too close, hands clasped, as they fell asleep that night.

The next day, as they rode out of Cold River, she urged her horse ahead of the others, and signaled for him to follow her. When he did, she said, "When we get to the Dronnegir village, we should be married."

He looked stunned for a moment. Then finding that same soft smile from the night before, said, "I'd like that."

41

"CAERWYN!" BARAMI RAN OVER TO CAERWYN AND SWEPT HER up in a bear hug nearly as soon as she'd dismounted.

Hildr was not far behind Barami looking tall, strong, and round with child.

Volf watched from his mount as the village of Dronnegir came out to greet the old friends and new strangers. His feelings were mixed at their arrival. He was so very glad to be off the road and at their destination, but would this mean an end to their travels and adventures all together? It was something he'd wondered but hadn't brought up to anyone but Mirala. She'd informed him that the adventure of being a father would occupy him for some time to come.

That had been how she'd told him she was pregnant.

She'd said she was fairly certain it had happened when they'd been in Cold River… with a warm bed to share.

Volf was still giddy from the news.

Barami looked from Caerwyn to Jais. "And Brakka! I did miss you too." Sweeping a look between the two of them, Barami added, "Did you two finally get your acts together and realize you were perfect for each other?"

Caerwyn looked over at Jais and smiled. "We did," she said lightly.

Jais nodded, returning her smile.

Hildr was as stern as ever when her gaze swept over Mirala, Andrei, and Astria. "I see you've shared our secret with even more strangers?" Yet Volf sensed a bit of dry wit to her words. The smile she gave them all the next moment gave away her true feelings. "It be good to see you all. All friends be welcome!"

"Is everyone here so... tall?" Mirala asked in a hushed voice as they dismounted. For a moment they were together between their horses, their mounts walling them off from everyone else. She took that moment to steal a kiss.

Volf could never quite understand how he'd gotten as lucky as he had. In the fading light of this late spring day, Mirala was radiant, a stunning beauty. She'd been letting her auburn hair grow out and it was nearly to her waist, flowing in silken waves... somehow pristine even after a day of riding. There was a sparkle in her blue eyes and a spring in her step. She seemed a little excited to be seeing this 'exotic' place.

"Pretty much," he said softly before kissing her in return. "These are legendary warriors. Even growing up just two weeks travel from here, the Dronnegir were stuff of legends and now you can see why." During their time in Cold River, he'd taken her to see the sights of the city. Though, he'd not shown her his old 'home'. The ramshackle hut in the alley that he'd called home for so long had been inhabited by a family of beggars. He'd gone to see it on his own and decided she didn't need to visit.

"Now where be the hero of legend? The one who slew the mighty wizard!" The voice was Hildr's.

"That would be me," Volf said with a grimace.

Mirala quirked an eyebrow. "We've been together for

months now, why have you never told me you are the mighty slayer of wizards?"

"It's a long story and not one I like to recall." He sighed. "But now that we're here I'm sure you'll hear all about it, probably over and over again."

Hildr came into view, pushing into the space between their mounts and she caught Volf in a strong-as-ever embrace. It was slightly awkward given the roundness of her belly. It was made even more so because of her height which meant Volf's head pressed into her bosom.

Once he was set down, he introduced Mirala. "Hildr, this is my wife, Mirala." They'd performed the rite to make it official privately on the journey north—the day she'd told him of their child.

"And, have you gotten her with child?" Hildr asked a little too directly.

"Ah, well, yes," Volf said with a shrug; it wasn't a secret.

"Good for you!" She slapped him on the shoulder.

"And for you," Mirala said with a bit of a bow. "You look like you'll be due soon?"

Hildr nodded. "In five to seven weeks, so the healers say. I will be glad to get rid of the blasted thing. It throws off my balance something fierce when I fight."

"You still fight?" Mirala seemed surprised. Volf wasn't.

"Of course." Hildr reacted as if she'd been asked if she still breathed or ate. "Now come, our scouts told us you were coming, and we've prepared a feast!" Hildr turned and strode away.

"They fight when pregnant?" Mirala whispered.

"They fight no matter what."

"Oh."

They were shown to an empty long house and they took a

bit of time to settle in. Tubs of heated water had been prepared for them to wash off the effects of their travel.

"They're not much for privacy, are these people?" Mirala looked at the row of tubs laid out down the center of the long house. There were no walls not even curtains between them. That and the doors at either end of the long house were still thrown open letting in a crisp evening breeze, which was a little on the chill side for spring.

"Not so much. No," Volf said. "Just look at this place. Imagine living with your family on one of those bunks with only a wall of animal skins between you and another family. You'd have to think they know pretty much everything about each other."

Mirala seemed a little shocked by all this, but shrugged. "Who am I to question their ways." A moment later she'd removed her clothes and was easing herself into the small tub.

Volf didn't mind the view at all. "Need any help?"

"I'm sure you'd love to, but I'll be fine. You're filthy too you know. Might as well find your own tub."

So, he did.

It was Andrei who balked the most at the open nature of the baths. He easily lifted his and carried it to the far end of the long house, then outside.

Once they were cleaned and ready, they joined the villagers in a celebration in their honor. Barami wanted to know everything about their trip and adventures. They were happy to oblige, telling the tale of Lucian and his cult. Though some of the more horrific details were omitted. Mostly it seemed Barami cared little for such things and was just glad to see his friends once again.

Volf could tell Caerwyn was glad to see her old friend as well. She practically glowed. She'd changed a lot on the trip north. She'd lost a sharpness to her, which she'd always had, and which had become worse after their encounter with the wizard here in the north last summer. She was easier on herself and others now, smiling more, lighter. Even with her dislike of the cold—which she'd made sure they were all well aware of these last few weeks—she was far happier these days, and particularly happy tonight. She was among friends... among family.

Volf was happy for her.

And he was happy himself.

He had his own family now. Mirala was glowing in a golden gown, outshining everyone else here. Astria had taken to him, referring to him as Father now.

And Mirala and Astria were currently getting an earful of his 'exploits' from last summer. Perhaps it was time he set the record straight.

He pulled his wife close and kissed her.

"That's not how it happened at all!" he said and began his retelling of events.

At the end of the feast, as the night drew late—after all the villagers had left and only their group of friends remained—Caerwyn raised her flagon of ale. "A toast! To the past, and the regrets we all must face, and a future of hope to help us do it."

Everyone pushed their mugs together in a clatter of wood and metal.

"To the future!" Volf joined the others in saying, and sincerely hoped it would be a bright one for all of them.

42

JAIS COULDN'T SUPPRESS A SMILE AS HE BOUNCED LITTLE Sareline on his knee. She laughed and squealed, her tiny hands gripping his thick fingers for support, eyes wide as she enjoyed the ride.

"Pick a pretty, picket pony. Ride it round on river road. Stop to sleep under a shade-tree, then to the stable where she's stowed." Jais repeated the song in time with his bounces.

They'd named their child after Jais' Aunt Sarelle. Caerwyn had suggested it, and he'd loved the idea. She was a gem. The most beautiful child in the world. Soft brown eyes, a match to Caerwyn's, danced with glee as she played. A permanent tangle of soft brown hair sat atop her head. She was five months old. It had been fifteen months since they'd returned to the Dronnegir camp. It was summer, warm and lovely.

It had been an eventful time for new lives. First Hildr had given birth to a boy, large and healthy. They'd named him Tauwe, which was some large hunting cat from the southern deserts. Caerwyn had said it was a strong name. Then had come word from the cave in the mountains, the new dragon had been born, the egg had finally hatched. That

had been about a year ago. A truly joyous time for the dronnegir, as their purpose was renewed, they had a dragon to
protect. It had been a summer of celebration for these
people.

All of the drahksani had known the instant the dragon had
been born. They'd felt that new power emerge into the world.
Jais had reveled in this new connection, marveled at its inten-
sity. With his enhanced spirit-link he was able to sense the
beast far more acutely then the last time he'd been here.

Then, in the dark depths of mid-winter, Mirala had had
her child. The boy had been named Mirhk, which meant
'peace' in the southern tongue. He was a small child, with
Mirala's wavy auburn hair and Volf's deep blue eyes. Then, in
the spring, Caerwyn had given birth.

She and Jais had been married not long after they'd come
to the village and that evening, they had shared themselves
with each other in a night of exploration and intimacy. From
that, had come the child he now held.

And... another was on the way.

Caerwyn had done what the dronnegir women did and
kept fit—sparring and training—through her pregnancy. And
she'd felt a call for another child not that long after the first
had been born. She only just discovered she was pregnant
again and was overjoyed. She was truly a changed woman.
Much more content now, vivacious and exuberant. Jais was so
happy for her, and felt like the luckiest man alive.

At the moment, Caerwyn was up at the dragon's cave.
She'd gone with a group, escorting the three dronnegir who
would be the first to receive the dragons' gift. After just over a
year, the dragon was already large and wise, a reincarnation
of its former self with renewed life—if a lesser version of
what it had been, smaller and diminished. Such was the way
of dragon rebirth. The memory would remain but the body

would never be as strong or large, nor would this incarnation live as long as the last, or so it had told them.

Hildr, Andrei, and Astria had also gone along. Jais had chosen to stay here and take care of Sareline. Though he was thankful Mirala had also stayed as she'd been helping to feed Sareline. She'd also been helping with Tauwe, though he was old enough to be taking goat's milk. Barami, unfortunately, was next to helpless as a parent. The man had spent all his life being a warrior and fatherhood had come as a struggle.

Not for Jais though. His aunt had been the healer for their village, so he'd been exposed to a lot of children, healthy and not, and though he had never taken care of one for any great length of time, he at least had had some decent exposure to the trials and joys of parenting.

Oddly, Andrei took to all the kids with a certain zeal as well. He had thrown himself into his new life as a healer and truly seemed to enjoy working and playing with the young ones of the village. He had relented and relaxed a little in his time here. Even though he still wouldn't touch a weapon, he had agreed to teach the Dronnegir everything he had learned about war-craft and the fighting ways of the world. One of the reasons he'd gone to see the dragon—other than wanting to see a dragon—was in hopes of working out some of his lingering issues with his foster father. Mirala had done a lot of work helping him with his soul, but still he'd never quite gotten over the horrors he'd committed or been a part of. It sat like a stain on his soul and on his bad-days you could see it in his eyes, haunted.

Jais would go to see the dragon in time. Perhaps he'd take Sareline when she was older, but he was in no hurry. When he'd first come to this village and learned of the dragon, he'd been so hopeful it could shed some light on who he was and his heritage. He'd since learned all of that himself. Though he wouldn't recommend how he'd come to his own self-realization. In an odd way, he thanked Lucian for that time, as painful as it had been. There might be more to know, but he was in no hurry. He wasn't going anywhere, and neither was the dragon most likely. He knew who he was now. He was a father, not only of little Sareline here, but now another on the way. They didn't yet know how large a family they wanted, but Caerwyn had been adamant that one wasn't enough.

"Hello, lover!"

Jais looked up from playing with Sareline to the wondrous sight of his wife approaching him. He hadn't known exactly when they'd been returning, but he had felt her drawing near for some time. His play with their child—and concentration on her shining spirit—had distracted him enough that Caerwyn's arrival came as a pleasant surprise.

He rose, lifting Sareline easily as Caerwyn drew near and they half-embraced, with their child between them.

"How is my little Sara?" Caerwyn waved a finger, touching the girl's nose. With rather astonishing reactions, Sareline reached up and grabbed the finger, giggling.

"You're just as quick as your mother, aren't you?" Caerwyn said with a smile. Looking up at Jais the smile grew. "I've missed you." They kissed. "I missed both of you." She kissed the top of Sareline's head as their child laughed some more. "And your grip is getting so strong!"

"That's true enough," Jais said. "My fingers are a little sore from another round of 'pretty picket ponies.'"

"She loves that so much. I'm sure she's going to be a great rider someday." They stepped apart and Caerwyn offered to take Sareline. Jais handed her over, watching his beloved coo and coddle their child. It was a beautiful sight.

"Did I miss anything?" Caerwyn asked.

Jais drew himself up a little. "That you did. I'm fairly certain she said 'dada' at me."

"Oh, did she? And not at her toy bird or her little wooden people... or the sky, or the fire pit... or..."

"Nope, it was definitely me."

Caerwyn smiled and leaned in to kiss him on the cheek. "I'm so very glad for you both, then."

Jais watched her for another long moment before asking. "How was the dragon?"

She shook her head in wonder. "They grow even faster than our little one here. Those who tend to the beast say they're still growing. Though Twilight—as Astria calls them— assures us they're nearly full size now." It was still odd to Jais' ear to hear the dragon referred to as 'they' but it made sense since the dragon had no gender, and it was far too grand a creature to refer to as "it".

Caerwyn went on. "When they hunt, they bring back full-grown bear or moose, and those big things don't last long. There's quite a collection of bones." Another shake of her head. "Yet as much as they claim to be fully grown, in many ways, they seem like a child, much less serious and solemn, almost playful. They actually offered to fly us around. Only Astria took them up on it and came back with wild hair and eyes the size of apples. She decided to stay up there for a while with the dragon. The two of them seemed to share a connection."

"Truly?" Jais was not surprised. Somehow the thought of Astria and the dragon together seemed, right. The girl's spirit had grown over the past years since the events in the south. She was a puissant force now. Jais suspected she hadn't lost as much as many of them had assumed when he'd kicked the gods essence out of her. Yet she seemed in every other way like a normal child. So, it made sense that these two powerful 'children' would get along.

Caerwyn smiled. "Astria seems more herself when she's with the dragon, more relaxed. It's odd. Everyone else is a little on edge, except for her." Caerwyn seemed lost in that thought for a moment before shaking her head and breaking away from her reverie. Then she made a face as if smelling something unpleasant. "After the trip down from the mountain, I'm quite warm and smelly, I'm going to have a bath." She looked at him with a mischievous grin. "Would you like to join me?"

He raised a brow. "I'd love to." He took a step toward her.

"Great, then you can wash up Sara here." She handed over the baby just as Jais smelled what Caerwyn had a moment before. Sareline had apparently filled her rabbit-skin wrappings.

"Oh." He took Sareline. "I see."

Caerwyn laughed. "What did you think I was offering?" she asked with a rather good impression of an innocent look. "The river is far too cold, even this time of year, to linger for too long." She wrapped her arm around him as they made their way out of the long house. Leaning her head closer, she whispered, "But perhaps I'll let you warm me up when we get back."

He put his arm around her waist, giving her a gentle squeeze. He carried Sareline cradled in his other arm.

Caerwyn's next whisper was even softer, her breath hot on his ear, sending a pleasant shiver down his spine. "Perhaps we can even leave Sara with Mirala for a while."

Now that sounded enticing indeed.

Jais turned and kissed her cheek as they walked. "That sounds quite nice."

"I thought you might say that."

They laughed, and when the laughter slowly faded Jais gave a heavy, contented sigh.

He knew who he was and where he belonged now. He was a father, a husband, a protector, and a healer. His place was here, at the side of his wife, with his friends—those who may not be blood but had become his family.

Someday, he might want to seek adventure once again, but for now he was as happy as any man could be. With a beautiful child and a loving wife, he had everything he needed in life, right here in his two arms.

To learn more about R. Michael's books and to sign up for his newsletter to receive exclusive announcements and new release notifications visit: www.rmichaelcard.com

ABOUT R. MICHAEL CARD

R. Michael Card has loved fantasy since he read his first Dragon Lance book so many years ago. He has been writing for twenty years but has only recently decided to start sharing his work with the world. He has always enjoyed the lighter side of epic fantasy, the grand adventure, and has infused that love into his works.

He lives near Toronto, Ontario with his beloved wife and their cat. He has had a plethora of careers, working in software, insurance, trades, and education, with jobs ranging from washing cars to career counseling.